JOVE
The Human Chronicles

By AJ Aarts

First Printed: 2013

ISBN: 978-0-9945994-1-4

Published by AJ Aarts

This book is dedicated to my high school friends
"We were, We are, We will…"

This series is dedicated to the late
Thomas Arthur Driscoll Taylor
Beloved Teacher, Linguist, Story-teller and, most importantly to me,
Grandfather

Contents

Prologue

Thousands of metres under the surface of the Atlantic Ocean, a fleet of war submarines closed in on the ancient city of Atlantis.

"Captain Mendoza, we've locked onto the target." A voice crackled in the ear of the singular man floating ahead of the armada. He was wearing a pressure suit specially designed to protect him from the elements. All of them.

"Good work. Hold your positions and wait for my signal." He answered by pressing the receiver on his neck. "We're about to meet some resistance."

Captain Mendoza had been waiting for this day a long time. It was the day he would acquire the power to permanently remove the hidden world.

As he had anticipated, a dark figure emerged from the ocean depths. Its body was silhouetted by the shimmering lights glowing within the city below. The Captain suddenly felt a sharp pain in his head as the creature attempted to invade his mind. He immediately put up his mental defences and spoke using only his thoughts.

Triton, come to fight us alone? How heroic of you.

The figure paused, surprised at the human's response. It blinked its large yellow eyes as the spotlights from the submarines revealed its naked alien body.

Unlike the fleet captain, the creature was wearing nothing to protect it from the immense water pressure. In fact, its body was already conditioned to survive within the harsh environment.

As much as this *Triton* looked human, there were many drastic differences. For starters, there was no clear sign to show whether the creature was male or female. Instead its body was smoothed over, flawless. Folds of skin stretched between its fingers and toes, blending in with the dark blue ocean and keeping the creature stable as it hovered in the water.

Its strangest feature, however, was the lack of a mouth upon its alien face. Except for a set of gills on either side of its neck and two thin slits for nostrils residing beneath its eyes, its features were blank.

None of these strange features deterred the Captain and he stared at the alien creature with malice.

I was expecting to fight some kind of Merpesces army. Mendoza taunted further. *But I guess I'll have to settle for the Incarnate itself.*

What do you want Human? Triton projected back threateningly. Although they were underwater and neither could speak aloud, the two managed to converse quite clearly with their minds.

I think you know what I want. I am here to extract the fifth element. With it I will have the power to rid the world of you and your vermin.

A slight twinge of fear flickered through Triton's thoughts and was concerned at how the captain knew of this information. It tried to scan Mendoza's own thoughts but his defences were stronger than he had expected.

You seem quite educated about the hidden world. Triton continued. *But there is still a great deal that you do not know, nor can handle…*

I know exactly who and what you are Triton, the Captain interjected harshly. *Today the Incarnate of the Merpesces shall fall, finally allowing Humans to conquer and triumph as the superior race.*

If you truly know who I am then you must know that you and your fleet stand no chance of defeating me. Triton projected back with equal malice.

Mendoza merely scoffed. *Surely you of all creatures know that everyone has their weak points. Even you.*

Your own weaknesses far outweigh any the Incarnate could ever hold, Captain.

Don't count on it. Mendoza projected.

There was something about the tone in the Captain's last thought that made Triton twitch uncomfortably. It glanced at the glowing city below them. The alarm had been raised and Atlantis' inhabitants were preparing for the oncoming attack while the younger spawn were being evacuated. If Triton did not act to hold off the fleet now they would not stand a chance; and these humans seemed to know too much already.

In the blink of an eye; Triton shot forward towards Mendoza, but he was already in action. With a single motion of his arm the submersibles honed in on the Incarnate with incredible speed. Each of them shot a torpedo aimed directly at the blue creature's body.

Instantly reacting, Triton froze the water around each of them, stopping the missiles merely metres from its body. In return, the Incarnate shot jets of pressurised water toward the machines, forcing them backwards. For a second, all appeared to have been thrown off course, but they quickly recovered.

Not wanting to give them a chance, Triton froze the water around their motors and encased the hulls in ice. This seemed to work.

How could you even think of defeating me in my own territory? Triton taunted back. *Such insolence. Even for a human.*

The ice suddenly exploded off the submarine shells and they gained full motion again.

So quick to assume the end, Mendoza responded through the shards of floating ice. *Do you really think that I would not have come prepared?*

Triton was starting to get worried, quickly thinking of another weakness the humans possessed.

Contract, pressurize and explode.

The Incarnate focussed on the air supply within the submarines and within the Captain's lungs. He choked slightly at the movement.

Triton was about to release the final action when the energy was blocked and forced back in full force. An electrical surge shimmered in the water.

How? ...*well if air won't work, maybe heat will throw them off*. Triton thought privately.

Directing all energy to the centre of its body, Triton converted its emotion into a heat that immediately affected the surroundings. The water bubbled and warped as the temperature quickly rose. If Triton's skin was not already conditioned for every environment on the planet, its body would surely have been cooked through. The water was almost at boiling point when Triton focussed even more intensity at the submarines to melt their systems.

But to no avail.

Glancing at Mendoza, the Incarnate was surprised to see that he was calmly treading water as if enjoying the sensation. The thermal energy had no effect on his pressurized suit.

Angry, Triton shot a burning jet of water at Mendoza. The Captain saw it coming and managed to avoid it easily. In retaliation, he raised his hand signalling for his fleet to make their move.

A powerful electronic pulse emitted through the water and Triton immediately grabbed its head.

A high-pitch screech ruptured its thoughts and pain coursed through its blue body draining its energy and making it seemingly impossible to maintain focus.

In an act of desperation, Triton launched its body toward Mendoza at breakneck speed, but he was ready. Triggering something in his suit, another powerful electrical current emanated from his body and surged through the water. Triton immediately tensed and began to twitch and seize uncontrollably. The Incarnate was helpless as Mendoza descended through the water. He pressed his finger onto the speech function on his neck so his prey could hear aloud.

"I know how you function." Mendoza's voice crackled through the water as he circled Triton. "Although as the Incarnate you have attained the attributes of each race, you are still of Merpesces origin. You solely rely on electric pulses within your brain to communicate and survive. I believe we humans have harnessed and made great accomplishments in electricity and technology over the years."

What . . . are you . . . getting at? Triton's projection was scrambled as the electrical pulses in its brain gave out. Its entire body was paralysed and could do nothing as the fleet started moving downward towards Atlantis.

"We humans have proven superior to you and the other races. We are truly the dominant species."

Mendoza moved in on Triton's alien face until their eyes were just inches apart. Although the Captain was wearing a thick diving mask and suit, Triton could sense his eyes glaring with revolt.

Its body continued to writhe and twitch with pain.

"Once I destroy your dismal city, I will uncover and master the fifth element and use it to eradicate the four hidden races for good. Their safety that you have spent so many years protecting will all have been a waste. They will die and you, the Incarnate, will cease to exist."

The Captain released the electrical field and forced Tritons limp body downward in the water. He pulled a large harpoon gun from the pack fastened to his suit. It was attached to a compact generator that Triton figured was the source of the electrical pulse. As Mendoza pressed his finger around the trigger, Triton saw his chance.

The moment the field was relinquished Triton seized control and managed to force his mindstream back into Mendoza's, taking over his brain function. The Captain's body froze in the water.

You say you know us Merpesces? Triton projected as Mendoza fought to regain movement. *Then surely you have not forgotten our strongest point and greatest weakness. Our ability to read minds and project thoughts is yes, powered by electric currents. A single pinch of these pulses anywhere in your body can cause permanent damage. One in your brain is almost certainly fatal.*

Mendoza froze and Triton sensed fear flood his thoughts. He couldn't even signal for the fleet to assist him. All he could do was project back to Triton.

No Merpesces has ever mastered the movement pulses in the brain. Doing so means blocking your own pulses. Even if you could, you cannot stop my fleet.

Now it was Tritons turn to take on the mocking tone, *There are many benefits to being the Incarnate and having my power. I am no ordinary Merpesces. You stand no chance.*

Mendoza fought desperately for control and his body thrashed about in the water but the Incarnate's hold was too strong. He made another desperate projection.

Even with that power, it will kill you.

Then I shall be reborn again, and my cycle shall continue. You, fortunately for all, will not have the same fate.

I can survive you. Mendoza projected threateningly, *Once you die, myself and my followers will find you and end you.*

Then so be it. Triton projected one last time. *Let the search begin.*

Triton reached for every mindstream in the vicinity and felt the panic of each of their final thoughts. Mendoza fought with every ounce of energy for his hand to reactivate the electrical field. But Tritons mind moved faster than the Captain's body ever could.

Mustering all the energy in its own mind, Triton bridged the connections and readied to block them once and for all. Just as the Incarnate was ready to shut them off, Mendoza tried to sever the connection, but not quickly enough.

In an instant, every living organism within a one mile radius fell silent. An eerie sense of death floated through the water above Atlantis. The city was safe; their secret was safe; the entirety of all the other races was safe. For now.

Amongst the dead limp bodies and floating masses of metal, a single body started to twitch. A spark of life returned to Mendoza's brain. Feeling returned to only some parts of his body, but it was enough to slowly help him move through the water. Using the little energy he had left, he struggled upwards toward the surface before his body gave out from exhaustion and lack of oxygen.

The next Incarnate would now be born as a Human. This would either confirm the success or failure of Mendoza's vision.

The search was on…

The Average Jove

-Present Day

Left punch…

Right punch…

Left punch…

A group of teenagers were practicing their karate sets in the local park. The early morning sun had just broken over the horizon and cast a warm light over the class. Their instructor, dressed in a long white karate robe, walked up and down the line of students, counting them in for each punch. He stopped in front of one of the older teenagers.

"Very good Jove." He grabbed the boy's fist and showed the rest of the class his stance. "Keep your arms steady and level with your legs." He shifted in an attempt to knock the boy over, but the teen remained standing. "This strengthens your stance and makes it harder to overthrow your opponent."

Jove Boyd felt proud of himself. He had been taking karate lessons since starting high school and was now one of the more senior students gathering in the park most mornings before school.

It was his mother's idea initially; something about discipline and being able to protect himself against danger in the real world. Not that he minded. He enjoyed the idea of being able to kick someone's arse if he needed to.

"Good job all of you. A couple more months and some of you will be ready to go for your black belts." The instructor glanced at Jove before dismissing the class. The students bowed and proceeded to grab their things before heading home to get ready for school.

"Show off." Ben, one of the other students, commented as he walked up to his mate.

"Hey, don't complain." Jove retorted. "You're already good at every other sport. Give me something to be proud of."

Ben was in the same grade as Jove and often beat him both in class and on the sports field.

"I suppose. Make the most of it until the Phys Ed exam this arvo. I'll see you at school." Ben winked before disappearing around the block. Jove continued in the opposite direction towards home.

Like every other normal school morning, the house was silent as Jove walked in. His mother had already left for work a few hours earlier.

She was a single parent with a modest nursing job at the local hospital. It was enough to put food on the table and keep a roof over their heads, but the shift work meant Jove was often home alone.

Jove's father, on the other hand, had been out of the picture for as long as he could remember. His mother had told him that he died shortly before Jove was born. She never talked about him much, so he decided not to dwell on the subject.

Jove grabbed his uniform and headed for the shower. As he washed himself, he went over his school timetable in his head.

Tuesday… Tuesday… Damn, double Maths first up. He thought as he stepped out of the shower and inspected himself in the mirror. His hazel eyes stared back at him underneath a sheet of messy, dark brown hair.

He wasn't a well-built kid. In fact, from his physical appearance he might have been considered a bit of a geek. He had been trying to bulk up by taking a few extra karate classes and protein shakes, but there were more important things for the soon-to-be graduate to worry about at present. It was only a few months until graduation and Jove still had no idea what he wanted to do after school finished.

He tensed his muscles in his reflection to see if the extra work and bulk-up shakes had been working. Apparently not, so he continued to dry himself off.

This process usually took longer than it would a normal person. For some strange reason water had some sort of attraction to his skin. Any tiny drop of water in the air stuck to his body in the same way that it would a cold glass. This had been going on for as long as Jove could remember and, as a result, he had always been scared of going to school on a rainy day as he never stayed dry.

After getting dressed, Jove made his way into the kitchen to make up a protein shake and a bowl of Weet-Bix before sitting in the lounge to watch the morning news. The newsreader flickered into life as she read the latest report.

"…*In local news, Boonda residents are cautioned to be on the lookout for suspicious characters believed to be involved with gang activity. These individuals may be seen in dark, concealing clothing and are believed to be armed and dangerous. If anyone…*" Click. Jove changed to the weather as an image of the gang members flashed across the screen.

He had heard of this mob the previous morning. In fact, they had apparently been skulking around the area for some time now. Jove was lucky enough not to have seen them in person. At the moment, however, he was more concerned about the rainclouds looming outside the window.

"…*Thunderstorms and heavy rain predicted for the afternoon…*"

Damn, he thought not wanting to walk home in a downpour after school.

As usual, Jove lost track of time and a quick glance at his watch told him it was after eight. His mate Cameron would already be waiting on the corner so they could walk to school together.

Jove guzzled down the rest of his breakfast and rushed out the front door, stuffing his books and sports clothes in his bag as he went.

He had barely made it to the corner when Cameron ran up from the next street, also running late. His bag and untucked shirt flapped in the wind behind him.

"Mornin' mate." He panted when he stopped beside Jove. "Had to wait for my sports shirt to dry. Forgot we had PE today."

"Well it's good to see you actually remembered this time." Jove joked as they started to walk.

"Yeah, that would've been convenient for ya." Cameron said nudging him.

"Whatdya mean?"

"Well, I could have left you alone to do some fitness trainin' with Tia. I'm sure she'd love that."

"Shove off. You know she'd be more interested in talkin' to her mates about Home and Away last night or somethin'."

"Whatever. You know you gotta make a move sometime yeh? She's not gonna stay a bachelorette forever."

"Shut up will ya?"

As Jove and Cameron walked through the gate and went to meet their group at a nearby bench, the bell rang for home room.

"What!? We just got here!" Cameron groaned as another of their friends came running up behind them.

"Hey Mitch." Jove greeted him.

"Mornin all." The boy panted back. "You'll never guess who Pa and I had to bring to school this morning." He paused and nudged Jove in the ribs.

14

"That misty-eyed chick Jovesy's got his eyes on. Somethin' bout car troubles."

"Are you two conspirin' against me or somethin'?" Jove replied dryly.

"What? Don't you want me to put in a good word for ya?" Mitch nudged him again as the group started to break up and make their way to their respective home rooms. Jove and Mitch started moving to the building on the far end of campus as Cameron walked toward the adjacent stairwell.

Within the group, Cameron and Jove had known each other since primary school and had become firm friends. Mitch was then introduced to the group through Jove when they met on their first day of high school and had been in the same home room since.

The conversation between Jove and Mitch continued through home room. Mitch lived just down the street from Tia and had given her a lift to school a couple of times now. Like the rest of their circle, he knew of Jove's crush and hardly passed up the opportunity to annoy him. He kept it up until they were seated in the back of their Maths class for first period and Jove was starting to get irritated.

"You need to strike up a conversation with her somehow." Mitch persisted. "Add her on Facebook or something."

"She's not on Facebook."

Mitch raised an eyebrow. "How do you know that?"

Jove's face flushed guiltily. "Already looked."

"Alright you stalker. Well, that's weird anyway. Wonder what she's got to hide?"

"Well she's the new kid. Maybe she wants to start fresh. Besides, I bet I'm not the only one who has a crush on her. She's smart, good at sport and looks like freakin' Miranda Kerr."

"An albino Miranda Kerr." Mitch added, trying to lighten Jove's mood.

"Albino means red eyes you idiot." Jove said sharply. "Besides, there's nothing wrong with having white pupils."

"I never said there was anything wrong with white pupils! I reckon it adds to her… mysteriousness. Not to mention it isn't her only distinguishing feature." Mitch winked as he moved his hands in a curvaceous manner, outlining a woman's figure.

A smirk ran across Jove's face. "Yeah I know." He noticed a few nosy faces turned around to see what was so interesting. Luckily, the teacher was more engrossed with writing math functions on the board than paying attention to what was going on behind him.

"Let's finish this later. I need to get this stuff down if I'm going to pass this next exam." Jove said as he picked up his pen and started copying the functions into his book.

"Yeah, 'cause everyone needs to know how to do linear equations." Mitch replied sarcastically.

Although Jove was serious about needing to get his work done, the deep monotonous tone of his teacher's voice made it hard for him to keep focus. Before long, his mind started to wander as he thought about Tia, picturing her in his mind.

Tia Favon was a pretty girl, good at sport and seemed to get along well with everybody. She was an only child who had apparently travelled around most of Australia with her father. They had only just arrived at the small east coast suburb of Boonda a couple of months ago to complete her senior schooling. Not much was known about her life before moving into town, but no-one really took much notice. They were far too occupied with their studies.

Along with a lot of other guys in the school, Jove had taken an instant liking to her. She had the slim yet slightly muscular build of an athlete that he guessed was a result of her phenomenal sporting abilities.

Her long, sandy brown hair flowed to her shoulder blades and always seemed to be caught in a gentle breeze, even if there wasn't any wind. Her tanned skin revealed no flaws, which was unusual for a teenager, but her most distinguishing feature was her deep brown eyes. Her pupils were not plain black like they should have been; instead they were tainted with swirling shades of white that seemed to glow when she smiled.

Rumour had it that they gave her super powers like x-ray vision. To everyone's disappointment, however, she admitted that it was simply a birth defect.

"…Alright, make sure you all finish the problems in Chapter Twelve for homework. I'll see you again tomorrow." The teacher's voice came back into focus as the lesson ended.

Jove swore silently as he realised most of his page was still blank. He was already struggling to keep up with his schoolwork and his lack of focus was not helping.

"I see you didn't get much work done either." Mitch commented as they walked into the courtyard for lunch.

"Mmm." Jove answered as they headed towards the stone tables and sat with the rest of their mates.

"Hey." Everyone greeted them in unison as they sat in their usual spot. Most of them already had their lunch bags open comparing food and swapping meals.

"What did you get?" Mitch leaned over the table to see if Jove had anything to swap.

"Nothing today." He replied. "I didn't have time to pack anything. I'll just get something from the tuckshop."

"Wait up. I might grab something as well." Cameron followed while searching his pockets for spare change.

"Oi you got two bucks I can borrow?" He asked as they got in line.

"You scungy bastard, you already owe me five from yesterday. Why do you always ask *me*?" Jove reluctantly pulled out a two dollar coin from his pocket.

"'Cos you're the only person with money who's generous to his mates." Cameron grinned innocently, holding out his hand.

"Well if that's the case do you mind if I borrow some too?" A soft voice butted in from behind them.

Jove's stomach churned as he turned and saw Tia Favon smiling back at him. He stammered for a moment.

"I-I would but I gotta get something for me as well, you know."

"Relax, I was only kidding." She winked a misty eye. Jove smiled uneasily in reply.

They endured an awkward moment and Cameron nudged Jove in the back.

"So," Tia tried to break the ice, "what are you getting for lunch?"

"Er, lasagne." Jove replied, his voice taking on a strange tone as he rubbed his belly. "Loooove my lasagne."

Cameron stifled a laugh behind them and Jove tried to ignore him.

"Any idea what we're doing for our PE exam this arv?" He quickly changed the subject.

"No, none at all," Tia shook her head, "but you shouldn't worry. You are passing aren't you?"

"Just barely, what about you?"

The question barely left Jove's mouth when he realised how stupid the question was. She was in the running for the school's sports award alongside Ben.

"Let's just say I'm satisfied with the mark I'm getting." She answered.

"Next!" The sound of the tuckshop lady's voice brought them back to earth.

"Umm, you can go first if you want." Jove stood aside and Cameron raised an eyebrow at him.

"Oh, thanks. Good to talk to you both." Tia said before turning toward the counter.

"Smooth move mate. Hope she likes lasagne as much as you." Cameron gave Jove another nudge.

"Shut up." Jove whispered back.

He noticed that Tia had bought a large steak sandwich and a bottle of coke before returning to her table.

"Least she eats healthy." Cameron commented.

"Yeah I wonder where she puts it all." Jove replied.

"Well judging by how tight her shirt is I guess it's going to her…"

"Next!"

"Man, I wish I had your talent." Mitch said in the middle of Manual Arts.

Jove had been working on a coffee table for his project and so far he seemed to be the only one in the class having any success. Mitch was struggling to attach the hinges on his cabinet while Cameron worked on a toolbox on Jove's other side.

Needing to weld some of the metal joints together on his table, Jove moved his project to the welding area, grabbing a mask as he did so. He placed the protective gloves on his person before picking up the welder and lighting it. Since it was old school equipment it didn't have much firepower so the flame was weak and welding the joint was a slow process.

"Nice table." The sound of Tia's voice next to him made him jump.

"Thanks." He pulled off the mask. "Wait, what are you doing here? You don't have Manual Arts with us this period."

"I'm on a spare so thought I might come down and finish off my bookcase."

"Bookcase? That one in the corner is yours?" Jove eyed the finely crafted piece to the side of the room. It was a slanted rectangular shape with tilted shelves that were cleverly fixed using complex joints. He had always admired it and wondered who had been working on it. He felt slightly ashamed of his own work now that he knew.

"That's a really ingenious piece of work. Is there anything that you're *not* actually good at?"

Tia giggled, "Well I can't do Drama to save my life."

"Really? I reckon you'd make a cool model, actress."

Jove immediately regretted saying that aloud. "What?"

"Ergh, never mind. Good job on the bookcase, really. I need to, um, keep going on my table here."

"Righto, catchya." Tia answered awkwardly as she walked away.

When she was out of sight Jove smacked his free hand on his face and his welding hand down on the table.

Dammit! You idiot! He thought angrily.

Jove suddenly he felt a hot sensation on his gloved hand and heard a crackling sound. He looked down, the welder had set it on fire!

"Whoa!" He instantly switched the welder off and threw off the glove, trying to stamp the fire out. It quickly spread along the workbench and set everything on it alight. The commotion drew the entire class' attention.

The teacher raced over wielding a fire extinguisher and quickly doused the fire.

"What happened?" He breathed when it was out.

"I dunno." Jove replied flustered. "The flame isn't strong enough to burn like that. And I thought these gloves were fireproof?"

"They are." The teacher gave him a quizzical look. "Maybe you shouldn't be welding for the rest of this lesson." He said before sending Jove back to his bench.

"Fine." Jove replied, thinking this might have been best. His face reddened as he passed Tia. She glanced from the welder to Jove again with a puzzled look on her face.

Cameron and Mitch came running after him to ask what happened, giving up when Jove couldn't give them an answer. After a time, the bell rang telling them it was time to get changed for Phys Ed.

The rest of the class had already gathered on the school oval by the time Jove and his mates arrived in their sports uniforms. Dark clouds had formed in the sky above them and looked as if they would unleash a deluge at any moment. Looking out beyond the grounds, the land slanted upwards with the houses looking down on the school. It was always really unnerving whenever a class was on the oval as they were in plain sight of the rest of the neighbourhood.

The Phys Ed teacher hadn't arrived yet and everyone was chatting in their groups. Jove spotted Tia with her friends doing warm up stretches. A knot formed in his stomach and he tried to hide himself from her view. Beyond them three foam mats sat side by side with a set of bars placed in front of them.

"Great." Ben groaned as he greeted them, "High jump."

Ben usually stuck with Jove in PE to give him pointers in return for the advice Jove would provide in their morning karate classes.

"This'll be interesting." Jove said with a bit of uncertainty. "I haven't done this since primary school."

"At least it's better than cross country," Ben replied, "which is next month apparently so plan your sickies."

"Well for now we're just gonna have to suffer." Mitch interrupted. "Here comes Londsy."

They peered over their shoulders to see the bulky form of their teacher, Mr Londs, walking towards them.

Cameron lowered his voice dramatically, "Prepare yourselves."

The rest of them snickered before breaking apart to await their instructions.

"Afternoon class. As you might have gathered, your exam today involves high jump as part of our athletics unit." Mr Londs' deep tone boomed over the oval. "Now, because of the weather and since we have a smaller group, we're going to test boys and girls together. So if you could all choose which side you're going to run from we can start the qualifying jumps."

Jove, Ben, Cameron and Mitch decided to jump from the left along with only a handful of other students. The rest of the class gathered on the opposite side of the field. They kicked off their shoes as Mr Londs spoke again.

"Ok, now I'm going to call you all up alphabetically. If you make this jump, you go through to the further rounds for marking. Everyone gets three attempts at the marking jumps. The higher the bar, the higher the mark."

"No pressure." Cameron remarked.

"… So if everyone's ready, we'll get started," Mr Londs finished, "Kirsty Ahmer."

A girl from the right broke out of the group in a sprint and cleared the bar with relative ease.

"Paul Beffer."

A boy of medium build stumbled for a bit after his name was called. He had been trying to catch the attention of the girls beside him. After making sure they were watching, he tore off toward the bar and cleared it, adding a lot of extra height and unneeded effort.

Show off, Jove thought while rolling his eyes.

"Jove Boyd."

He took a deep breath before setting off in a slow jog. As he approached the bar he quickened his pace. Unsure of how he had to position his feet, Jove staggered slightly before springing into the air. His legs flung upwards, nearly smacking him in the face and he barely scraped over the bar.

"Interesting technique Boyd, but I see it works for you." Mr Londs said as Jove stumbled over the mats and made his way back to his group. He quickly glanced over to the girls on the other side to find them hiding snickers, Tia among them. Once again, his face reddened.

"Nice form mate, but were you trying to go for a scissor kick or a frosby-flop?" Mitch commented as Jove approached.

"I guess it was a bit of both, I couldn't decide."

"Seriously, I think you might be more comfortable doing the scissor kick." Ben piped up,

"Might not be as pro as the frosby but it's a lot easier and your legs won't get in the way as much."

Jove turned to Ben so they were at eye level with each other. "Your expertise both amazes and disturbs me." He said with a hint of sarcasm.

"Well you can look like a real idiot when you stuff up a frosby." Cameron whispered as another person made the jump.

"But bugger up a scissor kick and you'll never live it down." Ben answered back.

"How the hell do you bugger up a scissor kick?" Jove said half confused and half amused.

"Well, with *your* legs you could smack yourself in the face with your own knees." Cameron joked from behind him. "It'd be an instant hit on Youtube." He pulled his phone out of his pocket and gestured toward its camera lens with a smirk.

"Shh, look who's jumping." Mitch nudged them. "We're about to learn how to properly master the ancient art of high jump." He added dramatically.

Jove turned around to see "Tia Favon" prepare for her jump. Apparently everyone else was interested too as a hush fell over the class. She set off in a graceful jog and cleared the bar in perfect form. Some students couldn't help but *ooh* and *aah* in awe.

"Well, if you could do it like that over and over again you'd get a top mark for sure." Mitch commented with envy.

"Well, let *me* show you how it's done." Cameron scoffed as he heard Mr Londs call his name.

They all raised their eyebrows as Cameron did an almost perfect scissor kick… about a metre before he was supposed to. His rear end clipped the bar making it quiver but it stayed put nonetheless.

"May I remind you, Mr Taylor, that this is *high* jump, not long jump." Mr Londs remarked while the rest of the class snickered. "And you might want to perfect your technique for that too."

Cameron rolled off the mat and tried to hide his embarrassment.

"No offense, but I think I'll stick with my own form." Jove said as he returned.

"At least I made it didn't I?" Cameron answered still unimpressed with himself. He turned around just in time to see the next girl crash into the bar.

"Which is more than I can say for her." Ben added with a wince.

The jumping continued for a few more rounds and as time wore on, more students dropped out of the running. Jove and his friends were still going strong along with Tia and her group. Paul Beffer was also holding his own quite comfortably.

Jove found his feet quickly and managed to clear the bar with as much ease as Paul and Tia. His confidence grew with every jump and excitement surged through his body making his muscles tingle.

His friends were becoming impressed, asking how he was doing it.

"Hidden talent I guess." He said proudly and he caught a hint of a smile from Tia on the opposite side of the field.

They had all made a passing grade and were now going to see how high a mark they could get. Their run of luck seemed to slow down when Cameron failed one round and Mitch followed soon after.

"Well at least I can say I passed now." Mitch said with a surprisingly upbeat attitude.

Satisfied with a B-grade, they both sat on the sidelines with the rest of the class to cheer on the remaining contestants. Up to this point, the crowd was coming up with different cheers for jumps that were successful, a failure, or just plain hilarious.

The bar quickly reached a record height with only a handful of students remaining and the pressure was starting to show. More and more faults were being made and the successful jumps were becoming all the more impressive. Jove and Tia were yet to fail a single jump and the rest of the class were now picking each of their favourites as they cheered them on.

At one point, when Ben started to struggle with a certain height, he approached Jove. "I think I might try your technique mate." He said curiously, "Seems simple enough."

Cameron and Mitchell gave a small 'woot' from the sideline as Ben sprinted toward the bar and attempted to mimic one of Jove's scissor kicks. He did it almost exactly how Jove would've done it, but he still fell short and collected the bar on his way down.

"Unlucky Mr Watson. Last attempts." Mr Londs announced as Ben made his way back toward Jove with a look of frustration on his face.

"Geez mate." He said after catching his breath and gave Jove a quizzical look. "How do you get the height? It's almost impossible to do!"

"Dunno," Jove shrugged, "but it works for me. Come on, you've still got another jump."

Jove wished Ben good luck with a pat on his back before he set off towards the bar. He appeared to have jumped with all his might. His body rolled over the bar leaving only a fingers breadth of space. The crowd gave a small cheer; compared to Cameron and Mitch anyway, and Ben rolled of the mat with a triumphant look on his face.

"Good on ya mate!" Jove gave him another slap on the back, "I didn't like the idea of being on this side by myself."

"Yeah, thought I might stick around for a little while longer." Ben replied with a smirk. As he finished talking, the last student to jump tried again to stay in the game. The crowd winced as he crashed, hard. Jove quickly glanced around the oval and noticed that there were now only four people remaining. Ben, Paul, Tia and himself.

"Okay, we have four of you left and you've each received an A-grade." Mr Londs announced as everyone started to calm down. "To decide a winner, we'll be moving the bar up two centimetres every round. I think we're going to be close to breaking the school record today."

He finished adjusting the bar to the new height and called for Paul to make his first attempt. Much to Jove's dislike, he gave Tia a playful wink before running off. He ran, jumped and failed. As he walked back, Jove could not help but smile as he saw Tia roll her eyes, unimpressed.

Now it was Jove's turn. He crouched down toward the ground before running off at his usual pace. As he jumped, his rear end collided with the bar and it was knocked off its perch.

Great, he thought, *guess this means I'll have to start trying harder.*

"Looks like the great Jove Boyd is human after all." Ben remarked as Jove walked back. He shrugged in reply and turned to watch Tia jump.

All the girls started cheering her on as she started her run. She jumped, twisted her body and moved her feet up just in time to clear the bar.

"Bet she felt that one. That was close." Ben commented.

"Mmm." Jove grunted in agreement but his mind had trailed. Now that he was getting a hang of the jumping, he started to pay more attention to everybody else's technique. He noticed that there was something odd about Tia's jumping. She slowed down way too much before the bar and he couldn't figure out how she was building her momentum up again to clear the jump. It was like she literally had a spring in her step.

"Oh well, my turn." Ben said just before his name was called. A pattern was forming and everyone was getting used to running off just as Mr Londs was announcing their names.

Much like the jump Ben had previously done, he jumped with all the effort he had but it wasn't enough to clear the bar.

"Oh well." He said after walking back, "Thought that last one was a fluke anyway."

They both turned to see Mitch and Cameron let out a cheer for no apparent reason. They still seemed to be really excited that their mates were in the final four of the competition.

It was now down to the three remaining boys to attempt their second jump with Paul starting them off. Although his next jump failed, he still milked it to try and impress Tia.

Now it was Jove's turn again, two particular fans started yelling louder than the others. He glanced over to the opposite side and unintentionally caught Tia's eye. Whether he imagined it, she winked at him, in plain sight of Paul. A strange feeling coursed through his body, seemingly charging his muscles.

He surged forward toward the bar at an exceptionally fast pace. At the last moment, he put all his might into pushing off the ground. Something felt different as he did so. It seemed like he was in the air for an eternity as he glided over the bar, still leaving a comfortable amount of room.

The rest of class applauded him as he stepped off the mat and walked back toward Ben. Cameron and Mitch seemed to be beside themselves. They were now turning to the people next to them as if to say '*we know him!*' Jove looked over at Tia who was also applauding and seemed fairly impressed by his jump.

"Ok, now you're just starting to show off." Ben brought him back to earth and gave him a suspicious look. "You sure you haven't done this before?"

"Not for a while." Jove smiled back. He was really enjoying having found a new talent to attract Tia's attention.

"Ben Watson."

Ben crouched low and looked as if he was gathering all of his focus before starting his run. As he approached the jump, his footing became awkward and his leg collided with the bar, bringing it down.

"Damn it." He came back shaking his head.

"At least you've still got one more." Jove reassured him.

It was now time for Paul to go for his final jump. All the girls in the crowd swooned as he did some last minute stretches. He seemed to focus all his attention on the bar. He ran, jumped, and the bar came crashing down after him. A disappointed sigh sounded from the girls on the sideline.

"About bloody time." Ben whispered as Jove thought the exact same thing.

"Unlucky Mr Beffer. Three contestants remaining. Ben."

Once everyone had calmed down, Ben started to prepare for his final jump. Mitch and Cameron started a clap that everyone else joined as Ben tore off toward the bar. The speed of the clapping increased as he approached and jumped with every ounce of strength he had.

But it wasn't enough. He flicked his legs up too high and his ankle came down on the bar with enough force that Jove was surprised the bar didn't snap in half. Everyone in the crowd cringed as he landed awkwardly and the bar fell on top of him.

"You alright Ben?" Mr Londs came over to help him up.

"Yeah, I'm good." He replied as he awkwardly rolled off the mat.

"Good. Awesome attempt by the way. You should be proud."

"Cheers." Ben answered as he walked back. There was a slight limp in his right leg.

Mitch and Cameron let out a triumphant cheer.

"You right mate?" Jove asked while handing Ben his shoes.

"Yeah I'll be fine. Looks like it's up to you to show her who's boss." Ben winked and hobbled off to join the rest of Jove's 'cheering squad'.

"Ok." Mr Londs caught everyone's attention after making further adjustments to the bar. "With just the two of you remaining, how about we change things up a bit? From now on, you just get the one attempt at each height. Let's see if we can finish this before the rain starts. Jove, you first."

Jove tried his best to shut out all distractions, including the overly loud cheering coming from his friends. He started running towards the bar at an even pace but suddenly got distracted as he felt Tia's gaze upon him. The same tingling feeling surged through his body just as he reached the bar and jumped. Surprised at how easy it was, he found himself on the mat with the bar still placed untouched on its stands. He had cleared it with plenty of room to spare.

The rest of the class let out a huge applause, impressed by the jump. Jove looked over at Tia, who was also applauding, but at the same time her face appeared deeply intrigued. Jove smiled at her smugly and strode back to his place, a small and familiar group *woot*-ed again as he passed.

Everyone fell silent and all eyes fell on Tia as she crouched low before setting off in long strides for her jump. She pushed off the ground with a bit more effort than usual and soared over the bar with enough grace to leave those watching to drop their jaws with amazement. Even Cameron and Mitch, who up until this point were only barracking for Jove, applauded her skill. Jove, on the other hand, stared at her intently.

Something wasn't adding up with the way she jumped. He couldn't quite put his finger on it. Tia turned to face him with a competitive stare.

Mr Londs raised the bar another few centimetres, clearly excited at the progress of his new star pupils. The rest of the class were growing more enthusiastic and competitive. The jump-off had now turned into a battle-of-the-sexes. The atmosphere even seemed to attract some local passers-by as they started to gather at the fence to look over the competition.

Being the only two left in the running, Jove approached Mr Londs and asked if he could swap sides to see if he might do better jumping from a different spot.

This was partly true; he thought that if so many people had initially jumped from Tia's side, it might work better for him as well. Also, he wanted to wish Tia good luck in her remaining jumps. It seemed like the responsible thing to do in the name of good sportsmanship. He heard Cameron give a taunting wolf whistle. Thankfully, it seemed that Tia did not hear it.

"Looks like you've got a bit of a fan club going over there." Jove said to her, trying to think of something witty. She looked back at him with an amused expression.

"Jove, your turn." Mr Londs interrupted and a loud cheer erupted from Jove's own squad.

"You too." Tia commented as Jove crouched down for his jump. He was partly trying to hide the fact that he was blushing.

As usual, he crouched down before setting off at a steady pace and speeding up as he got closer. He jumped and brought his legs up to clear the bar. The new height felt like it took its toll on Jove as his leg brushed against the bar, but it stayed put nonetheless.

He smirked daringly back at Tia but this time she didn't applaud. Instead she just stood there and eyed him as if she saw something that was helping him cheat. Jove interpreted it as a gesture of jealousy.

"What are you looking so worried for?" He tried to brighten her expression. "I know you're going to beat that."

She simply nodded to acknowledge him and started running toward the bar. Whether or not it was a change in his point-of-view, Jove noticed that she was running differently; slower it seemed. He saw her kick up an unusually large cloud of dust with her foot as she jumped. She soared over the bar and, after thinking how much better of a viewpoint it was, Jove noticed that she cleared the bar just as easily as he had been earlier.

She gracefully walked off the mat and Jove heard most of the girls scream with delight as she made her way back towards him.

"Beat that."

Mr Londs scribbled furiously on his clipboard. Excitement was splashed across his face as he went to adjust the bar. "This next jump will beat the school record. If either of you make this you'll be in our history books."

It took a few more moments before Jove was ready to take off for the jump. He felt Tia's eyes on the back of his head and was determined to beat her. He tried to focus all his energy into his leg muscles.

Okay, think light. You're a feather floating on the wind, yeah, he thought.

Setting off at a comfortable pace, Jove sped up as he came closer to the bar. He jumped and twisted his body, bringing his legs up as high as he could. Time seemed to slow down as he manoeuvred over.

He had cleared it. A roaring cheer came from his fan club. Even the girls seemed to be amazed by the jump. Tia wasn't the only one that was impressed at that moment.

"Congratulations Mr Boyd," Mr Londs came over and gave him a pat on the back, "you've just broken the school record! Tia, let's see if you can do it too."

"No pressure!" Cameron yelled at Tia across the field.

As Jove walked back toward Tia, he could see her glancing from the bar, to him and, for some reason, the crowd at the fence and the surrounding houses behind them. She had a strange look on her

37

face that eluded to something preoccupying her thoughts.

"Looks like it all comes down to this." She commented as Jove reached her. The expression on her face had changed. She seemed concerned all of a sudden.

Everyone held their breath as Tia went for her attempt at the jump.

She set off in her normal slow jog and sped up as she came closer to the bar before jumping in her usual technique. But Jove noticed something was different again, she didn't push off the ground as hard as she had been before. Her body twisted into a frosby-flop as she glided through the air.

Just as everyone thought she had made it, her foot brushed against the metal. She landed on the mats with a little less grace than usual and glanced back up at the trembling bar. It seemed like it quivered for an eternity.

Tia moved her hand in a strange motion and finally, to everyone's horror, it fell to the ground.

The roar from the boys was almost deafening, but none more so than Cameron, Mitch and Ben. The impossible had just come true; Jove Boyd had defeated Tia Favon in a sporting competition.

Jove had a moment of disbelief; *I thought she would have easily cleared that?*

He watched her glance at the bar in front of her and again toward the audience gathered at the edge of the school grounds. Her mind seemed to be wandering. Jove tried to follow her gaze, seeing a brief flash of black beyond the fence before returning his attention to her.

Maybe I've embarrassed her, he thought. He walked over to the mat to help her up. Tia snapped back to reality and suddenly her misty eyes were gleaming back at him.

"Congratulations." She said while shaking his hand, "Looks like you're not *just barely* passing."

She gave him a final grin and turned to walk toward her group of girls, who seemed a little distraught by the turn of events.

Jove stood there for a while wishing he could have thought of something more intelligent to say before his mates came running up behind him. They, unlike the girls, were rejoicing and running around in circles as if they had just won the lottery.

"Good on ya mate! Who'd of thought?" Cameron said giving him another slap on the back, "You, a high jump champion!?"

The euphoria had died down a bit by the time they headed back toward the change rooms. They made it to shelter just as the first wave of rain started to sprinkle across the oval.

To Jove's surprise, Cameron was over ecstatic while Mitch seemed a bit reluctant all of a sudden. But Jove finally understood as he saw Mitch pull a ten dollar note out of his pocket and handed it to Cameron.

"Oh, real mature guys." He said with a smirk as Cameron snatched the money from Mitch's hand, "Hey, I did all the work. You gonna split that?"

The Storm

In the short time it took for them to change and get ready to head home, word of Jove's victory spread throughout the school. As was the daily routine, Jove's group met at the front gate before parting ways. Today, however, everyone crowded under the roof as the rain changed from a light sprinkle to a heavy downpour.

Jove ran up to his friends and saw that Cameron was already giving the rest of the group a recount of what had happened. He was even trying to imitate Jove's unusual jumping style.

"Here's the hero of the hour!" He yelled as he noticed Jove. "I've organised a little get together at mine this arvo to celebrate your win if you're interested."

"Any excuse for a party at your place." Jove replied with a raised eyebrow.

"I just sent Dad a text. He's comin' round with the four-wheel drive so he can pick everyone up. No point walking there in the wet."

"Alright, count me in. I'll just let Mum know." Jove answered and pulled out his phone to send a message. She would be fine with it. Going out after school for a couple of hours was a regular thing, so long as it didn't interfere with his studies.

Mitch and Ben also agreed to go while the rest of their group raced to their rides as they pulled up on the curb.

Soon enough, Cameron's dad pulled up in the four-wheel drive. By the time everyone had made the quick dash from under the eaves to the car, Mr Taylor had already put up his sons learner plates and was in the passenger side of the car.

"G'day mate." He said as Cameron climbed into the driver's seat and everyone else piled in. Water dripped from their hair and uniforms. As usual, Jove was wetter than the others as the water clung to his skin. He tried to dry as much off with his shirt as he could so nobody would notice.

"Hi all. Make sure you buckle up, this kid is a maniac on the road." Mr Taylor turned around with a smirk that strongly resembled Cameron's on his face.

"Gee, thanks Dad." Cameron jeered as he started the car and put it in gear, "That's all the support I need right there."

"Nah, you'll be right. I put on those all-terrain tyres last week so you shouldn't spin-out. Your mother wouldn't let you drive otherwise." he added on a serious note. "Oh and watch the gears. In this weather they're as stiff as a teenager on viag…"

"Yeah I know Dad I've driven this thing before." Cameron interjected.

The rest of the car snickered as Cameron indicated to leave the curb. Jove peered out the window and watched the other student's race to their cars trying to stay as dry as possible.

His attention was quickly drawn to a short, stubby man dressed in a black trench coat walking on the opposite side of the road. Jove couldn't make out any of his features. He appeared to be searching the school for someone. Jove felt a shiver run down his spine as the man seemed to turn eyes on the four-wheel drive. The figure was slightly familiar, but Jove couldn't remember where he knew him from.

"I'd hate to be their kid and have my parents out in public in that kind of get-up." Mitch chuckled as he caught sight of the same man.

The car lurched as Cameron found a gap in the traffic and pulled out, scaring another unsuspecting learner.

"It's okay mate, you had right of way." Mr Taylor instructed.

Mitchell and Jove glanced one last time at the stranger before losing sight of him in the rain.

"Boy, don't envy everyone who has to walk home today." Ben said from the other side of the car. The rain was streaming down the windows making tiny gushing rivers on the glass.

"You said it." Jove replied still trying to dry himself off.

A few minutes later, they pulled into Cameron's driveway.

"You all alive back there?" Mr Taylor joked.

"Hey, I didn't do too badly this trip, especially considering it's raining." Cameron retorted while taking down his learner plates.

"You kidding? My life flashed before my eyes!" Mitch joked.

Everyone laughed as they piled out of the car and ran for shelter.

"Ok, shoes and socks off before going in the house boys, or the missus will be onto you like flies on a pile of ..."

"We get it Dad." Cameron kicked off his shoes alongside everyone else's before leading them into the lock-up garage. It had been rebuilt as a games room for visitors. Cameron often had people over to enjoy it as his Dad had put in a movie projector and a pool table.

"So have you guys decided what you're gonna do once we've graduated?" Mitch asked a couple of hours later as they played a game of doubles.

"Well, I've applied for the armed forces next year." Cameron replied while inspecting the table, deciding what kind of shot to take. "I go for my tests just before Christmas and find out if I'm in or not in the New Year. Guess we'll see how that goes."

"What about you?" Mitch turned to Jove now, who had been leaning on his cue watching the table.

"I still dunno yet." he answered with a shrug, "I'm going to see the careers advisor next week. I'm thinkin' of doing somethin' at uni though, for sure."

43

"I reckon you should go into politics or law or somethin'." Cameron said as he finally leaned over the table to take a shot.

"Why's that?" Jove asked.

Cameron finished his turn, narrowly missing a corner pocket before answering. "Well, you've always been very opinionated. You make a point if something's wrong or unfair but keep your yap shut when something's ok, even if you don't agree with it."

"Yeah, you need to work on your lying though." Mitch added as Jove prepared to take his turn, "They'll never let you into politics otherwise."

"Yeah, but I don't like the idea of being behind a desk for the rest of my life." He leaned over the cue and lined up the shot, "I wanna be out in the world doin' good and stuff, you know?"

"Well, you could always do the celeb thing and do missionary work in some third world country." Cameron shrugged as Jove took a moment to snicker. He took aim and struck the white ball, skilfully ricocheting a coloured ball into the next pocket.

"Fluke." Mitch commented with a grimace.

"You're just jealous you don't have my skills." Jove stood up grinning and moved to the other side of the table, leaning over it again. "Nah, I don't think I wanna go that far." he said taking another shot. "Leave that to genuinely nice people… and celebrities. Like you Ben, I reckon you'll be some kind of famous athlete or somethin'."

"Not likely after being shown up by you today." Ben answered jokingly.

The shot missed and Mitch made another comment about Jove's so-called *skills* before taking his turn.

"Well, we'll have to wait and see what this advisor reckons then." Cameron said coming to stand beside Jove.

"That's the idea." Jove replied, "And hopefully it'll be somethin' I enjoy too."

They kept playing pool for a few hours until Ben mentioned he had to leave early for some kind of training. As it got late, Mitch offered Jove a lift home.

"Nah that's ok. I'm only three blocks over and it's out of your way. Besides I could probably use a rain shower after today." He joked.

The rain had become significantly worse and turned into a storm by the time Mitch's parents came to pick him up. Lightning cracked every so often and thunder rumbled quickly afterward, telling them the worst of it was nearly upon them.

"You sure you'll be right getting home by yourself?" Mitch asked again.

"Yeah I'm fine, really. It's only a few minutes' walk." Jove replied as he grabbed his bag and shoes.

"Ok, well see ya tomorrow then." Mitch waved before getting in the car and disappearing into the deluge.

"You know, it's getting pretty heavy. You're welcome to stay until it lets up a bit." Cameron offered as thunder cracked in the distance.

"Nah Mum's got a roast on tonight and I'm pretty keen for it. What's a bit of water in the streets?" Jove replied. Water was already starting to cling to his skin and he didn't want Cameron to notice.

"Ha, so sports star *and* invincible, eh?" Cameron joked, "Well I'll see you tomorrow then. Be sure to bring some of that roast for lunch."

"Scungy bastard." Jove waved as he jogged down the driveway and into the rain. He pulled his backpack over his head for protection.

Good thing this bag's waterproof, he thought as he felt his textbooks press against his skull. A couple of strides brought him to the edge of the driveway and he turned onto the footpath towards his house. He was careful not to run too fast along the rain-slicked concrete as small puddles and rivers formed along the walkway.

A stitch started to form in Jove's chest as he rounded the first corner. He slowed down a bit and figured there was no real need to hurry. The water had already seeped into his skin leaving him completely drenched.

I should probably get this checked out, Jove thought as he inspected the flecks of water gathering on the back of his hand. Some of them even seemed to have frozen into flakes of ice. Although he was used to this uncanny 'defect', it seemed to be getting worse lately. He could even see the raindrops curving in towards him as if he was a magnet.

He shrugged it off and continued around another corner. A sudden flash of lightning illuminated the sky and seemed to strike somewhere behind him. Reacting instinctively, Jove spun around to see how far away it had struck.

Instead, his eyes fell upon a strange, dark silhouette that quickly retreated around the corner he had just rounded. He didn't get a good enough look to see what it was but figured it was just a dog wandering around, scared by the storm. Jove turned again and started walking towards his house as the thunder from the lightning reached his ears.

He had only taken a few more steps along the path before he heard another sound that made him whirl around. The silhouette had stepped in a puddle and seemed to be surprised by the fact it made a noise. It was obviously trying to remain unseen and Jove could only get another quick glance at it before it darted out of sight.

He stood there for a while staring through the rain hoping it would come out again. When he figured it was not going to willingly show itself, Jove slowly turned around and started to make his way across the road. He turned the corner and hid under the shelter of a bus stop behind a nearby fence to see if the creature would follow him.

Making sure that he was hidden from view, Jove peered around the fence and watched for the figure. After a while, he saw its head appear from behind a parked car before completely emerging from its hiding spot. It wasn't an animal, as Jove saw, but his eyes widened with horror and the hair on the back of his neck stood on end as he recognised the person.

The short, stubby man from the front of the school was swiftly making his way over the road. His black trench coat flapped about in the wind as he clutched it around his body, covering his face. He didn't notice Jove watching him.

For a moment Jove thought of confronting him but another flash of lightning lit the street and he realised where else he had seen the man.

"Suspicious characters in black streetwear... Potentially armed and dangerous." The morning newsreader's voice echoed in his head.

Fear surged through Jove as he watched the man come closer. Realising that he would be seen when the figure turned the corner, Jove set off in a sprint down the footpath. He hoped to get as much distance between him and the stranger as possible. As he ran, he noticed that he was making more noise as his feet hit the pavement and sloshed in the puddles. He figured the stranger would have realised that he had been discovered and that Jove was now trying to evade him.

This assumption was confirmed as Jove turned his head about thirty metres away from the bus shelter and saw the black figure turn the corner, also in a sprint. Despite his stout stature, the man was moving fast, keeping at an even distance behind Jove.

In an attempt to lose him, Jove darted across the road and ran down a nearby alleyway that connected with another street. It was a detour in getting back to his house, but Jove figured that it would not be a good idea for this guy to find out where he lived.

He could feel a giant bruise forming along his back as his bag thumped against it with every stride. The stitch tightened in his chest but Jove still ran as fast as he could. He was halfway down the alley and turned his head again just in time to see the figure run in behind him.

What the hell does this guy want!? Jove thought in panic as he remembered the man standing out the front of the school.

Is he searching for someone to mug? Is he a serial killer? Jove dismissed all these thoughts and that he just had to focus on losing the man.

Jove reached the end of the alleyway and darted to the right. He hoped that somehow, the rain might have blurred the man's vision. He ran another few metres before diving behind one of the parked cars in the street.

Crouching low to the ground, Jove felt the gushing water from the gutter run up his legs and seep into his shoes. Putting his head down close to the ground and shielding his eyes from the rain, Jove watched the alleyway opening through the underside of the car.

A few moments later, the stranger burst onto the street. Jove held his breath and watched in silence as the man stopped and looked around desperately to see where his target had gone.

Taking a moment to think, Jove slowly reached into his pocket and pulled out his phone to call the police. He took his eyes off the man for a second to check his phone so he could dial the number. His heart sank, however, as he saw a splotched water mark on the screen. It was waterlogged.

Jove swore under his breath as he returned it to his pocket and turned his attention back to the man. He paced along the street as he became more aggravated.

An eternity passed as the icy rain lashed Jove's body. Although his heart was racing, he was careful not to move or make a sound in case it attracted any attention.

Every few seconds, a bolt of lightning would strike around them, illuminating the street and refracting off skin the man hadn't covered. Dark red flecks of light scattered across the wet bitumen with every flash. As odd as Jove thought this was, he remained fixated on the characters movements rather than his strange appearance.

The figure turned suddenly in the opposite direction as he decided to cross the road. Jove kept his eyes on him and edged around the side of the car, balancing his bag on his back as he did so. He cringed every time his hands and feet made a sound through the water, but the man didn't seem to notice the extra noise over the pouring rain.

Manoeuvring himself away from the gutter, Jove pushed himself up and saw the stranger's top half through the car windows. He was looking up and down the street and getting increasingly frustrated, forcing Jove to stay in his hiding spot. Jove knew he would have to attempt an escape any moment now.

Keeping his eyes on the stout figure, he waited for the perfect moment to run for it. That moment came as the figure heard a noise from the other side of the street. In an instant, Jove hitched his bag, twisted his body and made a break for the corner.

THUD…SPLASH… He was barely a few metres away from the car when his feet slipped from underneath him. His hands and face landed hard on the wet concrete and he grazed his front as he pushed himself back up out of the water.

What the…!? Jove swore as he tried to figure out what brought him down. He glanced back at the gushing river of water coming from the curb. A blocked storm drain in the gutter was causing the water to back up and form a gigantic puddle on the footpath.

Jove swore again and struggled to find his footing. He could feel his face and hands sting from the combination of gravel, water and blood that now covered the entire front of his body. All the commotion caught the attention of the man who realised what had happened and started running menacingly toward Jove.

Finally, Jove managed to stabilise himself and with a sudden burst of energy, launched himself out of the puddle. As he did so, an unusually cold chill ran up his legs and through his hands. He ignored it as he saw the stranger advance upon him, pulling something out of his coat pocket.

Not wanting to find out what it was, Jove went to sprint toward the corner. But something quickly stopped him. The ground became extra slippery underneath and he heard a sickening crack followed by a *thud* come from behind him. The distraction caused him to fall to the ground once again. Thinking it was all over, Jove closed his eyes and waited for impact, but it didn't come.

Still panicking, he turned around to see what had happened to his attacker. There in front of him, where he had been only moments before, lay the stout stranger sprawled unconscious on the footpath. However, the puddle that Jove had fallen in had frozen into a solid sheet of ice.

The man lay unconscious on the cold surface while blood trickled from under his dark trench coat. His feet were encased in the solid puddle, causing him to fall forward and knock himself out.

Keeping his distance, Jove stared at the strange image. He noticed a knife poking out of the sleeve of the man's coat. The blade was singeing the fabric and steamed in the rain as if it was burning hot.

What the hell just happened!? Jove sat in shock, his body rooted to the spot.

The man's body suddenly started to stir but Jove was unable to move. He saw a pair of squinty yellow eyes flicker underneath the black cloth hiding the man's elongated face. Of the patches of skin that were uncovered, Jove saw that they were deep red in colour and reflected the light from the lightning.

What a weird mask, he concluded after inspecting it from a safe distance. It looked like the face of a large, grotesque lizard. He burned the image in his mind so he could give an accurate description to the police later.

Without warning, the man gave a loud groan and started thrashing about. He shrieked with pain as his ankle gave a sickening *crack*. The sudden movement triggered something in Jove's brain and he gained control over his limbs again. The man shot him an angry and frustrated look and threw himself about in an attempt to break free of the ice. He continued to yelp with pain.

A strange heat started to fill the atmosphere and Jove could almost swear he saw steam emanate from the man as his anger increased.

Taking the chance to get away from the strange man, Jove took one last look at his attacker before turning away. Ignoring the stitch in his chest, he sprinted to the corner and rounded it toward home. An angry yell sounded in the distance as he disappeared from sight.

Jove didn't slow down again until he turned into his own street. An eerie chill surged through his body and he shivered uncontrollably. He moved his bag into a more comfortable spot and winced as it brushed against the bruise swelling on his back. He glanced at his arm and noticed, among the blood and gravel rash, that large shards of ice had formed on his skin. Curious, he gently rubbed at them, wondering if there was any connection between them and the frozen puddle.

By the time he had warmed his hands and rubbed most of the ice off of his arms, Jove had reached his driveway. He looked up and saw that the kitchen light was on through the window. Peering behind him to make sure he wasn't being watched or followed, Jove made his way up to the front door.

The warmth of the house welcomed him as he heard his mother talking on the phone in the kitchen. She sounded deeply engrossed in conversation.

Jove silently kicked off his drenched shoes and placed them outside before shutting the door. The sound was enough to attract his mother's attention.

"Hi Darl, be with you in a minute!" She called.

As Jove passed the kitchen he noticed her back was turned with the phone to her ear. In her hand she skilfully twirled the blade of a large steak knife through her fingers as she usually did when she was deep in thought or anxious.

Jove trudged to his room, dumping his bag on the floor and shutting the door. He searched desperately for a dry towel so he could clean off the blood and gravel before his mother walked in. She had enough to worry about with all the bills without this on her mind as well.

Just as Jove started scraping the excess gravel from his skin, he heard her hang up the phone and walk toward his room.

"… Just got off the phone with Mr Favon, Tia's father, and he was telling me of how you won the…" She paused as she opened the door and her eyes widened with horror when she saw him.

"Are you alright!? You're bleeding! What happened!?"

Jove sighed as he realised he couldn't hide what had happened from her.

"I think I nearly got mugged Mum."

The Favons

The next couple of hours involved Jove giving a recount of what had happened to two policemen while his mother tended to his wounds. He winced in pain a few times as she sterilised his cuts and grazes with strong antiseptic.

As Jove spoke, the policemen gave him strange looks and raised their eyebrows as they took notes.

"It definitely sounds like one of these gang members." One of the officers stated once Jove finished. "Although, it is quite an unusual story. We will require a full statement. Ms Boyd…"

"Sandra." Jove's mother replied politely. Her eyes remained fixed on her son even after she finished bandaging him up.

"Sandra." The officer repeated, "Would you allow us to accompany your son to the station?"

"Don't you have enough information?" Sandra hesitated. "Can't you just go off what you've got?"

"Well it is an unusual turn of events. We want to make sure we record the whole incident accurately."

Sandra seemed very reluctant but relented.

"Is that okay with you?" She gently asked her son.

Jove looked from the officers to his mother and back before nodding slowly.

Once Sandra was satisfied with Jove's condition, they were accompanied to the police station. Upon arrival, Jove was immediately seated in an office where a senior officer was waiting for him.

"I'll just be in the next room if you need me." Sandra put a comforting hand on her son's shoulder before leaving him with the policeman. Once the officer was satisfied they were alone and ready, they started. This time Jove was asked to repeat everything in more detail.

When it came time for Jove to explain how he had escaped, he paused for a moment. No matter which way he looked at it, a puddle that suddenly froze and immobilized his attacker seemed stupid and unlikely.

"The water froze around his feet?" The officer looked at him curiously. Jove nodded.

"Are you sure?" He pressed again.

"I know it sounds weird and I don't know how it happened but that's definitely what I saw."

"Did you see anything else around that would explain how this could have happened?" The officer said sternly.

"No. Is something like that even possible?" Jove asked hoping for a satisfying answer.

"I'm sure there's a reasonable explanation." The officer shrugged and continued, "So this is how you managed to escape?"

"Yes," Jove nodded in reply, "the fall knocked him unconscious, I got a good look at him and I left as soon as he started to wake up."

"Alright, from what you saw, what did he look like?" The officer pulled out another sheet of paper and waited for Jove to answer.

Again, Jove found it difficult to give an accurate description. All he could remember was the dark red reptile mask burned into his mind.

"So all you could see of him was that he is about five feet tall, medium to large build and yellowish eyes?"

Pausing to take it all in and realising just how ridiculous it sounded, Jove nodded. "Yeah, that's what I remember."

"Any other distinguishing features?" The policeman asked again in an authoritative tone.

"Well, if it helps, his skin must have been badly sunburnt."

"How so?"

"Some parts of him seemed to glisten and were bright red. Like a recent burn maybe?"

"I'll make note of it." The officer answered and scribbled it down. Jove could sense a hint of scepticism in his tone.

"As I said before," he tried to assert himself, "he was mostly covered underneath a black trench coat, a hat and that mask over his face."

As he finished Jove heard the door swing open and turned to see his mother walk into the room with another officer in tow. Jove couldn't help his relief at seeing her, despite the stern expression on her face.

"I think my son has had quite enough." She addressed the senior officer. "If you don't mind I will take him home now so he can rest."

The officer closed his notebook and put down his pen. "Very well, I am sure we have everything we need. Thank you for your co-operation."

Without a second glance the officer dismissed them in such a way that Jove felt foolish. Walking out of the office, Jove noticed a clock on the wall showing it was nearly midnight. They walked out into the car park where the rain had temporarily subsided.

"You ok, Darl?" His mother asked in a soothing voice, her eyes riddled with worry.

"Yeah, I'll be right." Jove replied as they reached the car. Pain and exhaustion surged through his body as he sat in the passenger seat. It subsided into a dull ache as he settled into its warmth.

"You're having the day off tomorrow." Sandra said as she sat in the driver's seat and inspected the grazing on his arm. "You're going to be very sore in the morning and you'll need time to let everything sink in so you can recover properly."

"Ok." Jove nodded in reply. A short pause fell between them as she started the car and drove away from the station.

"Hey Mum, you believe me don't you?"

She turned and her brow softened.

"Of course I do. Every word of it."

Jove was not convinced, he could tell that something else was bothering her. If he had more energy and his story was more believable, he would have pressed the issue. However he decided to ignore it and lay back in his seat, almost drifting off to sleep as they drove home.

It was nearly noon the next day when Jove awoke to the sound of rain drizzling on the roof. Pain still throbbed throughout his body as he tried to get up. He let out a strained groan as he remembered what had happened the night before. Giving up on his attempt to get out of bed, he rolled into a more comfortable position.

"Hey, how are you feeling?" his Mum quietly walked in holding a wet cloth and some breakfast. She placed the food on his desk and sat on the edge of the bed.

"Sore." Jove replied with a groan as she put the cloth on his arm. The warm water seeped into his grazes and stung for a bit before giving him some relief. He cringed every time his mother moved the cloth and disturbed his skin.

"Well, I've rung the school and told them what happened and that you're not going in today."

Jove simply grunted in reply.

His mother made him sit up and moved his bacon and eggs onto the bed. She opened her mouth to say something but struggled to speak.

"You're special darl," she put her hand on his cheek, "and you are so important to me."

Jove looked back at her after stuffing some bacon into his mouth. "What brought that on?"

"Well I guess after last night I realised that I don't tell you that enough." Her eyes started to glisten. "And you're all I have."

Before Jove could say anything in reply his mother stood and composed herself.

"If there's anything else you need just give me a yell." She said softly before leaving the room.

Jove replied by giving her a 'thumbs up' before digging into the rest of his breakfast. He was surprised by his sudden appetite, but exhaustion quickly set in as his skin started to tingle. His mind, however, was still ticking as he tried to remember the previous day's events.

Images of the incident flashed across his mind and he wondered how and why any of it would have happened. Eventually, his head and body started to ache and he dozed off again. The images still played around in his mind and distant voices spoke about him as he slept.

A few hours passed leading into mid-afternoon before Jove felt he was well enough to get up. After enduring a bit of pain, he got to his feet and walked out of his room toward the lounge.

As he trudged down the hallway, he overheard his mother talking to someone at the front door. He stopped, hiding behind the wall to eavesdrop.

"…Well thanks for coming around. I appreciate it."

"Thanks for seeing me." Jove heard a gruff voice reply, "I'm glad to hear he's alright. And you too."

There was an awkward silence at the door and Jove tried to peer around the corner to get a look at the visitor.

"Well I better get going. Tia will be wondering where I am."

Jove could feel the blood drain from his face as soon as he heard the name 'Tia'.

The man continued. "I'll be in touch again soon."

There was another silence before Sandra answered. "Ok."

Jove heard the man's footsteps disappear down the driveway and his mother close the door behind him. Hearing her walk into the lounge, Jove discreetly tried to backtrack to his room out of view. He waited until he thought the coast was clear and walked back down the hall as if he had just woken up.

"Ah, someone's looking a lot better." His mother said unusually cheerfully when she caught sight of him. The lines on her face, however, made her appear weary.

"Yeah, I think the bruising is starting to go down a bit." Jove said pointing out the black and blue blotches on his arms. They were considerably smaller than before. His cuts and grazes also looked as though they were healing faster than usual.

"Really?" His Mum leaned over to have a look for herself, "That was quick. I guess the rest and warm water is working well then."

"Mmm." Jove grunted in agreement. He took up his usual spot on the couch and turned on the television. Curiosity quickly got the better of him.

"So who was that you were talking to at the door before?"

Sandra's face went slightly pale. "That was Auster Favon. Tia's father."

"How do *you* know Tia and her father?" Jove couldn't help himself.

"Oh, well, Auster came through the hospital one day. Broken arm or something." She explained slowly, "We got to talking and found that we had a lot in common. We each had a child the same age and happened to go to the same school. You'd be surprised the kind of people you get acquainted with just by being a parent."

"Ok." Jove replied, satisfied with this answer, "So what did he come by here for?"

Sandra stuttered guiltily for a moment, "Well I figured that you probably didn't want anyone else to find out what happened yet. But Tia went home during lunch today and told her father that she was worried you weren't at school."

"Really?" Jove said with a tone that made his mother raise an eyebrow.

"Yes," she replied, "and Auster grew concerned as well. The police put out a statement on this morning's news explaining the attack on an unnamed teenager. When you weren't at school today I guess he put two and two together."

"Oh."

"You know what else he told me?" Sandra sat back with a look of amusement. "Someone beat his daughter in a high jump competition yesterday."

"Oh yeah." Jove couldn't help but smile.

After a couple more hours of watching television and Jove telling his mother about Tia and the high jump contest, they decided it was time for an early dinner and bed. The cuts and bruises on Jove's body had gone down even further and he was sure he would be well enough to go back to school the next morning.

Once his alarm was set for the next day, Jove lay down on his bed and, for the third time in the last twenty-four hours, dozed off within moments of his head hitting the pillow.

The next morning, Jove's alarm went off and his morning ritual was back to normal. He decided to skip morning karate for the day, just to be on the safe side. After enduring a few more aches and pains he rolled out of bed and headed for the shower.

Like the day before, Jove felt his skin tingling under the warm water. Curious, he crawled out of the shower and inspected his bruises and grazes in the mirror. They had almost completely disappeared! Other than the big mark on his back and the occasional scrape on his arms and legs there was barely anything at all.

Satisfied with this progress, Jove dressed and continued getting ready for school. His skin was still burning and itching but he figured it was because of the remaining grazes.

His mother had already left for work a few hours earlier. She had left a note on the kitchen bench reading 'Hope you're feeling better'. After fixing himself some breakfast, Jove sat in the lounge and turned on the television.

The stories were not anything out of the ordinary, but Jove nearly dropped his bowl of cereal when he saw the headlines blaring about a 'nameless' seventeen-year-old being attacked by one of the local gang members.

He felt foolish as he once again realised what a peculiar description he had given. The headline ended with the reader informing everyone to keep a lookout and that the authorities were trying to apprehend the attacker.

Eventually, Jove decided that he should head to school. He waited on the corner where he usually met up with Cameron. A few minutes passed before he came running up from the next street.

"Mornin'." he said in a cheerful mood, "What happened to you yesterday?"

Jove figured there was no point in hiding what had happened from his mates. "You mean what happened on Tuesday afternoon." He corrected him and started to explain what had happened.

During the recount, Cameron's expression switched between curiosity and concern. Jove made sure he was a little vague on how he got away. It still did not make sense, especially to him.

"So that news story this morning," Cameron said when Jove had finished, "that was you?"

"Yep," Jove replied, "but don't get too excited about it. It's not exactly something I want everyone to know about."

"You sure? You were on TV!" Cameron replied as they approached the school gates. "Well, sort of."

They were just about to walk in when they saw a strange, old model car pull up at the school. Faded yellow paint was peeling all over its body. It was a car neither Cameron nor Jove had seen before. Jove felt a knot form in his stomach when he saw who was inside it.

In the passenger seat was Tia. She was in a deep and serious conversation with the man behind the wheel. He seemed to be giving Tia a lecture of some sort. Jove and Cameron slowed their pace, nosing in on the scene.

The atmosphere changed, however, when Tia suddenly caught sight of Jove and instantly brightened, waving at him. Jove's stomach gave another lurch and he caught Cameron giving him a suspicious look.

The man in the driver's seat also turned his attention toward Jove and his eyes briefly fixed on him. Tia's father was a fit, middle-aged man with dark hair that had streaks of grey running through it. Unlike Tia, his eyes were dark and his pupils were the normal jet black.

Auster Favon exchanged curious glances with Jove for an awkward moment before farewelling his daughter.

"Is there something going on that I don't know about?" Cameron queried.

"Apparently." Jove answered as Tia climbed out of the car, "I know about as much as you."

They were both surprised to see that instead of walking towards her friends, Tia headed towards Jove and Cameron with a cheery expression on her face.

"Morning." She greeted them as if this was normal.

"Umm…hi?" Jove and Cameron awkwardly replied.

An uncomfortable moment passed where the three of them stood at the front gate before Tia finally broke the silence.

"I heard about what happened on Tuesday, are you alright?" She questioned Jove in a soft tone as they walked into the school grounds.

"Yeah, I'm fine. It could've been worse."

"I saw the news report this morning." She interrogated him further. "Are you sure that was a good description of the attacker?"

Jove paused for moment, "Yeah. Sounds stupid, I know, but that's all that I saw of him."

"Right." Tia gave him a stern look. She was either unsatisfied or discomforted by his answer, Jove couldn't tell.

"Yeah, there are some freaky people out there." Cameron made an attempt to be involved in the conversation.

"I couldn't agree more."

Something about Tia's tone made Jove give her a funny look.

The three of them made their way to where Jove and Cameron usually met with their mates. Everyone turned around and seemed taken aback by the fact that Tia was with them. They were equally eager to hear why Jove had been absent and quickly converged upon him.

"Is everyone else here allowed to know what happened?" Cameron whispered in Jove's ear.

"Hey Jove ol' buddy, you alright?" They were interrupted as Mitch and Ben ran up behind them. "We saw the news this morning and figured it was you."

"Sounds like they already do." Jove answered bluntly.

Jove allowed Cameron to recount the story of his attack. Everyone, including Tia, gathered around and listened intently, glancing at Jove with concern as Cameron confirmed some of the details. All the while he could sense Tia observing him, her pearlescent pupils swirling with concern.

The bell rang just as Cameron finished his version of the story. Everyone gave Jove their sympathies before they split up and left for their home rooms. Eventually it was just him, Mitch and Tia walking towards their block and respective home rooms.

"Well it's good to know you came out of it alright mate." Mitch commented from Jove's right side.

Jove felt Mitch's hand give him a hard slap on the back and flinched as he waited for the pain from the bruise, but it never came.

"You right there?" Mitch stopped and eyed him.

"Yeah." Jove replied puzzled. He moved his hand behind his back to feel for the bruise, but it was gone. His skin was back to normal.

"What's wrong?" Mitch asked as he saw Jove's expression. Tia stopped as well and gave him another worried look.

"There used to be a bruise on my back there. It was about the size of a cricket ball when I had a shower this morning." Jove answered. "Must've healed already."

"What!?" Tia immediately stepped behind Jove and lifted the back of his shirt. Mitch took a step back, his eyes popping at the strange picture. Jove gave him a similar look as he stood there, feeling vulnerable while Tia inspected his bare back. His face flushed bright red.

"You sure?" she asked as she put his shirt down again.

"Yeah, it's been healing really quickly actually, used to be huge."

"Well woddya know? Our Jove's a miracle child!" Mitch exclaimed, giving him another slap on the back.

They took another few steps toward their building before Tia broke away and headed toward her home room up the stairwell.

"See you in Physics!" She waved back at them.

"Sure." Jove waved back and both he and Mitch walked through the doorway to their home room.

"Does someone wanna tell me why she's hangin' 'round us all of a sudden?" Mitch asked as they sat down in their usual spots.

"I have no idea." Jove shrugged back at him, "I'm not complaining though."

"I bet you're not!"

For once Jove was looking forward to going to Physics for first period. Usually he sat up the back of the class so that he had less chance of drawing the teacher's attention and also so he could watch Tia from behind without her noticing. She had always seemed to breeze through the classwork as if she already knew most of the subject matter.

Hey!" She greeted him enthusiastically outside the classroom. "Wanna sit together and swap notes? You normally sit up the back yeah?"

"Oh, yeh, sure." Jove stuttered. He didn't think that Tia even knew he was in the same class before today let alone where he sat.

Since it was nearing exam time for the seniors, the teacher had dedicated this particular session for the students to review what they had learnt over the semester. Jove felt a bit nervous opening his book of notes beside Tia's. It looked like she had scribbled something in every possible space on the page.

"And you're asking to swap notes with me?" Jove said dryly. He flicked through her book and came across a whole lot of information on stuff he didn't remember covering in class.

"Well I guess you're going to get more out of this than I am." Tia smiled.

"Where do you learn all this stuff?" He was reading over her work about magnetic and gravitational relationships. After flicking through a few more pages he also came across some notes on the characteristics of fire.

"A little bit here and there." she answered modestly, "I've always had an interest and Dad's mad about learning all this kind of thing as well."

"Liar." Jove smiled back. "You're a nerd, admit it." He came across another section in her notebook that showed some useful information about the elements of flight and air currents.

"You should become an aeronautical engineer or something. You'd earn heaps." Jove added admiring her work. He started copying the notes into his own book.

"Nah, I'm more interested in travelling overseas, doing good for all the people of the world."

They continued back and forth for the rest of the lesson, even drawing a few curious glances from their classmates when they made too much noise.

The lesson ended sooner than Jove would have liked but was excited to hear that Tia wanted to sit with his group for lunch. He was happy to oblige.

Mitch, Cameron and Ben's jaws nearly dropped when Jove approached their table accompanied by Tia. They still hadn't gotten over the shock of her sudden interest in them.

Midway through the lunchbreak, Tia's phone rang. Her face immediately darkened as she pulled it out of her pocket.

Jove curiously glanced at the screen and saw the word 'Dad' flash across it. Without a word, she got up from the table and walked out of the courtyard pressing her phone against her ear.

"Methinks someone's grown a little crush on ya mate." Ben nudged Jove in the ribs when Tia was out of earshot.

"Yeah maybe you should ask her what she's doing on the weekend or somethin'." Cameron added.

"Not with you lot hanging about." Jove replied defensively. "You're like social vultures."

"What do you expect? We've got nothing better to do with our lives than watch you struggle with your love life." Mitch said after taking a swig of soft drink and letting out a large belch. "Tell ya what, if you get the guts to ask her out before lunch is over, us boys'll pitch in for a movie date."

"Hmmm, tempting." Jove pondered sarcastically. He pretended to look into the distance as he considered the offer but something in the corner of his eye made the hairs on the back of his neck stand on end.

Through the trees looking over the courtyard, Jove thought he could see a familiar black cloak move beyond the grounds. A second glance assured him that it was merely a black tarp that had blown off one of the buildings damaged in the storm.

"You alright?" Cameron snapped his fingers and brought Jove's attention back.

"Yeah."

"You look like you've just seen a ghost."

"It's nothing. Guess I'm just nervous, that's all." He lied.

"Well keep your cool. She's coming back." Ben said softly as Tia approached them.

"Hey Jove what are you up to after school this arv?" She said as she sat at the table again.

"Er, nothing yet." Jove stuttered. "Why?"

"Would you like to come 'round to my house this afternoon?"

Cameron and Ben's eyes widened with shock and Mitch almost snorted soft drink out of his nose.

"Umm…yeah." Jove stuttered again. "Sure."

Tia's misty eyes started swirling with excitement and they all jumped as the bell sounded.

"Great! Meet me out the front of my home room after the final bell okay?" She winked before gathering her things and walking off to her next class. Jove and his friends simply sat there in shock.

"That was unexpected." Ben said as they got up.

"Yeah, I'll say." Jove added.

"Well at least you don't have to worry about asking her out now." Mitch chuckled. "You probably would've stuffed it up anyway."

"I wonder why you got her attention all of a sudden." Cameron added. "Has something else happened that I don't know about?"

"Not that I know of." Jove shrugged. "Maybe she's always had a crush on me and it wasn't until after the other night that she's decided to make a move."

"Sure." Mitch rolled his eyes, "'Cause who can resist *this* man of modesty."

Code Black

For the rest of the day Jove found it difficult to keep focus in class as he looked forward to his afternoon with Tia. The more he thought about it the more excited he became that maybe she liked him in return.

After a lifetime, the final bell sounded and Jove raced from the classroom for Tia's home room. He passed through the courtyard where students bustled around trying to leave for the day. Amongst the crowd, something caught his eye.

A flicker of black dashed beyond the gate. All colour drained from Jove's face as he whirled round, trying to find its source. His heart pounded in his throat as he scanned the scene for any sign of a hooded figure. He jumped as a crow flew past and perched on a power line above the gate.

I'm getting paranoid, he thought as his heart rate returned to normal.

Tia was already standing on the balcony outside her home room slinging her bag over her shoulder. Jove caught her eye from across the courtyard and waved. She gave him a small smile and returned the wave before her gaze fell upon something in the distance behind him.

A look of horror quickly replaced her smile and Jove could see her misty pupils contract.

In an instant, she disappeared from view heading towards the stairwell as the fire alarm rang. An announcement suddenly blared over the speakers.

"Attention students and staff. Code black. Code black. Man on grounds with a weapon. This is not a drill. Find cover immediately. Code black."

Immediately, the courtyard was filled with screams and everyone madly dashed for cover.

Not realising what was happening, Jove fought amongst the panic to make it out of the courtyard. Students pushed and shoved around him, almost knocking him over.

"Jove!" He heard a girl screech as she came sprinting down the stairwell. He spun around to see Tia running towards him at an incredible speed, but she wasn't focussed on him. Instead she was glaring at a man standing on the other side of the courtyard.

Following her eyes, Jove turned and saw the man dressed in his black trench coat and dark red reptile mask. Fear raced through him, constricting his muscles and rooting him to the spot. The stout man was walking towards him with a look of fury in his squinty yellow eyes.

For the first time, Jove was able to see the mask clearly in the sunlight. It looked eerily like a mutated crocodile head. The crowd parted around him and soon nobody else was left in the clearing.

Still glued to the spot, Jove watched in horror as the man jerked his arm as if he was brandishing a weapon. A stream of fire burst out from what must have been a compact flamethrower aimed directly at Jove. He closed his eyes and held his own arms up ready to be engulfed in the flames.

But they never came.

Instead, he felt a huge gush of air rush by from behind followed by heat that surrounded his whole body. Opening his eyes and lowering his hands, he tried to figure out what had happened.

Tia had jumped just centimetres in front of Jove, blocking the line of fire between him and the stranger. She was waving her hands and arms in quick sweeping motions, somehow deflecting the flames.

The man started to try different tactics by changing angles and giving different bursts of intensity. But Tia was ready for him. With every move he made trying to get to Jove, Tia deflected the jets of fire with another sweep of her hand.

"How are you doing that!?" Jove called over the commotion. She didn't answer. Her entire focus was devoted to defending the both of them. Still confused by what was happening, Jove desperately surveyed the rest of the courtyard in the hope for answers.

Through the flames he could see bewildered students peering out from the buildings and bag racks. Teachers stood around the outside trying to decide whether they should interfere. One teacher, which Jove saw to be Mr Londs, attempted to sneak up behind the stranger but quickly retreated as a warning flare was shot in his direction.

The man was now circling both Jove and Tia, getting more infuriated at the resistance and shooting wild bursts of fire. Tia's movements were becoming erratic and Jove saw the strain showing in her face.

Maybe if I could lead him away from her. It doesn't look like she can last much longer... whatever she's doing.

Jove waited for a moment where he would be able to break away. Sweat dripped down his forehead and stung his eyes as the hot air swirled around him.

Finally, the moment came when Tia was able to throw the man off balance. Jove stepped out to start running, but the attacker quickly found his footing and manoeuvred another blazing jet of fire directly at him. Tia only just managed to deflect it, leaving a scorch mark on Jove's arm.

"Don't run! He'll catch you!" She yelled as he stumbled back behind her. Her pupils swirled angrily.

"What do I do then?!" he shouted back, annoyed that he was just standing there doing nothing.

"Just wait. I'll think of something." She spun on the spot in an attempt to retaliate. Beads of sweat ran down her face as well. She put her wrists together forming a '*v*' shape before thrusting them in the man's direction.

Jove thought he saw something warp around Tia's hands. A moment later, the man stumbled backwards as if he had been pushed by an invisible force. A column of fire erupted from his hands and flew in random directions before disintegrating into nothing.

At once, something appeared to click in Tia's brain as her pearly eyes sparkled.

"I have an idea. Get behind me and get ready to run for the front gate." She called back at him.

The stranger found his footing again and prepared to lunge another fireball at them. At the same time, Tia crouched down placing her hands in the same '*v*' shape as before. Jove stood directly behind her, ready to run at her signal. He felt a gush of wind rush past him like a vacuum, sucking him back towards Tia. He noticed the space around her hands starting to warp again. The same was happening with the stranger, a ball of flame somehow forming in his palms.

How is he doing that? Jove thought briefly. He now realised that he saw no evidence of a flamethrower.

"Now!" Tia shouted and Jove instantly made a break for the gate with all the strength and speed he could muster. The stranger saw this and hurled the ball of fire at him.

Tia was ready. At that same moment, she lunged forward stretching her out hands like before. The fireball stopped just inches from her fingertips. The strain showed as she tried to keep the blaze at bay.

She spun on the spot, bringing her hands close to her body before suddenly thrusting them away. Once again, Jove saw the same warping around her hands as a huge gush of wind emanated from the centre of the courtyard.

The fireball swirled and expanded, engulfing the entire scene in a thick cloud of smoke. From somewhere within the haze, Jove heard Tia yell and he saw the man hurtle backwards in a sudden gale. His body crashed into one of the concrete bag racks and he lay dazed amongst the rubble.

The courtyard disappeared in a large plume of dark smoke and Jove's terrorized classmates were trying to run away from it as quickly as they could.

Just as he started to wonder if Tia was okay, she materialized out of the haze running full pelt toward him. As she closed the gap, he saw that her face had become extremely pale and she was panting heavily. Although fatigue looked as if it was taking its toll on her body, Tia managed to catch up to Jove easily by the time he reached the street.

As they ran down the road they passed the oval and Jove could hear the fire alarm blaring over the school grounds. Students and staff were frantically gathering on the grass as per the fire escape plan.

"Behind here." Tia grabbed Jove's arm mid-step and yanked him down a nearby alleyway. Slowing down, she led him behind a large dumpster and crouched down.

"What the hell was that?" Jove panted. But she quickly cut him off by pressing a finger to her lips, telling him to keep quiet. Sirens sounded just beyond the alleyway and Jove peered around from behind the dumpster. A line of police cars and fire engines raced down the street towards the school.

As the sound of the sirens died away, Tia grabbed Jove's arm again and yanked him upwards.

"Follow me," she puffed while leading him down the alley, "and try to keep up. He's probably hot on our trail already."

"But the police can help…" Jove argued but Tia was already racing down the footpath. Although he was running as fast as his legs could carry him, Tia still seemed to be effortlessly pulling further and further ahead. There was something odd about her running style. Noticing Jove's struggle, Tia slowed so that he could catch up.

"Put your arms behind you like this." She cupped her hands and moved her arms in a fluid motion behind her body. Once again, Jove saw something warp around her hands and her body lunged forward with an extra burst of speed. She seemed to lean forward so much that she would have fallen over if it weren't for her incredible pace. Her legs were almost a blur.

As confusing as this all was, Jove figured it was best to simply go along with it rather than questioning her. For now. Mimicking her movements, he cupped his hands and thrust them behind his body. He lunged forward and the imbalance sent him stumbling a few metres.

Regaining his stability, he tried again. Tia had slowed down in the distance, anxiously waiting for him to catch up. This time, he was ready for what was coming. Still running, Jove cupped his hands in front of him, feeling a strange sensation around them as he did so. They then started warping like Tia's did. Forcing them backwards, he felt a strong wind rush past his body. The force sent him flying forward in an abnormally fast sprint.

Jove staggered a few more steps but managed to gain his balance at the new pace by copying Tia's pose and leaning forward. His feet were pounding the bitumen in a blur as he ran. He found that if he leaned further forward, it prevented him from falling back in the wind and allowed him to move faster still. Jove also realised that if he moved his hands behind his body, he could control the airflow to steer and maintain balance. His mind started to race as he tried to figure out how this was possible.

She'd better have a good answer to all this, he thought as he quickly caught up to her. She stayed a few feet in front of him, manoeuvring through streets and alleyways away from the school. A few times, Jove made the mistake of running directly behind her and almost got wiped out by a powerful slipstream.

He managed to catch quick glimpses of houses as they flashed past and realised how fast they were really going. They ran through empty streets until Tia eventually brought her arms up, slowing herself down. Following her actions, Jove slowed as well and they came to a stop out the front of an old, run-down house with a familiar yellow car sitting in the driveway.

"Ok, now that we're far enough away, can you please tell me what the hell is going on here?" Jove stopped beside her and tried to catch his breath. He felt more drained than he would have expected.

"I'll explain…once we're definitely safe…" Tia panted and jogged up the front steps to the door. Jove followed, dissatisfied by her answer.

Without even knocking, Tia burst through and called for her father. Jove filed in cautiously behind her. The inside of the house seemed just as old as the outside. Paint was peeling off the walls, the ceiling was riddled with cobwebs and there was barely any furniture in the rooms that Jove could see.

"Dad, they've found us and they know. We've got to leave now." Tia called as her father came running towards them. Jove just stood there as the man glared at him with great intensity. His eyes were very different from Tia's friendly and welcoming ones. They made him feel quite vulnerable.

"How many were there? Where are they now?" His attention turned to Tia. His voice was very gruff and coarse. If his eyes were not already intimidating enough, his voice certainly was.

"Just the one." Tia answered. "He attacked at the school. I was able to hold him off for short while but he's probably recovered and retreated far enough under the radar by now." She walked over and collapsed onto a nearby chair. "I'm pretty sure we weren't followed."

Jove remained standing in the doorway in shock, unsure whether he should be doing or saying anything.

"Good. They must be getting desperate if they dare to go out during the day. Not to mention somewhere so public." Mr Favon knelt beside his daughter. "You didn't overexert yourself did you?"

"I'll be fine. It took a bit to hold him off and run back here but I should be fine in a couple of hours."

"Ok, let's get out of here then." He stood up and came to stand in front of Jove.

"Jove Boyd, it's an honour to finally meet you." Tia's father said in his gruff tone as he grabbed Jove's hand and shook it firmly. "I am sorry we are not meeting under better circumstances."

Jove apprehensively withdrew his hand. "Would you mind explaining to me what is going on?"

"All in good time. For now, we need to get out of town."

Hearing this answer sent Jove over the edge. "No, I'm not going anywhere until someone tells me what the hell is happening!"

Tia turned around at the sudden outburst while her father tried to calm Jove down.

"I understand that you are confused but it will all make sense soon. In the meantime, it is essential that we leave immediately."

"What if I don't want to leave?" Jove yelled back. "You expect me to leave town with you? I barely even know you! And you're not even telling me what's going on! How long does it take to fill someone in?"

Tia now moved to stand in front of him too, "Jove, I know you're frustrated but you have to trust us." She put her hand on his shoulder but he shook it off. Her misty eyes gave him a sympathetic look.

"It's long and complicated." She tried to comfort him.

"Just give me the basics then." Jove retorted, almost yelling at her.

"We don't have time for this." Mr Favon was getting anxious and pulled a mobile phone out of his pocket. "Tia, calm him down."

"But…" Tia seemed reluctant but she appeared to have no choice. She turned toward Jove, "I'm sorry. I promise we'll explain everything as soon as we're away from here."

What? Jove gave her a baffled look as she stretched out her open hand, stopping an inch from his chest. Her fingers twitched and Jove felt his chest tighten. He was about to knock her hand away when a strange force constricted his lungs and he became short of breath. Tia's hand motioned up towards his throat and he began to feel dizzy. He started to choke as he became starved of oxygen.

Jove looked into Tia's face and saw that she was clearly disturbed by what she was doing.

"Who are you?" He managed to gasp before he blacked out.

Jove woke a few hours later lying uncomfortably on a rigid, uneven surface. He felt queasy as he realised that wherever he was, he was moving.

Groaning and opening his eyes, he found that he was lying over the back seat of a car. The cushioning had lost most of its padding so the only source of comfort came from an old pillow that had been carefully placed under his head.

It took a few moments for Jove's brain to catch up. He noticed that it was dark outside and the car he was in was, in fact, Mr Favon's old yellow sedan.

"Where are we?" Jove asked in a groggy voice. "What's going on?"

"Oh, you're up." Tia's soft tone came from the front passenger seat as she turned around to face Jove, "We're about three hundred kilometres up the Queensland coast."

"What?" Everything came back to him and panic started to set in. "Where are we going? How long have I been out?"

Tia opened her mouth to answer but her father beat her to it.

"A few hours. We're going up to a small town on the northern coast where we'll be safe and you can be educated without anyone finding us."

Tia gestured to Jove's sports bag in the back seat. "We stopped by your house to pick up some essentials and explained everything to your Mum."

"What? When are we going back to see her?" Jove was still feeling slightly disoriented. His head was starting to ache from confusion.

Tia had hesitated so Mr Favon broke the news instead.

"We're not going back."

Jove immediately snapped to full attention, "What!?"

"I'm sorry Jove." Tia put her hand on his knee in an attempt to comfort him but he pulled away.

"But, what's going to happen to my Mum?" Jove interrogated her, "I can't just disappear."

"You can, and she's safe." Mr Favon answered him. "As we speak, a Ventieran escort is meeting with your mother and taking her to Fervune in South America."

This answer made absolutely no sense to Jove. "What?"

"Dad, he doesn't know yet remember?" Tia said softly to her father.

"You promised that you would explain everything to me!" Jove pushed himself forward so that his head was protruding through the gap between the front seats. He gave each of them a demanding glare and lowered his voice into a more threatening tone. "What is going on?"

Mr Favon took his eyes of the road for a moment and met Jove's. They softened as he nodded.

"Very well." He said turning back to the road. "You may call me Auster if you wish. We're going to be too well acquainted to have to worry about such formalities. I was going to wait until we'd finished travelling before I started your induction, but I guess we've got enough time before we get there."

"Thank you." Jove retreated to the rear section of the car and folded his arms. Tia gave him a weak smile and turned back around as she waited for her father to speak.

"Make yourself comfortable Mr Boyd," Auster Favon shifted in his seat, "I am going to tell you everything."

The Truth

"You may have figured out by now that there is a lot more to this world than first meets the eye. As such, the world has evolved to the point where the truth has been completely hidden and forgotten in today's society."

Auster glanced at Jove through the rear-vision mirror. "Many thousands of years ago, there were actually five different races that shared this planet, not just humans. The other four races were known as the Olderak, the Draagni, the Merpesces and the Ventiera. Each of these peoples stood for different beliefs and cared for the earth in different ways in order to keep balance."

Great, I've been abducted by conspiracy theorists, Jove thought.

He looked questioningly at Tia. She simply nodded and put a single finger to her lips as her father continued. Somehow, this comforted him.

"These different beliefs were mainly to do with how each race was created and how they lived their lives. Eventually, as time progressed and evolution kicked in, they learned how to control and manipulate the respective elements that they lived amongst."

"How do you mean?" Jove asked curiously.

"Well, I'll start with the Olderak. They have simple beliefs in which all their resources and everything they need in order to survive can be drawn from the earth. So, over time, they developed the power to control and shape the earth around them at will."

Auster paused and looked back at Jove again. He still did not understand. As perplexed as he was, he listened intently as Auster continued.

"The Draagni are a proud and fierce people who saw power and life in fire. So, just as the Olderak can control the earth, the Draagni can create and control the element of fire and variations of it such as heat."

Jove's mind started racing as thoughts started triggering in his head. He remembered the strange man who had been attacking him over the past few days.

"So, that guy that's been attacking me recently, that's one of these dragon creatures, isn't it?"

"You catch on pretty quick. That'll make life easier." Auster commented before continuing. "And yes, Draagni. The one that has been attacking you is named Gahnarg. He is the equivalent of a soldier to his race, and a particularly dangerous one at that. I thought he lost our trail about a year ago but he seems to have tracked us and you down. He has been quite intent on killing you. The Draagni are not fond of humans."

Jove felt a sick feeling surge through his body as he heard this, "But why?"

"I'll get to that." Auster tried to say kindly.

Jove now fought back the urge to throw up but he listened on nonetheless.

"The Ventiera are a predominantly female race that believe in freedom for all creatures. They became free-spirited like the wind and, as such, learnt to manipulate the wind and air around them at will. They are also closely related to humans, baring almost exactly the same appearance. The most obvious thing that sets them apart, though, is their eyes. Their pupils are pure white."

Immediately Jove spun to face Tia, who met his gaze. His jaw dropped as he stared into her misty eyes which were gleaming back at him. She nodded.

"Tia's mother was Ventieran." Auster said, noticing Jove's reaction.

"Where is she now?" Jove asked, curious to hear about Tia's unusual heritage. He realised he had hit a delicate spot as he saw Tia drop her head.

"She passed away when I was born." She answered solemnly. "Ventiera are able to live for almost a thousand years as they lead very healthy, carefree lifestyles. However, this makes them more prone to illness and death. It is not uncommon for Ventieran women to die when they give birth. My mother was one of them."

"I'm sorry." Jove felt a wave of sympathy toward her as the car fell silent.

"So do you have any other traits of the Ventiera?" He continued again. "I guess you can control the wind like they can."

Tia nodded. "Yes, that was how I was able to hold Gahnarg off for so long. Though, since I'm not of pure blood my abilities are fairly limited. I've also inherited their longevity but still age more quickly because of Dad being human… Not that that's a bad thing." she quickly added, glancing at her father.

"Age quickly?" Jove asked, slightly confused.

Auster answered this time. "Because they can live for so long, the Ventiera age extremely slowly. As Tia is part…"

"I'm actually twenty-two, in human years." Tia interrupted quickly as if she was bursting to say it.

"…Oh… Right," Jove sat back in his seat. Something inside him felt slightly betrayed. He was not sure he liked this Tia, the real Tia. Auster turned to look at both of them, frowning before he changed the subject.

"Lastly are the Merpesces. They are the most isolated and I suppose you could say *alien* of the five. They are an ocean dwelling people who have learnt the ways of water by understanding its gravitational and magnetic relationship with the moon."

"So they can control water," Jove translated for himself to understand.

Auster nodded. "In all its forms. As a liquid, ice and even vapour. They have also gone further in the evolution chain regarding their abilities."

"How do you mean?"

"Since their abilities in controlling water are based on magnetic and gravitational pulls, they've extended further to also manipulate small electric pulses. This allows them to communicate by creating electrical messages in another's brain and nerve system... They don't have mouths." Auster added as he noticed Jove's confused expression.

Jove tried to picture a mutated person without a mouth. He got a creepy shiver down his spine as the image formed in his head.

"They also have healing abilities. Have you heard the saying that water is the liquid of life?"

Jove nodded.

"It's true. They figured out how to harness the beneficial properties of water and use them to speed up the healing process. They can even manipulate blood in the body in order to cure debilitating illnesses and conditions."

Jove became intrigued. Biology class always fascinated him. "So they would be able live for ages too, wouldn't they?" He whispered.

"Not exactly. Healing takes up a tremendous amount of their energy so it's like a double-edged sword. The Merpesces actually have one of the shortest lifespans of the five races."

An idea was starting to form in Jove's head. He thought of the strange power he also possessed over water.

"I'm connected to these…" he struggled to get his mouth around word, "Merpesces, aren't I?"

Tia and her father turned to face Jove, both with impressed looks on their faces.

"For as long as I can remember, I've had this strange magnetic effect on water and when I got attacked by this... Draagni thing… I froze a puddle of water in order to get away."

"I know." Auster turned back toward the front, "Your mother told us. You also have their healing abilities, apparently." He raised an eyebrow in Tia's direction. Jove gave her a confused look.

"Remember this morning when you said you had a bruise on your back, but it mysteriously disappeared?" Tia stared at him.

"Oh…" Jove started blushing, remembering what happened and, "Oh!" when he finally clicked. He had realised that between every time he checked his scarring, water was involved.

"And it's not just water you have power over." Tia piped up as she adjusted her seatbelt so she could face him. "You also have influences over fire and the wind. I've seen you."

"What? When?" Jove frowned.

"Whenever you exert yourself." she answered, "Remember the other day when the spot welder caught fire and you nearly set the whole building alight?"

Jove nodded.

"You must have built up some kind of energy or emotion in your body which manifested in the welder's flame."

"So that was me?"

Tia nodded. "And the average human isn't exactly capable of doing that. Also, that high jump contest the other day?"

Jove nodded again.

"Well, a gift that the Ventiera have that I've sort of inherited is the ability to read air currents. That is why their pupils are pure white, and mine to a degree."

Jove looked into her misty eyes, finally realising what they were for.

"Anyway, when you were jumping, you were giving yourself extra lift by creating small gusts of wind as you ran. This allowed you to soar over the bar. Every time you did so, I saw the air around your feet warp."

Jove was beginning to understand. "Just like your hands when you were fighting that dragon-something,"

Tia gave him a curious look, "You saw that?"

She adjusted her seatbelt so she could move into the back half of the car. Her face stopped just inches before his and she stared into his eyes. Her pupils swirled with curiosity. After a moment she let out a squeak of excitement and quickly retreated back to the front seat.

"Dad, the process is starting already!" She squealed.

"What?" Auster turned for a brief moment, "I didn't think it would start so soon."

"What are you talking about?" Jove was starting to feel nervous.

Tia pulled her sun visor down so that Jove could see the mirror. He edged closer to get a look at himself. His eyes stared back at him, but something about them was different. They seemed to be normal, but his pupils had subtly changed to a dark tinge of swirling grey rather than the normal jet black.

He sat back in shock, blinking madly and wiping his eyes trying to get rid of the strange colouring. But it did not change.

"I don't understand?" Jove said with panic. "How can this be happening to me? I haven't even heard of these other races before tonight."

Tia made an attempt to calm him down before Auster spoke again.

"Because they are all a part of you."

Jove became both confused and fearful.

"Let me explain. Hundreds of thousands of years ago, when the five races were still at peace, there was a council that consisted of five representatives, one elected from each race. Their duties were to address matters that arose amongst their peoples."

Auster paused for a moment to make sure Jove was keeping up. "At some point in history, nobody knows when, this council sensed that there was dissension forming amongst the five races. Eventually, they decided that something should be done so that everyone's way of life would not be threatened. They figured that if there was one being who could understand and was a part of each race, it alone could take care of all global issues and keep the world at peace. So the council of that time came together and created this being, designing it to have the traits and abilities of each race. They also gave it the ability to be reborn again and again in a cycle. Remember how we said that the Ventiera can live for up to a thousand years?"

Jove nodded and Auster continued, "Well they passed on their gift of longevity so this being could live for so long and with so much vigour thanks to the Merpesces traits of healing. It would be born as a Ventiera, then a Draagni, followed by Olderak, Merpesces and finally as a Human. This cycle was to repeat itself for the rest of eternity."

Jove's eyes widened again, he had a gut feeling he knew where this was going.

"Anyway, soon after this being was created, the Incarnate as it came to be known, the humans started to feel isolated from the other races and quickly became jealous of their abilities. Humans have always been extremely creative and resourceful. They could fend for themselves and change their surroundings to suit so they could survive. Because of this, they didn't develop any special abilities as they didn't need them. However, they became greedy and fearful that the other races would overthrow them so they declared war. They tried to eradicate the remaining four races and very nearly succeeded. But in the end they were only able to force them into hiding, driving them all to near extinction."

Jove could imagine a gruesome war in which his own kind had wiped out everything in their path.

I wish I could find that harder to believe, he thought.

"Since then, it has been the Incarnate's job to make sure that the humans didn't kill off the other races for good, no matter how bad things became. Often, they have been enslaved and tortured by humans, helping to build their empire across the globe as their population increased. Around five thousand years ago, the last Human Incarnate managed to break the last of the other races out of slavery and into hiding. Since then, almost all evidence of their existence has been lost in human society and everyone has gone along with their lives without much confrontation."

Jove started to feel sick as he started taking all this information in and certain parts were starting to add up in his mind.

"However, over the last hundred years or so, humans have made outstanding progressions in technology and the population is growing to the point where staying in hiding is getting almost impossible for the other races. The last Incarnate, a

Merpesces, died just over eighteen years ago holding off a human military fleet from the Merpesces capital of Atlantis. Since then, the exiled races have come to realise that the next in the Incarnate's birth cycle is a human and parties have been sent out in search of him. Some, like the Draagni, believe that a Human Incarnate will set out to finish off the other races once and for all. They have made it their mission to kill him so that he will be reborn as a Ventiera, skipping the human stage entirely. However, the rest of us believe the next Human Incarnate can prove to play a vital role in the fight for freedom and peace."

Jove wasn't sure he wanted to hear whatever was coming next.

"The other races can't stay in hiding for much longer. When they're discovered, the world will fall into chaos. A human with the knowledge and power of all the races can turn the tides and ultimately save everyone's way of life as we know it. So the hidden world has been searching, Jove, for the past eighteen years. As of today though, the search is over. We've found him, we found the Incarnate."

Mr Favon looked at Jove through the rear vision mirror. "We found you."

Grendun Court

The entire car remained silent. For a while, the world seemed really distant as Jove tried to make sense of everything he had just heard. He could see Tia trying to bring him back to reality but he wasn't registering. Auster was looking at him worriedly from the front seat.

"Jove?" Tia waved her hand in front of his face. "Jove! Are you alright?"

"I think I'm going to be sick."

"We're about to pass through a town." Auster replied quickly, "I'll pull into a servo there."

"No. Now!" Jove started to panic and became short of breath. He fumbled with the door handle while the car was still in motion. Auster noticed and immediately pulled over. The second they stopped Jove managed to open the door and he launched himself out of the car. He had only stumbled a few steps before he doubled over and threw up in the bushes.

He wanted to yell as loud as he could into the cold night air but his body wouldn't allow him to. Instead he started to breathe heavily as his mind raced. It was a dream. It had to be. Hidden races all around the globe with magical powers? What a load of crap.

On the other hand, thinking of all the events that had taken place over the last few days, it all started to add up. The more he thought about it, the more he wanted to get out of there and forget about it all.

Jove jumped as a hand clasped his shoulder.

"Come on. I'll stop in the next town and you can take all the time you need." Auster said as kindly as his voice allowed. He handed Jove a bottle of water so he could wash the sick out of his mouth.

Without looking Auster in the face, Jove got up and walked silently back to the car. Climbing into the back seat, he didn't even make eye contact with Tia. He simply stared out the window into a far off place as Auster started the car and they continued into the night.

After a short while, lights appeared in the distance and Auster pulled into the service station just outside of town. It was eerily deserted except for the cashier bustling about inside.

"Do you want to get out and stretch your legs for a bit?" Auster asked as he opened the door.

Instead of answering, Jove merely turned his attention to the flickering lights above the bowser as if he hadn't heard him.

"Very well. Will you both be alright?"

Tia nodded in reply before her father stepped out of the car. Her eyes remained fixated on Jove.

After a time, she unbuckled her seatbelt and shuffled into the back seat.

"Jove?" She said softly, nudging his leg. He slowly shifted his eyes from the lights to meet hers. He became mesmerised by the depth in her misty pupils now he understood why she had them.

"I know this all sounds really daunting and it must be hard for you to take in. I can't imagine what's going through your mind." She said softly.

She was right, even Jove wasn't entirely sure how his mind was working at the moment. It was racing with visions and thoughts of everything strange he had ever seen and experienced in his life. They all seemed to have some sort of connection with everything Auster had said.

"Are you sure it's me?" His mouth was dry.

Tia nodded and put a caring hand on his shoulder, "And something tells me you know it too."

Another silent moment passed as Jove continued to process the news. Finally, he built up the courage to speak again, "So what are these other races like?"

Tia's eyes started to sparkle and a smile broke across her face. She started a huge speech about each of the races and their cultures and beliefs. Jove merely laid back and listened to her words.

Auster finished fuelling the car up and after a short while they were driving into the darkened landscape ahead. Jove closed his eyes and tried to picture the races as Tia explained. He shivered as he thought of a mutant human fish with no mouth and webbed hands and feet. Apparently they were asexual creatures who were able to change their gender as needed to reproduce.

He also cringed as Tia described the Draagni as stout reptiles with beady eyes and large scales. Jove immediately pictured his attacker, whose yellow eyes glinted with anger. It turned out Jove had seen the creature's real face instead of a mask like he had originally thought.

Lastly were the Olderak who Jove imagined to be overgrown mole-people as Tia described them. Their bodies had evolved to the point where they lived solely underground and nobody had seen one on the surface for decades.

An hour went by before Tia started explaining the different environments each of the races lived in. As Jove figured, they each lived in a place that attributed to their respective elements. The Ventiera lived in colonies built high in the canopies of forests around the world that would normally have been thought to be uninhabitable. After asking further, Jove learned that the city where his mother was being escorted to was located deep within the Amazon Jungle in South America.

Volcanoes were home to the Draagni, which Jove thought made sense because of their relationship with fire. Tia also made mention that eventually Jove would have to travel to their main metropolis in order to learn their ways.

Great, Jove thought sarcastically while wondering if all Draagni wanted him dead.

Originally, the main Draagni colony lived deep within the bowels of Krakatoa. They destroyed it in a massive eruption when humans started forming colonies around the volcano. Since then, they had been rebuilding their home that was now dubbed Anak Krakatau, son of Krakatoa.

Jove tried his best to keep listening, but his mind was starting to become overloaded. While Tia started talking about the Olderak colonies under Stonehenge and the Himalayas, Jove succumbed to her soothing voice and nodded off into a deep sleep. He drifted off into a distant world filled with these mysterious creatures in strange and isolated places.

Jove did not stir again until just after sunrise. He propped his head up and looked out the window. The car slowed and turned down the streets of an unfamiliar town. For a moment, Jove believed that everything that happened the night before was merely a vivid dream. But all doubt disappeared as reality came rushing back to him.

He sat up groggily rubbing his eyes. Tia had fallen asleep opposite him with her head resting against her seatbelt.

"Where are we?" He grumbled as he stretched out across the back seat. His leg accidentally brushed against Tia's and woke her as well.

"Mornin'." she yawned.

"Mornin'." Auster said to both of them before answering Jove's question. "We're high up north on the Queensland coast in a town called Driscoll. We will remain here while I educate and train you."

Jove simply slumped back in his seat. His mind was still weary and he didn't have the energy to answer.

Once Tia found her bearings, she wound down her window so that fresh air hit her face. Her hair cleared away and danced behind her head while the cool morning wind brushed her skin and flowed through the rest of the car.

"That's a nice ocean breeze." she commented.

Jove had also noticed a faint ocean smell as he watched Tia and rolled down his own window. Sure enough, a blast of cool and slightly salty air struck his face and blew his hair back. It was quite a relaxing and refreshing sensation and he started to understand why the Ventiera were so fond of the wind. The car rounded another bend and Jove noticed an outline of trees covering the horizon ahead of them.

"That's part of the Daintree forest." Tia explained as she noticed his puzzled expression, "The town itself is wedged between the southern tip of the forest and the sea."

"So what makes here so special?" Jove asked.

"It's our base. I was sent back here while Tia was still very young after the Ventieran city in the Daintree was destroyed. We've been coming here from time to time over the last eighteen years as a break from our travels." Auster replied and Jove noticed the fatigue in his voice.

The car turned into a dead-end road on the outskirts of town and Jove looked at the corroding street sign; Grendun Court. All the houses in it seemed run down and uninhabitable except for the one at the end. They slowed and pulled into its driveway and Jove saw a rusty number nine swinging from the letterbox as they drove in.

It was a low set brick house that looked as if it had not had any maintenance done in years. The lawn was wildly overgrown and appeared to have a whole other ecosystem living within it. The outer brick walls were covered in a dense layer of moss and dirt giving the building a dark, dank look. Beyond the side of the house was a thin line of trees that seemed to get thicker the further Jove peered into it. The salty smell of the ocean was more distinct in the air.

"Alright, we're here." Auster said pulling the handbrake and turning off the car.

Tia was the first to get out and stretch with her father soon following suit. It took a little longer for Jove to open the door and step out of the car himself. He was not sure he liked the idea of this place being his new home, however long his stay.

Auster made his way around to the rear of the car and popped the boot to get their bags out. He threw Jove's bag to him and carried the rest himself.

"The bare essentials." He said as he saw the confused look on Jove's face. "We only had enough time to grab the basics. Your mother was very obliging."

Jove zipped open his bag to see what had been pre-packed for him. He tried to picture his mother's reaction when Auster showed up on her doorstep. The contents seemed to have been packed in a rush. A small bundle of clothes lay snugly beside a small toiletries bag.

"Tia, do you want to give Jove a quick tour?" Auster said throwing the house keys to his daughter.

She nodded and took Jove by the arm, giving him barely enough time to zip his bag back up before leading him to the front door. Pushing aside the torn, rusted screen, she inserted the key into the main lock. She had to jiggle it a bit before Jove heard it click and they stepped inside.

Dust filled the air obscuring Jove's vision and rays of light spattered through the windows. It was obvious that nobody had lived there in quite some time. The furniture and the structure of the house barely seemed to be intact. The only solid piece of furniture he could see was a large bookcase fixed to the main wall in the lounge.

Tia took a few steps inside the house ahead of Jove and opened one of the windows. She turned back around and extended her arms.

"What are you doing?" Jove eyed her curiously.

"Watch." She answered with a smile. Her misty pupils sparkled and the dust that filled the house started swirling around her body. Slowly moving her arms in circular motions, the dust followed and gathered into a single cloud in the centre of the room. Jove watched on in awe as she suddenly extended her arm in a quick movement with her open palm facing the window. Immediately, the dust started streaming out the window, clearing the room. Tia's eyes stopped swirling and she lowered her arms.

"Am I gonna be able to do that too?" Jove said, thoroughly impressed.

"In time." she replied with a grin. "Come on, I'll show you your room."

He followed her down the hallway until she stopped in front of the first door on the left. She pushed it open and motioned for Jove to enter.

It was not a very large room. There was only enough space to fit an old single bed against the wall and a small desk next to the doorway. The walls were bare except for a thin layer of dust and old faded blinds covering the window. A single, blown light bulb dangled from the ceiling.

Jove dumped his bag on the bed and opened the blinds to let some light in. From the window he had a full view of the backyard.

He saw a rusted swing set he assumed was Tia's from when she was a toddler. A large shed took up most of the space in the backyard which was about half the size of the house. Beyond the wire fence that marked the boundary Jove could see an overgrown path leading down toward the beach.

He could faintly hear the sound of waves crashing on the sand.

"If you want to have a shower, the bathroom is at the end of the hallway on the right opposite Dad's room." Tia was still standing in the doorway. "Feel free to go have one now. The water should be on and you probably want to get out of those clothes."

She gave him a gentle smile before leaving to assist her father. Jove looked down at his clothes. He was still in his school uniform which was dirty and even charred in places. He could only imagine what he looked and smelt like to Tia.

Dumping the contents of his bag onto the bed, Jove grabbed a pair of shorts and his toiletries and headed towards the bathroom. He had to give the shower head a fair whack before the water gurgled and spilled out. It was a bit chilly at first but he didn't mind. It was significantly warmer here in the tropical climate.

Jove sat in the shower and let the cool water run over his body as he gave himself a moment to ponder everything in his mind. His friends were gone. His mum was gone. Life as he knew it was gone. Everything he had to go on now was the word of the two people that had just abducted him.

So I'm supposed to be the link between the five races, Jove thought as visions of creatures from the other races flashed through his mind.

What makes them so sure that I am who they say I am? A sudden fear surged through his body and he started to feel completely isolated from the rest of the world.

What if I don't want to be this Incarnate person? He thought angrily, *What makes them think that I, of all people, can fix everything? I don't know anything about these other races! This is so screwed up!* Jove clenched his fist and punched the wall out of frustration.

He slowly withdrew his hand. A tiny, barely noticeable dent was now imprinted in the shower wall. He started to take slow, deep breaths to calm himself down.

Raising his hand in front of his face, Jove watched the water trickle down his fingers into his palm and down his wrist. An idea came to him.

Focussing his energy, he tried to see if he could move the water like Auster had explained in the car.

Nothing.

Opening his palm again, Jove tried to see if he could turn the water pooling on the bottom of the shower into ice like he did the night he was attacked. He moved his hand in a sweeping motion.

Still nothing.

Maybe it has to be turned on and off or something, he thought.

Jove let a few more minutes go by before he decided to finally get out. He felt the hot air hit his body as soon as he drew back the shower curtain. The water particles clung to his body now more than ever.

Eventually he completely dried himself and got dressed. Reaching into his toiletries bag to find some deodorant, he realised the bag was empty aside from some swabs, his toothbrush and some toothpaste.

Bugger, he thought. He would have to ask if Auster could go down to the shops for him.

As Jove walked out of the bathroom he heard noises coming from the next room. Knocking on the door he heard Tia's voice beckon him in.

Her room was slightly larger than his and looked as if it were better suited to a small child. Although the room seemed fairly aged, the curtains and bedspread shone a bright yellow as if they were still new. Much like Jove's room, there was not much furniture other than the bed, a desk and a wooden dresser.

"Thought you drowned yourself." Tia grinned as she sat on the edge of her bed unpacking her bag. "Dad's just ducked down to the shops to get some supplies. What's up?"

"Umm." Jove was a bit nervous asking about his toiletries, "I was just wondering if he would be able to pick up some deodorant for me. It seems like Mum may have forgotten a few things."

"Oh, hang on, I think I might actually have some in here." Tia dug through her bag and pulled out a clear travel case that held a full range of men's toiletries. "I always carry spares for Dad. You know, just in case."

"So I guess you're an expert when it comes to travel then." Jove gratefully took the bag.

"Yeah well you get used to the lifestyle. I haven't known much else growing up."

"What's it like?"

"Well it sucked that Dad and I never really knew when and where we would go next. You'd get to know people in one place for only a short time before having to pack up and move again. But because of our mission we couldn't really get too attached to anybody anyway. We couldn't afford to leave a noticeable trail." She sighed slightly.

"So how did it all start? I mean, if the other races are supposed to be a secret and all, how did you and your Dad get caught up in things?"

"Dad actually used to be in the army when he was around my age." Tia explained. "He was on a training mission in the Amazon one time that went wrong and he ended up being stranded in the jungle with one of his colleagues. The way he tells it, they were hopelessly lost and after a few days of trekking around in circles they were on the brink of death. Just when they thought it was all over, they were found by the Ventieran sentries. Instead of executing them, the Ventiera allowed them to stay in the city and learn their culture. Dad immediately fell in love with the people and their way of life. He's been working for them ever since."

"Wow." Jove was impressed. "Well that explains a lot. He seems like a real military buff."

"Yep."

"And so what, they've covered for you guys and your travels?"

"The Ventiera have always had their inside people within human society over the centuries. Guess that's one of the benefits of being able to live for so long. Over time they've been able to build up small fortunes to cover whatever expenses necessary to keep them hidden and surviving."

"Shame no-one can survive without money." Jove scoffed. Tia mumbled in agreement.

"So is this what my life's going to be like now? Some vagabond living as a shadow from human society?"

"Only for a short while." Tia looked at Jove and noticed the worried look on his face. "It's got its upsides you know." She reassured him. "Every day is a new adventure and you know that you're doing something for the greater good. You get a sense of what really matters and you don't worry about the little things."

Jove wasn't fully convinced.

"You'll adjust to it Jove. I know you will. There's a large world out there you'll get to experience and I have no doubt that you are going to change it for the better."

They became quiet for a moment. Realising Jove was still unsure, Tia decided to change the subject.

"I'll text Dad and see if he can get you some more clothes and stuff. It didn't look like you had much in your bag there."

"I guess it was the best Mum could do on such short notice."

Tia fell silent and they broke eye contact.

"How did she take all this by the way?" Jove asked. The question had been bothering him for a while now. He noticed a confused look on Tia's face.

"Surprisingly well from what I know."

"What do you mean?"

"Well, I only met her briefly when we arrived at your house. Dad made me guard the car while you were unconscious in case Gahnarg managed to track us down. I thought he would take ages trying to tell your Mum what was going on but I guess he must have sounded really convincing."

"That doesn't make sense." Jove looked at her accusingly. "Mum's always been a bit… overprotective of me and almost scared of the outside world."

"And I bet getting attacked the other night wouldn't have helped." Tia added, "Not to mention you being passed out in our back seat. But she seemed to trust us ok."

"Hmm…"

"You don't have to worry about her you know." Tia could tell what Jove was thinking. "She's going to one of the safest places in the world and the Ventiera in Fervune are really friendly and accommodating. She'll be just fine."

"It's still hard to just give up everything and go."

"I know, but believe me things will become easier. Sure, there's a long road ahead for all of us but we'll get there. You just have to trust us."

"Right." Jove found it hard to look her in the eye. It was weird seeing Tia like this outside of school.

"Well thanks for the stuff." He nodded his head and walked out without another word.

Retreating back to his own room, Jove sprayed himself with the deodorant and threw the new toiletries case into his bag. He picked up the rest of his clothes to put away when, to his surprise, a loosely folded piece of paper fell to the floor.

Curious, he picked it up and inspected it. The paper had been folded a couple of times until it was the size of a playing card and was slightly crinkled from travelling in his bag.

Sitting on the bed, Jove unfolded the paper. A note was scribbled across the page as if it was written in a hurry. A nervous lump formed in his throat as he recognised the wavy handwriting;

Jove,

I haven't got much time to write this, Auster has just come 'round and explained to me that we all need to get out of here. He has already informed me of the outside world. By the time you read this letter, you will know what I am talking about.

You must put your complete trust in the Favons, as I have. I have no doubt that they will be able to protect you until we meet again. In the meantime don't worry about me. I have been told that I'm going to be well taken care of.

I want you to know that I am so unbelievably proud and love you so much. I always knew you were destined for great things.

> *Much love,*
> *Mum*

Jove finished the letter and allowed the words to sink in. He saw there were small watermarks smudging the bottom where she had signed 'Mum'. He quickly realised they were from her tears.

He read the letter again and again to the point where he had practically memorised it. His mother sounded so trusting and calm. In all his years, Jove thought her to be more critical of people. Her apparent reaction did not make sense.

Jove snapped back to reality when he heard the front door open down the hall. Leaving the letter on his bed, he walked out of his room and came face to face with Tia.

"Dad's home." She said awkwardly as they met.

"I gathered." Jove replied.

They walked down the hall and saw some grocery bags on the dining table. Auster had left them and moved into the lounge adjusting the knobs on the old style television. It made loud static noises as he tried to get it to work.

Tia eagerly picked up the bags and took them into the kitchen to unpack and scavenge for food. She retrieved a large, glass fruit bowl from one of the cupboards and emptied one of the bags into it, grabbing a large apple to snack on while she unpacked the rest. Jove was about to go in and help her, but something in the lounge room caught his attention.

Two large cabinets stood against the far wall of the lounge containing a variety of swords and spears seemingly taken from different cultures of the world. He peered into one of them and saw different forms of small metal armour, maces and broadswords. Some of them appeared to be hundreds of years old and taken from different cultures. Awe and intrigue got the better of him.

"What are these?" Jove asked curiously.

Auster peered up from the television. "Those are weapons from each of the different races, including humans. I've made a bit of a collection over the years."

Jove gazed back into the cabinet and Auster came to stand beside him so he could point out each artefact. "This cabinet contains most of the typical artillery of Draagni warriors. They are brilliant blacksmiths and exceptional weapons artists. See those mesh gloves hanging there?" He pointed them out to Jove. "The metal is mined from igneous rock and can withstand even the hottest of fires a Draagni can create."

"What are the holes for?" Jove inspected them and noticed small gaps in the mesh around the joints.

"To fit around their talons." Auster explained. "Draagni grow sharp talons on their knuckles from a very young age." He clenched his fists to demonstrate. "They're used as an extra form of weapon in hand to hand combat, usually in a duel against another Draagni."

"Ouch." Jove winced slightly as he imagined getting struck by a sharp set of knuckle busters.

"Look at these ones." Auster continued, trying to move Jove's attention.

He had pointed toward the other cabinet. It was full of more delicate instruments that seemed to be made of wood and other raw materials. Jove instantly recognised one of them to be an archer's bow propped up against a quiver of arrows.

"These are pretty standard forms of weaponry you would find in a Ventiera's arsenal. Although most of these instruments are mainly used for hunting food as they are not usually a violent people." Auster explained. "The bow and arrows may not seem as lethal as other weapons but are fatal if the user is very skilled at manipulating air currents. They can adjust the airflow around the arrows, controlling their angles and speed."

Auster motioned toward another weapon which was coiled underneath the bow like a snake.

"This is an air whip." he opened the cabinet and uncoiled the whip to show Jove. It extended to a couple of metres in length between Auster's hands while a small handle dangled from the thicker end.

"What's it made of?" Jove asked as he noticed its length consisted of woven bands.

"Wood and sap." Auster replied. "The wood has been stripped from forest trees into long slivers. Then they're soaked in a sap mixture to give them both strength and flexibility before being woven together to make whips such as this one and other useful tools. The Ventiera are excellent weavers you know."

"I can see that." Jove agreed as Auster coiled the whip again and placed it back in the cabinet.

Jove also noticed a thick and sturdy stick propped up against the wall. It had next to no dust on it and seemed to have been used more than the others.

"What's this?" Jove asked, picking it up.

"My bo-staff." Tia's voice came unexpectedly from behind him.

"I've been training Tia on the bo-staff since she was little." Auster explained. "Just as we will both be training you."

"With one of these?" Jove twirled the staff in his hands before Tia came up and gently took it from him. She was afraid he might break something with it.

"Eventually." she said.

"We'll probably start you off on one of these first." Auster picked up a set of wooden broadswords from a holster in the corner of the room and handed one to Jove.

"Wow." he ran his hand over the dulled surface of the blade which had been carved from red oak. "Where are these from?"

"Ebay." Auster answered bluntly, "They're basic training swords. I bought them last time we stayed here."

"Oh." Jove gave the sword back. Tia snickered silently before retreating out of the room, her bo-staff still firmly in her grasp.

"How come there aren't any weapons here from the other two races?"

Auster took the swords back and placed them in their holsters before answering. "The Olderak and the Merpesces are generally a kindly people. They're not accustomed to combat. However if the situation calls for it, they are able to control their respective elements to shape weapons at will and enhance their fighting ability. The Olderak, for example, can summon large bodies of earth and rock to slingshot towards opponents and can also shape them to form defensive barriers."

He paused for a second and motioned for Jove to follow him back to the television so he could continue fixing it.

"The Merpesces are a strange bunch when it comes to battle. They have many different ways in which they can take down their opponent. Along with using water to fight, they can also call upon the use of ice to create blades, spears and other such weapons. However, they can also harness another technique which is used only when circumstances are extreme. Do you remember me telling you last night how Merpesces have the ability to manipulate both the blood and the electrical nerve pulses in another's body?"

Jove nodded.

"Well, if need be, they can instantly kill their opponent by constricting blood vessels or blocking nerve systems. Basically they can shut your body down from the inside in a quick and often painless death."

Jove suddenly felt vulnerable and shifted uneasily.

Auster noticed his discomfort, "But accounts of that happening are almost unheard of. Having the power to control the life of another being has allowed the Merpesces to develop a respect for it. They believe it is totally immoral to control or take lives. Besides, the power of taking one's life can also come at the cost of their own. So really it's a double-edged sword, so to speak. It's incredibly risky."

"Well that's a comforting thought." Jove replied sarcastically.

"Mmm." Auster grumbled as he continued working on the television. Eventually, he stood up after he finished connecting the aerial and leads.

"That should be right to go now." He picked up the remote and pointed it at the television just as Tia walked into the room.

"Hopefully we can catch the last of the morning news." she sat down in an armchair.

The television clicked on and warmed up before the morning news showed on the screen.

"…Finishing our news today, a code black was called at Boonda State High School yesterday after an intruder threatened staff and students with what is believed to be a flamethrower."

Jove sat up immediately and Tia was on the edge of her seat.

"Turn it up." She ordered but her father was already fiddling with the button on the remote.

"…At 3pm the individual was witnessed entering the premises where he caused severe damage to buildings and school property, fleeing while staff and students evacuated. None of the three hundred staff or students suffered serious injuries. Details on the cause of the attack are currently under investigation…"

Auster turned the volume down again as the story ended.

"They left out the fact we fought him." Jove commented.

"It's best that they missed that." Auster replied as he placed the remote on the coffee table. "Drawing any kind of attention to yourselves is exactly what we don't want."

"But what about giving details on the Draagni that attacked us?" Tia piped up.

"The police had already warned the community not to approach dark and suspicious characters. Then Jove got attacked and they were officially deemed dangerous. Let's just hope Gahnarg's had the sense to leave town and cover his trail like we have ours."

"Wait," Jove interjected, "if the news mentioned that this *Gahnarg* is part of a gang does that mean there are other Draagni out to get us?"

"Possibly," Auster answered grimly, "and now that he knows who you are, he is likely to regroup even more Draagni to hunt us down."

Jove instantly went pale and he could sense Tia's worry. Auster continued.

"Don't worry, in all my years nobody has ever found us here. So long as we keep a low profile, things will stay that way."

Jove and Tia still remained silent.

"I'm going to go deal with some personal matters." Auster continued as he got up and prepared to go out again. "I'll see you both soon."

He walked out of the front door without another word and left a surprised Jove and Tia sitting on the couch.

"Come on, we should keep unpacking and clean up." Tia finally said.

She got up and turned off the television. Jove quickly followed suit and walked out of the room behind her.

"Welcome home, by the way." She said with a hint of playful sarcasm.

First Day of Training

The sun had not even broken over the horizon when Tia gently shook Jove awake the next morning.

"Oi, wake up." She said softly. "Time for your first lesson."

Jove let out a groan and opened his eyes to Tia sitting on the edge of his bed, already fully dressed.

"You're insane." He rolled over and pulled the pillow over his head.

"Come on, have a shower and I'll meet you in the lounge in ten." Tia grabbed his pillow and threw it back at him as she got up and left the room. It was a short while before Jove groggily rolled out of bed, grabbed a set of clothes and headed for the shower.

"About time." Tia greeted him half an hour later snacking on a large plate of toast. "Here, the rest is yours but eat it quickly. You're already late."

"Late for what?" Jove took the plate from her.

"For what I'm going to teach you."

After wolfing down the couple of slices left, Tia led Jove out the front door and into the crisp darkness of early morning.

"So where are we going to train?" Jove queried as they turned onto the footpath, "Might be a bit obvious to anyone who stumbles across us."

"I know. That's why we have to start early. There's nobody walking through the woods at this hour."

"I wonder why." Jove mumbled sarcastically.

Walking to the end of the road onto the grass, Jove could smell the early morning ocean spray over the dunes. Although he was still sour about getting up extra early, he enjoyed the refreshing sea breeze brushing against his face and watching the first rays of sun peer over the ocean in the distance.

Tia led him through the grass and soon into the forest. A thin layer of frost coated the foliage of the trees and Jove felt the air grow cooler as they ventured further in. Tia finally stopped in a clearing baring fewer trees. The ground was damp and covered with a layer of mist.

"This'll do. You stand there and I'll face you from over here."

"What exactly are we doing?" Jove queried as Tia walked a few paces away before stopping and turning back towards him.

"Well, I'm going to start you off slowly." She raised her arms. "At first you'll learn some basic movements so you can get a feel for the air around you and how it moves. Like so."

She slowly waved her arms in a large circular motion and Jove observed how smooth and fluid-like her actions were. A slight breeze picked up around her and Jove saw the mist swirl and dance in the wind as it followed Tia's arms.

"Like this?" Jove copied Tia's stance and awkwardly mirrored her actions.

"More smoothly, and loosen your body up more. Before you can move any wind, you have to warm up by getting your energy flowing and a feel for your surroundings. Think of it as a tai-chi exercise."

Thinking back to the very few televisions excerpts he had seen about health and tai-chi, Jove tried to incorporate it into his movements as best he could.

"Wind is created through the displacement of air." Tia continued. "Normally, anybody can cause this displacement when they run, clap, fan themselves, you get the idea. Air rushes in to even out the difference in pressure. We have the power to exaggerate these displacements and pressures through our movements."

"Right." Jove tried to focus on what she meant.

"Your body must be moving freely and fluently in order to control and maintain a constant stream. Naturally, the wind is free-spirited and is always moving in endless streams. Any obstruction in your movement will likewise obstruct this stream and block your control over it."

Jove continued following Tia's instruction but quickly grew frustrated. The movements made him feel like an idiot and he seemed no more likely to control any air currents than he did making friends with a Draagni.

"I'm not getting this. How am I supposed to exaggerate my movements in a way for it to achieve anything?"

"It's all about focus," Tia could see his growing angst and stopped. "Maybe we should try another way. Stand still and close your eyes."

Jove did so and heard Tia walking towards him. His heartbeat quickened as she walked in a slow tight circle around him.

"When I was first learning as a child, I found that I had to empty my mind of all thoughts and distractions and completely focus on my surroundings through my senses. The same should go for you. Relax your muscles and breathe slowly. In. Then out."

Inhaling and exhaling at the sound of Tia's footsteps, Jove did as she said. His breathing combined with the sound of her voice was almost hypnotic and Jove quickly found himself completely relaxed. His breathing formed a slow rhythm synchronised with his heartbeat.

"Good. Now focus on your own body. You should feel the blood pumping through your veins and into your muscles, enriching them with the energy to move."

Blocking out all but Tia's voice, Jove focussed on his heartbeat. Blood was surging throughout his body and feeding his muscles and movements.

"Wind is all about kinetic energy. You must extend your own movements and senses. Concentrate on the energy pulsing through your body. Build this energy. Listen to your surroundings and focus on where you want it to go."

Once again, Jove started moving his arms in circular motions around his body. Though this time it felt more natural and he did not fight it. Slowly he could feel the air pressurising around his body as he maintained a constant stream. With every heartbeat, power pulsated from his palms. After a long minute of this constant movement, Jove felt he had built up enough energy.

"Good, now guide the stream of air to where you want it to go. When you are ready to release, push away as forcefully as possible with your palms, using your fingertips as a guide."

Still focussing on his breathing and opening his eyes, Jove focussed on an area in the canopy. Bringing all the built up pressure to his hands, he widened his stance and pushed it away from his body with as much force as he could muster.

In an instant, all the pressure left through his outstretched hands and the wind pushed itself upwards into the trees above. The sudden gale briefly shook the tree branches and startled a couple of finches that were nestling among them. The leaves on the entire tree rustled for a moment before becoming silent again. The gust was a lot weaker than Jove had hoped.

"Brilliant!" Tia squealed with excitement from behind. "That was awesome for a first try. Don't worry about power yet. You still need to master the basics. Eventually you'll be able to build up the pressure much more quickly and focus it on more precise targets. It's all going to become easier as your body and mind get used to it."

"I hope so." Jove looked at his hands in awe.

"And that's just the beginning." Tia slapped him on the shoulder.

"So what else are we able to do?" Jove asked curiously.

"Well, obviously displacing the air to cause wind streams and bursts are the basics. Depending on how much focus and power you put in, you can do practically anything. A skilled Ventiera can do things like building gale force winds as a constant stream, extract air out of the atmosphere like a vacuum, and concentrate bursts of air that have the same impact as a bullet. Also, and only an expert Ventiera can achieve this, you can build up so much pressure in the atmosphere around you that you can actually solidify the air into an impenetrable barrier."

"Wow." Jove looked at her in amazement, "Like a force-field?"

"Sorta," Tia snickered, "if you're into the whole *super powers* kinda thing."

"Are *you* able to do anything like all that?"

"I wish." She replied with a hint of cold sarcasm. "I'm still training myself remember?

Besides, I'm only half Ventiera so my abilities are very limited. Human blood is very dominant and unfortunately taints my power."

Tia was looking at her hands as if she had a disease running through veins. It was obvious that she desired the full power of her heritage. Jove felt her dejection and tried to cheer her up.

"Well I think you're pretty amazing." He blurted.

She raised her eyebrow and Jove blushed.

"Your powers. You blow me away every time I see you use them." He covered and Tia smiled.

"Just wait until you learn from a real Ventiera in Fervune. They will quite literally blow you away." She winked back at him. "My job is just to get you started on the basics and to prepare you for what's to come. Believe me, once you undergo proper training within all the races, your own power is going to grow and surpass anything you could ever imagine."

Jove couldn't help but grin as excitement welled in his stomach, "Ah well, bring it on."

"Well slow down a bit," Tia doused his spirit slightly, "you need to keep focus and be patient. This process happens over years, not days."

They spent another half hour going over movements and technique rather than actual air streaming, much to Jove's disappointment. However his mood did improve every time Tia gave him a compliment or words of encouragement.

They ended the lesson once the mist had fully dispersed and the air was starting to warm up from the morning sun. Jove was looking forward to having a bit of a break.

"Hurry up. Dad's waiting." Tia said as they walked through the trees and back onto the street.

"Waiting for what?" Jove had a sinking feeling.

"Well it's his turn to train you now."

"What, more training?" Jove groaned.

"Of course." Tia replied. "You didn't expect this to be like a holiday did you?"

"Well no." Jove said disheartened, "I didn't really expect all this, period."

"Oh, right, yeah." Tia stammered awkwardly. "Well you're here now so you may as well make the most of it. There's a lot you have to get your mind and body used to before you're near enough to being ready to be introduced to the real world."

"Yeah I know, just don't break out that *it doesn't happen overnight* bull on me." Jove said cynically. "It's hard enough adjusting to all this as it is."

"Well count yourself lucky," Tia snickered, "you're in pretty good shape already."

Jove raised an eyebrow and his stomach tensed.

"Meaning you're already fit and know a bit of martial arts." She clarified. "Plus from what I've seen you're also a quick learner. Although you could stand to bulk up a bit. You're a tad on the scrawny side."

131

"Gee thanks." Jove's hopes from Tia's first comments were instantly shot down. They remained silent for the rest of the walk home.

"Mornin'." Auster greeted as they walked through the front door. He was on the couch watching the morning news and had just polished off a plate of toast. "Have a good session?"

"Yeah, he's a really fast learner," Tia replied collapsing on the couch and grabbing the remote from her father, "looks like doing karate through school is going to make our jobs easier."

Auster stood up, surrendering the couch to his daughter. "Well I'll have to see about that for myself, now won't I?"

"Make sure you're careful with the little princess." Tia winked at them and Jove retorted with a rude hand gesture.

"Oi, saw that." Auster interjected, "Play nice. Have you ever been to the gym Jove?"

"Er." Jove hesitated and felt a bit guilty. "Not really no."

"Didn't think so." Tia teased.

"Well this is going be a shock to your system. Follow me."

Going out the back of the house toward the shed, Auster slid open the steel door and Jove realised why the structure was as big as it was.

Inside was a fully stocked gym with a wide variety of weights and equipment. In the centre of the shed was a large sparring mat covered with a thin layer of dust as if it had not been used in years.

Immediately Jove was hit with a wave of heat that had been encapsulated within the steel walls from the sun. The only source of fresh air seemed to come from the front door and a single circular vent in the roof.

"You will probably spend most of your time in here. You need to build your physical strength so you can withstand your further training and the extreme conditions of everywhere you travel."

Jove scrunched his eyebrows with disapproval.

"Aren't I supposed to take fitness slowly?" He argued, "I mean, I'm no health expert but aren't you supposed to take time off to allow your muscles to repair themselves?"

"Fair point," Auster replied with an almost devilish grin, "but there are many advantages to being you. Your body has certain traits that are exclusive to only the Incarnate and the Merpesces."

Jove groaned to himself as he figured where this was going.

"As you have already noticed, your body has an intense reaction to water which quickens your healing process. A bath or swim at the beach will well and truly be enough to compensate for a day's rest."

"Oh the joys of being me." Jove answered sarcastically. "What's the sparring mat for?"

"As its name suggests. I know that you have already undergone basic training in martial arts so fortunately we have a head start."

"We?" Jove questioned.

133

"Yes, *we*." Auster repeated, "For the remainder of our time here I will be your sensei and broaden your fighting abilities across the arts."

"You?" Jove did not mean to sound so doubtful. He wasn't entirely convinced that his new master was an experienced black belt. Let alone a fit one.

"Again yes, *me*." Auster was becoming slightly annoyed. "Believe me when I say that I am a worthy opponent. Remember, I have been part of this world for many years now and I am more than capable of passing on my knowledge and skills."

"Well you should know that I've been in training to become a black belt. I would have been due for my exam in a couple of weeks."

"Really?" Auster's expression was mocking and he motioned for Jove to approach the sparring mat. Something about his tone made Jove feel uneasy.

"Well I think *I* should be the judge of that."

Suddenly, Auster came at him with incredible speed. In the blink of an eye, he made two swift movements and Jove found himself flat on his back. Auster's fist hung an inch from his face.

"A black belt doesn't mean anything here. All it will do is keep your pants up." He unclenched his fist and offered Jove a hand off the floor.

Jove's face went red as he took Auster's hand.

"We'll start off easy. I need to see what your technique is like. Take a stance. Basic five step sparring. Don't hold back." Auster said sternly. He

134

stood in front of Jove in the centre of the mat, "On my count... One!"

Eager to prove himself, Jove thrust his fist forward at Auster's face. With one simple movement, he had deflected it.

"Two!"

Jove aimed a punch at Auster's stomach. He easily brushed it aside.

"Three!"

Jove launched his leg upwards to kick at his side. Auster stopped it with his forearm.

"Four!"

Launching himself off his other foot, Jove tried to kick Auster in the stomach. He blocked it with his wrists and Jove stumbled slightly.

"Five"

Giving it everything he had, Jove spun and lifted his leg so it would hit Auster in the side of his head. But Auster was ready, with one swift movement he caught Jove's foot just before impact and pushed him backwards. Stumbling again, Jove fell with a painful amount of force.

"Your balance and timing need a fair bit of work." Auster looked down at him. He offered Jove another hand up.

"Again."

They continued for hours until Jove felt the heat of the shed start to get to him.

"Is this really all that necessary?" Jove panted after another set and leaned against the wall, "I mean, if I'm going to learn how to control the elements wouldn't hand-to-hand combat be a little redundant?"

"Martial arts is about more than just proving physical strength." Auster replied, fetching his towel from the sideline. "It also trains your mind to be more resourceful and creative under pressure. This will benefit you when you learn to control the different elements and even when making decisions that will affect the other races."

"I suppose." Jove relented. He didn't want to admit it but deep down he was actually looking forward to learning more about karate. At the very least it might change Tia's opinion on his abilities and physique.

"Besides, learning more about human combat and abilities will actually help in further improving your own development and understanding of the other races. Plus it will build your pain threshold so that when your body starts to change, it won't be such an agonising process."

"Um, what?" Jove thought he misheard.

"When your body changes." Auster repeated, "You've got a bit of each race wired into your DNA remember?"

"I thought it was just their powers!" Jove's eyes widened with horror. "Are you saying I'm going to look like a little bit of the other races as well?"

"Basically yeah. After all, your body has to be able to cope under the same circumstances and environments as each of the other four races."

"So I'm going to look like an alien lizard with no mouth!?" Jove yelled, shuddering at the thought.

"Not to that extent. You'll still be human. Your body will just adapt to all the different environmental conditions. Your skin will harden like scales to deal with heat and pressure like the water and fire dwellers. Your hands and feet will become more sensitive in order to feel the energy in the air and earth. In a nutshell, your body will be the epitome of evolution."

Jove collapsed onto the floor as his mind tried to process this information.

"Count yourself lucky." Auster continued. "The metamorphosis is much easier and less painful for a Human Incarnate. Our physique bears no biases to any of the physical elements, so it's easier for your body to adapt and develop to all of them."

"Well that makes me feel *sooo* much better." Jove replied sarcastically. He wasn't sure he could take much more of this 'Incarnate' stuff.

"I think we'll finish up early for today." Auster could sense Jove's lack of focus. "I'll leave you to process everything, but be ready for tomorrow. There will be no special treatment."

Jove couldn't bring himself to answer so he simply sat on the sparring mat as Auster left. The shed fell silent and dust was still floating through the air, stifling the light.

Conflicting thoughts ran through his mind. It would be cool to be a kind of superhero that had all the powers in the world. On the other hand, people and creatures alike would look up to him and expect him to solve their problems. The idea of all this pressure was starting to sink in.

He sat there for what seemed like hours thinking about it until he eventually got a headache. Since the heat in the shed was starting to get to him as well, he decided to walk down to the beach for a relaxing swim to hopefully clear his head.

The cool water lapped at his feet and the beach was completely deserted. Taking off his shirt, Jove waded into the ocean until he was submerged up to his neck. He could feel his body pulsate as he relaxed and the water worked on his muscles. His skin started to tingle and within minutes he felt completely refreshed.

Jove lay back in the water and his body bobbed up and down in the waves. He closed his eyes and for the first time, everything hit him. He wished he was back at home and that none of this had ever happened. Images of his friends and mother smiled back at him. They seemed so distant. His normal life was long gone.

What if I'm not good enough? Fear coursed through Jove's body as he rolled over in the water. Tears began to well in his eyes. They mixed with the saltwater and started to sting. He couldn't remember a moment where he had ever felt so alone. Feeling helpless, he started to thrash about under the water as if he was trying to ward off all these fears. Wearing himself out and starving for air, he returned to the surface.

"Jove!" He heard a girl calling out to him.

He looked up and saw Tia standing on the shore. She was waving a towel around in the air madly trying to get his attention. Quickly washing all evidence of tears from his face, he waded back to shore. His eyes were still stinging.

"It's nearly time for dinner. I was starting to worry about you. Here I brought you a towel."

She noticed Jove's expression, "Are you alright? Your eyes are all puffy."

Jove nodded and took the towel from her, wiping his eyes. "It's just the seawater."

Tia wasn't convinced.

"Here." She grabbed the towel back and wrapped it around his body. Keeping her arms around him she pulled Jove in for a hug. "I'm not going to pretend that I understand exactly what you're feeling. But whatever you need, just know that Dad and I are here for you."

Jove didn't answer. Instead he wrapped his arms around her and returned the hug. He let out a silent sob on her shoulder.

They stood there for a while without speaking before Jove finally broke away and composed himself.

"Thanks." He whispered. Tia simply nodded.

"Come on." She led him back up the dunes, "We've fixed up something special for dinner."

"What?"

"Lasagne." she smiled.

Sand, Surf and Secrets

After a few weeks of the new training regime, Jove's body had started to adjust. It was getting easier for him to wake up early and his growing strength and endurance was helping him handle more in a day.

Auster was pushing Jove to the limits and he was moving and fighting with more skill and agility. Quite soon they were training with the wooden broadswords and Jove often left their sessions battered and bruised. Over time he found that Auster had a strong pain threshold and was able to take hard hits even without Jove's healing abilities to help him.

In Tia's sessions, Jove had started to master air currents and could maintain a constant stream of wind with ease. The early morning mists made it easier for him to read the wind and understand how it moved and acted.

One day, after a particularly productive session, Jove and Tia walked back into the house to find Auster sitting on the lounge focussed to the television. A well-dressed young woman occupied the screen above a *'breaking news'* icon.

"Is everything alright?" Jove sat on the recliner opposite the television. Tia took up the spot next to her father.

"Watch." Auster replied and turned up the volume. The newsreaders voice echoed around the room.

"World Leaders are considering propositions from the U.S. Military to form a one party global government. Allied forces around the globe have been petitioned to participate in the scheme in a bid to move towards world peace, combining global technologies. Australian and Russian forces have begun negotiations, forming a defence team to promote the scheme…"

Auster turned the volume back down, "It's a reel that's been going for the last hour."

"What does it mean?" Jove queried.

"It means someone high up might know about the other races and they're preparing for the rest of the world to confront them."

"Could that be a good thing or a bad thing?" Tia chimed in as she got up to make herself some lunch.

"I'm not sure, although I would have heard of it before now if it was a good thing." Auster replied fumbling with the remote.

"Remember how I told you that the last Incarnate died while protecting Atlantis?"

Jove nodded, recalling the story.

"The invaders were a military force of humans. It was the first known attack on a colony in thousands of years. Long overdue, if you ask me,

141

and it was planned. It's only by sheer luck that the media didn't catch wind of it. Since then it has only been a matter of time until another attack is mounted on another colony and their presence is broadcast to the rest of the world."

"Wait a minute." Something wasn't adding up to Jove. "If the Incarnate is the most powerful being on the planet, how could it have fallen to a party of humans?"

"Jove, I have been pondering that for the last eighteen years." Auster sighed. "The only conclusion I've come up with is that whoever was leading the invasion on Atlantis knew about the hidden races and their powers. They may have figured out how to hold their own against the elements. What's worse is that they had enough influence in our own government and military system to launch such a large attack."

"So you're saying what? That this global government is a front for an allied force that will take out the other races for good?"

"Maybe…" Auster sat there in silence for a moment before getting up and walking out of the room. "I'm going out. I might be a couple of days."

"What!?" Jove and Tia exclaimed. Tia had poked her head around the wall with a frying pan in her hand. Auster paused at their reaction.

"Jove, keep going with your training and Tia…" He glanced at the frying pan in his daughter's grasp, "…please don't set the house on fire. I don't want another incident like Alice Springs."

Tia shot him a dark look and opened her mouth to retaliate but her father interrupted.

"Take care of yourselves."

Before either of them could answer, Auster had grabbed his coat and keys and disappeared out the door. Jove looked puzzlingly at Tia as the car started in the driveway. She returned the look and shrugged before moving back to the kitchen.

Since they were apparently alone for the rest of the day, Jove decided he might sneak in some television before training. He sat on the couch and went to pick up the remote.

"Bastard!" He exclaimed and got up again.

"What?" Tia called.

"He's taken the remote."

"Well he's not stupid." She laughed. "He used to do the same to me growing up. Well, whenever we lived anywhere that actually had a television in the first place."

"Oh well, I guess I can help you cook then." Jove walked into the kitchen and saw that Tia was about to cook up some leftover lasagne and steak with tomato sauce.

"Oi!" Tia smacked his hand, "Get out of it. This is mine. Here you can have this stuff." She dipped her finger into the tomato sauce and smeared it on the side of his face. Jove moved to retaliate but she was too quick for him and blocked his arms.

"You've got training to do. Obviously a lot more than you thought if I can block you that easily." She stifled a playful grimace and moved her plate away from him.

"Fine." Jove sighed vigorously rubbing the side of his face to get the rest of the sauce off. "Don't burn the house down while I'm gone."

"Geez you and Dad are as bad as each other." Tia tried to push him out the door. "Now bugger off."

"I better not return to a burnt pile of rubble." Jove jeered and quickly disappeared out the door. An incoming tea-towel narrowly missed his head.

The shed was steaming hot as the daily temperature hit its maximum. Lately, Jove had been lazy and managed to convince Auster to let him have a fan in the shed. He had not yet mastered streaming his own wind currents to cool the shed down.

Jove walked inside and his forehead immediately started beading with sweat, even with the fan on. Peeling his shirt off and strapping some weights onto his wrists and ankles, Jove started his first set across the mat and on the boxing bag.

A few hours later, the final flurry of kicks and punches left Jove panting heavily on the floor. He realised he had lost track of time when the air was starting to cool down and evening started to set in. Lying back, he thought of the news story on the television earlier.

I hope there isn't a war coming, he thought.

Jove tried to picture each of the races in army gear. The image seemed really odd in his head as each of them brandished their respective weaponry. At first it would seem they have a distinct advantage with their abilities to manipulate the elements. But as Auster had said, if humans had figured out how to overcome them it may mean their end. Was there something else Auster knew that he wasn't letting on?

I wonder what he's doing, Jove thought of Auster involved in some kind of life-threatening mission only seen in spy movies. The idea seemed oddly realistic.

His stomach started to growl and Jove snapped back to reality. He wondered if Tia had left any food for him.

"Ready for a break yet?" Tia stood at the shed door, making him jolt.

"Yeah, you got any leftovers from lunch?" He got up and grabbed his shirt.

"Nah I was going to leave some but you didn't come back in for a while so I ate it." She shrugged. "I thought we might want to eat out for dinner instead while Dads not here."

Jove's insides fluttered at the thought but he heard Auster's gruff voice in his head like a guilty conscience.

"You think he'll pick up on it? He kinda has a sixth sense for when I'm slacking off."

"It'll be fine. One night off won't hurt. Come on, I know where he keeps some emergency money. I think we've earned it."

"If you say so." Jove smiled and followed her back into the house.

Once both of them were showered and dressed, they met at the front door.

"So where are we going?" Jove asked as they journeyed around the streets.

"There's a fish and chip shop a few blocks over that Dad and I used to go to."

"Yuuuuum." Jove's mouth started to water.

"Don't get your hopes up yet. We've gotta find the place first. I haven't been there in yonks. I hope it's still… ah there it is!"

They rounded a curb and Tia pointed out the modest shop on the corner. There were a couple of tables and chairs set up on the footpath and lights dangled from the eaves of the building. The smell of deep fried food filled the air and Jove's mouth watered even more.

"It's still like I remember it." Tia said as they stepped inside and glanced longingly at the food. Trays of hot chips and other deep fried food lined the inside of the glass counter. Jove was surprised that the place was so quiet.

Tia immediately walked up to the cashier. "Can we please get a large battered fish each and two serves of chips?" She ordered then turned to Jove. "You want some potato cakes too?"

"Yeah sure." Jove answered eagerly.

"Four please. And two drinks."

Jove grabbed two bottles of soft drink from the fridge as Tia paid for the meal. Once the cashier gave them their ticket number, they sat at one of the tables out the front.

"So when was the last time you came here?" Jove broke the silence as they waited.

"Years ago. I think it was just before Dad enrolled me in a school down in Victoria. I would have been about fifteen or sixteen."

"Wow that's a long time." Jove replied.

"Mmm." Tia nodded. "We kinda spent most of our time travelling."

"So how many places have you been to?" Jove asked curiously.

"Lost count." She shrugged. "Been to different suburbs in Melbourne, Perth, Darwin, Sydney," she counted them off on her fingers, "we drove through all these country towns as well and stayed in them for about a week before moving on. After a while they're all pretty much the same deal."

"What were you looking for?"

"Well Dad just mainly kept an eye out for anything or anyone out of the ordinary. He figured the new Incarnate would be school age so it was convenient that he could enrol me in schools as a guise."

"That would've sucked." Jove replied.

Tia gave him a questioning look, "How do you mean?"

"Well you were picked up and constantly dragged from town to town and school to school. Did you ever stay in a place long enough to make *any* friends?"

"Not really." She sighed, "I got to meet a lot of nice people though. Just don't ask me their names."

"So you couldn't even have a boyfriend?" Jove asked before he could stop himself.

"No." Tia raised an eyebrow, "I was never really interested in having one anyway. There was no point in ever getting attached to anyone. I wouldn't know them for long enough and we'd be dragged off to another town after a short time anyway."

"I suppose."

"It was ok though. I knew that what Dad and I were doing was more important. The idea of going to a new place, one where we might be able to find the Incarnate, was pretty rewarding. Even if we had a slim chance, the day was getting closer when someone somewhere would make the announcement that they'd found you." She paused for a moment and gave him a cheeky grin, "I was never really much interested in boys anyway."

"Right." Jove awkwardly took a swig of his drink.

"What about you?" Tia continued while keeping her grin, "Have *you* ever had a boyfriend?"

Jove shot her a sardonic glare. "No, and haven't had a girlfriend either."

"You weren't interested either?" She teased.

"Nah, you kinda have to have girls be interested in you in return before you can go out on a date."

"They may have been interested. You just had to ask." She paused. "You never asked me."

Jove blushed. "Was it that obvious?"

Tia nodded. "It was cute."

"Since when do you call anything a teenager does *cute*?" Jove retorted.

"Don't beat yourself up about it. Remember, I've had a couple more years of experience in the schoolyard than you have."

"You know somehow that doesn't make me feel any better."

Tia shrugged and the sound of the cashier's voice made them both jump.

"Number forty-two!"

"That's us!" Tia got up and they went to retrieve their food.

"Still got your ticket?" The clerk demanded.

"We're the only ones here." Jove muttered but the man ignored him.

"Ah yeah, right here." Tia opened her wallet and took out the ticket. Jove noticed another piece of paper fall out and float to the ground.

"Thanks." Tia retrieved the food and went to sit down again.

"What's this?" Jove picked up the folded card off the floor behind her.

Tia put the food down and turned to see what Jove was talking about. Her face went white.

"Er…private." She tried to snatch it back from Jove but he pulled away.

"Doesn't look it." He teased and went to unfold it. Tia lunged at him again.

"No seriously." She made another few grabs at it but Jove held it slightly out of reach. "You'll rip it. Give it here."

Jove detected the firmness in her tone and lowered his hand. Tia snatched the card back. Without a sound she turned around and unfolded the card out of Jove's view, delicately wiping the dust off. She then folded it up carefully and returned it to her wallet before quietly sitting down.

Jove stood there unsure of what had just happened. The clerk was giving him a funny look over the counter so he went and sat down again. Tia unwrapped their food and started divvying out each of their portions.

"I'm sorry." Jove said softly. Tia still didn't make eye contact. "You ok?"

"Yeah." She took a bite out of her fish. Jove could see her pupils swirling.

"I didn't realise that thing was important." He continued.

"That's ok. I overreacted."

They sat there quietly eating their food.

"So wonder what your Dad's up to." Jove attempted to make conversation. "He wouldn't be on some covert undercover mission would he?"

Tia gave Jove a strange look before a smile finally broke across her face. "You know, that probably wouldn't surprise me."

"Like something out of an Indiana Jones or James Bond movie." Jove continued.

"Who?"

Jove's jaw dropped, "Seriously?"

Tia shrugged.

"Have you watched any movies at all?"

"No, not really." She replied and laughed at Jove's shocked expression. "You should tell me about some."

Jove continued to tell her about movies he had seen while they finished eating. He was surprised when Tia started comparing some of them to real-life stories she and her father had heard and experienced on their travels. They sat there for quite some time before the shop assistant eventually told them that it was nearly closing time.

"So what say we take the day off tomorrow?" Tia proposed as they walked home.

"You sure?" Jove yawned in reply.

"Yeah." Tia said in a proudly rebellious tone, "What Dad doesn't know won't hurt him. Besides, I think we deserve a good sleep in."

"And here I was thinking you were a real Daddy's girl that did everything you were told."

Tia gave him a mocking '*as if*' look.

"Well I ain't gonna argue with that." He finished.

They got home and Jove could feel exhaustion set in. After bidding Tia good night, he went to his room and collapsed onto his bed, almost instantly falling asleep.

Even though he was used to waking up early, Jove found it very easy to lose track of time and sleep in for the majority of the morning. This was probably because nobody was banging on the door for him to get up.

Around late morning, however, Jove heard a familiar knock at the door. He grumbled and rolled over.

"Oi, you decent?" Tia called from the hall. Jove groaned again and she opened the door. He opened an eye and saw that she was already dressed with a bag slung over her shoulder.

"Come on, I thought we could spend the day down the beach. You keen?"

"Do I have a choice?" Jove answered groggily.

"Not really." Tia smiled. "I'll see you outside in ten."

After getting dressed, Jove followed her down to the beach and they picked a spot in the sand to sit. To their surprise, the beach was almost completely deserted except for a group of children playing with a Frisbee in the distance.

Tia dug around in her bag and pulled out two towels for them to sit on. She had packed some sandwiches for their breakfast followed by some old toffees she had found in the back of the pantry. Jove found he had to let them melt in his mouth for a while so to avoid breaking his teeth.

"Whatdya reckon? I couldn't find a use by date on the packet." Tia asked as she finished one. Jove's teeth were practically glued shut so he politely gave her a 'thumbs up'.

"You know you still haven't asked me." Tia said after a short silence.

"Asked you what?" Jove replied when his mouth became unstuck.

"Whether I was interested."

Jove looked at her confusingly for a time before he clicked. He nearly choked on the toffee and had to clear his throat before answering.

"Random much?"

Tia shrugged.

"Well it doesn't really matter now does it?" Jove answered defensively.

"Why's that?"

"Things have changed since we were back home when my life was, you know, normal. Since then I've been kidnapped by you and your father and found out that there's a whole new world out there that I'm apparently a part of. Now we're living together whether we like it or not and you're my trainer. Not to mention you're like five years older than me."

"True." Tia popped another toffee in her mouth while Jove sifted some sand through his fingers.

"Were you?" He eventually blurted out.

153

She shrugged. "Before I figured out that you were the Incarnate you were like every other guy. You were probably shyer than most though. You need to give yourself more credit. You're a lot more capable than you think you are."

"Thanks." Jove smiled weakly.

"Anyways." Tia packed up the remaining food back in her bag, "You wanna go for a swim?"

"Sure." Jove shrugged.

Tia got up from her towel and took off her shirt. Underneath she was wearing a bright yellow bikini with matching short pants. Jove hadn't seen this much of her slender figure before and he suddenly felt a lump form in his throat. Her tan had an even cover across her flawless body.

"Last one in is a shrivelled old Draagni." She grinned at him before pelting toward the water.

Jove did not answer. In fact he was struggling to even maintain eye contact. He bolted after her, hoping he would not get caught checking out the finer points of her physique.

They had barely made it into the water when Jove felt something hard hit him in his side. The shock sent him crashing into an oncoming wave.

"What the…?" Jove spluttered as he surfaced again. Tia turned around as she heard the commotion. The children that were playing further along the beach had moved closer toward them and had thrown their Frisbee a little too far. It floated in the water next to Jove.

"Oooh lovers." One of the older boys jeered and the others laughed along with him.

"Come here you little bastard." Jove caught his breath and ran out of the water. Tia quickly stopped him in his tracks.

"Let it go. They're just kids." She halted him but Jove shot the group a look that was enough to make them flinch.

Tia grabbed the Frisbee from the water and twirled it in her hands. A playful smirk broke across her face which caught Jove's eye.

"Hey guys go long." She tossed the Frisbee out over the beach beyond the children. They watched in awe as it glided over the dunes and curved back towards them. Jove noticed Tia's pupils swirling and her hand moving in circular motions behind her back as she controlled the Frisbee.

"Show off." He whispered.

"That's awesome." One of kids ran over and plucked the disc out of the air as it hovered back toward them. "How'd you do that?"

"Secret." Tia winked at them.

They ogled at her and handed over the Frisbee, begging for her to do it again. She playfully palmed the Frisbee over to Jove as if to challenge him. The kids dared him to match Tia's throw.

Jove was about to throw a high one when he suddenly felt a painful throb in the back of his head. Something about it made him feel vulnerable all of a sudden, as if something had intruded on his mind.

He looked over to Tia. She also had a pained look on her face and seemed equally confused.

"Dad's home." She said so the children couldn't hear.

"I know. He's early." Jove answered, wondering how he knew that.

"Sorry kids but we gotta go." Jove handed the Frisbee back to the taller boy of the group. He was giving Jove a slightly perplexed look.

"Umm, thanks." He took the disc. "Who are you?"

"Pardon?" Jove answered. He looked around the group and saw that all the kids were giving him and Tia looks as if they had never seen them before. Before the boy could answer, one of his friends piped up.

"Hey guys, lets head home. My mums just finished making lunch."

"How do you know?" One of the others questioned him.

"I dunno." The boy seemed puzzled for a moment but then smiled again. "Come on lets go."

Without even farewelling them the group took off up the beach leaving Jove and Tia standing there confused.

"Come on. We've gotta go too." Tia went to pick up their stuff.

He joined her and together they trudged back up the dunes toward the house. They saw movement through the screen door and noticed that Auster had returned. But he was not alone.

Tia opened the door and they were instantly hit with a strange smell that stung their nostrils. Jove was about to make a rude noise when he was jabbed in the chest by Tia's elbow as she realised that it would have offended their guest sitting proudly at the dining room table.

Maré

Jove and Tia stood dumbfounded in the doorway and stared at the creature sitting naked in front of them. Its piercing yellow eyes were already fixated on Jove as he walked in. It was roughly the same size and build of a well-toned human adult with seemingly powerful webbed hands and feet. The smooth skin that covered all of its body emanated a pale blue colour and had absolutely no trace of hair anywhere.

The most alien thing about this 'person', Jove thought, was the absence of a mouth on its face. Instead it had been replaced by gills on either side of its neck. After the awkward moment it took for Jove to take in this strange image, the Merpesces stood up and strode toward him.

Jove Boyd, Jove heard the sound of his own voice inside his head, making him jump. At the same time pain filled his head as if something was trying to invade his mind again and curiously probe at his thoughts.

I am Maré. Formerly of the Euxine tribe. The Merpesces held out a slimy webbed hand to Jove, *It is an honour to finally meet you, Incarnate.*

Jove reluctantly went to return the handshake but, to his surprise, Maré jerked away.

No young master, like this. and it instead proceeded to grab at Jove's wrist, spreading a slimy film underneath its webbed fingers. Trying to hide the fact that he was gagging, Jove reciprocated with a slightly less powerful grip.

After locking wrists for another second, Maré released. Trying not to seem rude, Jove subtly wiped his arm on the back of his shirt while the visitor greeted Tia in the same way.

You have a strong mind for a human your age. Jove's voice echoed inside his head again.

"Umm, thank you?" He replied awkwardly. It was a weird feeling having an audibly one-sided conversation.

I'm sorry, I should probably explain why I'm here. Maré's echo rang out again. Jove figured that everyone else had heard the voice as well since Tia seemed to be just as bewildered as he was.

I am here to train you, young Incarnate.

"Train me?" Jove felt his heart sinking. His current training regime was rigorous enough without cramming more into it.

"In the ways of using your mind." Auster confirmed.

"How do you mean?"

As you may have gathered by now young master, I have the ability to project and interpret speech through the electric pulses in your brain. It is an ability all of my people possess.

159

Jove felt slightly uncomfortable hearing his own voice take on such a matter-of-fact tone.

Sir Favon has already briefed you on this knowledge, yes?

Jove nodded nervously and Maré's eyes gleamed as if the creature was smiling.

As the Incarnate you will also attain these abilities. It is vital in your development and will contribute to your roles amongst the five races.

"Normally the Incarnate doesn't undergo mind-conditioning in the transformation process." Auster interjected. "But we, Maré and I, believe that we may have to change things up a bit. It would be useful for you to be able to navigate through another's mind for information."

"I don't think I'm ready for this though." Jove stood back nervously. "You've already got me training every hour of the day."

"It is a big ask of you I know but we can't afford to wait any longer than we have to. Anyway, the human mind is considered to be the most ingenious and strong-willed of the races so it can bear to start earlier conditioning."

Maré then cut in, *If you do not mind young master, shall we spend some time alone so that I may assess your potential?*

Eyeing the strange creature's figure and feeling its presence in his mind, Jove got the impression that he couldn't refuse. Auster gave him a reassuring look and motioned for him to accept.

"Umm, sure."

Excellent, excitement flared in Maré's eyes. This half telepathic conversation was starting to give Jove a headache.

If you can please follow me down to the beach we shall start immediately.

Maré turned and headed toward the back door with long graceful strides.

"Wish me luck." Jove whispered to Tia as he reluctantly followed.

You do realise I can hear you? A voice said sharply in his head.

"Er, sorry." Jove's face reddened. Tia snickered behind him.

Maré waited for Jove outside the door and together they made their way toward the beach. There was an eerie silence as they walked. Jove's mind was teeming with anxiety and he tried to keep his thoughts to a minimum in case they were being probed.

It is always so interesting when a human meets a Merpesces for the first time, Maré projected with a calm tone as they reached the sand dunes. *I can sense your discomfort but do not worry, it is nothing short of normal.*

Jove could not think of an answer. Instead he eyed Maré's strange physique and a question formed in his head. Before he could put it into words, the Merpesces was already answering him.

I am a male specimen presently, as you were about to ask. My people are able to change sex when it suits in order to provide offspring.

A creepy shiver ran down Jove's spine as they made it to the dunes. He peered down the beach to see if anyone had seen him with this alien creature.

Instead, he was surprised to see it was completely deserted. There wasn't even any sign of the children that had been playing with their Frisbee.

It is ok young master, the only life pulses I can detect are yourself and the crabs burrowing beneath the sand.

"You can detect life?" Jove asked curiously.

Of course. All living creatures give off an electrical signal that I am able to pick up. It is, after all, how my people interact with the world.

"Wow." Jove couldn't help but say this out loud.

They continued to walk down the sand toward the water at low tide. Jove expected to stop on the beach, however Maré continued to walk out into the ocean.

"Umm, am I supposed to follow you?" The water was lapping at Jove's feet. Maré turned. The water was already around his waist.

Of course, the fins on his body were starting to flex. *Electrical pulses and sound travel more efficiently through water. So it is beneficial that we are fully submerged.*

"Right." Jove answered apprehensively. He took off his shirt and made sure there were definitely no passers-by before wading out toward

Maré. Soon his feet were no longer touching the ocean floor.

How good are you at holding your breath? Jove heard his own voice ask smugly. Realising Maré was not expecting an answer, they both descended below the water's surface.

Immediately Jove felt the salty water brush over his face and it made him feel unusually relaxed. It was as if Maré's presence in the water gave off a soothing aura heightening the senses in his mind. This creature was definitely within its natural element.

Understand now? Jove's voice echoed so clearly it was as if the words had come out of his own mouth. *It is a lot easier to project your thoughts and to enhance your mind training down here. So there is no need to speak during these sessions.*

Jove stayed relaxed for only a few seconds before he realised he needed air. He panicked and quickly surfaced.

"So how are we supposed to do this if I have to keep coming up to breathe?" He coughed out a mouthful of seawater.

This exercise is all to do with the mind and disconnecting from your physical body. This is vital if you are to venture into another's mind and communicate with it. Maré replied. *You can trick the brain into thinking your body is without danger and your muscles are not in need of oxygen. For the moment, I will block these pulses for you and eventually you will be able to do this for yourself. We will have to keep these sessions short to start with.*

"Right." Jove's breathing returned to normal. He expanded his lungs and streamed as much air into them as he could. Once they were filled to almost bursting and his heart rate had slowed, he descended into the water again.

Immediately he felt Maré sever the connection between his mind and body and the world around him deteriorated into a black abyss. Whether or not it was because he was submerged in the water, Jove felt a strange sense of weightlessness.

Instantly, Jove was overcome by the thoughts and emotions bustling through his mind. It felt almost as if they were attacking him. They took the form of large orbs of colour and sound. After only a few shorts seconds, Jove felt them overwhelm his consciousness to the point where he thought something was going to short circuit. They darted about in front of Jove's eyes leaving him dizzy and disorientated.

"Whats going on!?" He started to panic.

Maré felt his panic and interjected, immediately silencing all the action around them. Artificial calm fell over Jove as Maré controlled his loose thoughts and feelings.

Everything is fine, The bulk of his minds contents fell away. *You just panicked. Your brain's natural reaction is to ward off intruders by attacking them with random thoughts and raw emotion.*

Well it works, Jove thought to himself. To his surprise he heard these words echo inside his head as if he had spoken them aloud.

In due time, you will learn to suppress all your excess thoughts, increasing your focus during future experiences.

Right, Jove thought and heard his voice ring out again. *So where are we?*

Your mindstream, Maré quickly answered using Jove's voice. *This is where all your thoughts, emotions and memories pool in your brain. Current and past.*

Maré allowed for some memories to bubble up from below. As they circled, Jove heard mottled sounds of cries and laughter depending on whatever bubble was closest to him. Familiar voices rang out, some of which he hadn't heard in many years.

This is a place where your subconscious visits whenever your mind is idling, especially during sleep. Dreams, for example, are a collection of these thoughts and are often blended together to form what you see when you are asleep. Some can be more prominent than others depending on your mood.

Jove remained fascinated with the floating bubbles around him while Maré spoke. He yearned to reach out and grab one.

Go on, touch it. Maré fuelled his curiosity, *Even though you do not have a physical body in here, you can still move about as if you did. It is all a matter of will.*

Jove reached out to the closest bubble. Just before he made contact it burst in a suddenly vast array of colour and an image projected around him. A young boy was crying on the ground next to a slide in a kindergarten playground. Five-year-old Jove clutched his knee and rocked back and forth crying in pain.

"I remember this." Jove stepped back out of the memory.

Evidently.

"I thought I might be able to fly. I wanted to feel the wind on my face and soar through the clouds. The other kids thought I couldn't do it." The sound of the crying child died away as the image faded. "They were right."

It sounds like you acquired Ventieran instinct very early in your development.

"I guess so." Jove answered thinking of the air creatures. Another bubble playfully approached them from below. Euphoria flowed from the membrane and urged Jove to touch it. He obliged.

Immediately a projection of Tia formed in front of him. Her features were flawless and her surroundings seemed to have faded from view. She seductively winked and beckoned for him to come closer. Jove felt his stomach churn.

A sudden jerk in the back of his mind reminded him of Maré's presence and Jove quickly shoved himself out of the bubble. Using all his will, he pushed it back down into the depths of his mind. It was replaced by a figure Maré conjured up, taking the form of Jove's physical image. It was an exact likeness. However this version seemed more dignified and confident while Maré possessed it.

"That was private." Jove said guiltily but his mirrored self raised an eyebrow.

Feeling slightly embarrassed, he changed the subject. "Why are we in here anyway?"

Jove watched himself open his mouth as if replying to his own question.

Well, Young Master, I am presently assessing the state of your mind. The figure circled Jove and became fixated on random objects floating around the mindstream.

It is fascinating to study the mind of an adolescent human. There is usually a lot of depth to the human mind and it is most complex as it matures into adulthood.

There was silence and the figure suddenly darted about through the void.

But there is more to your mind young master. You are dealing with more issues at the present and so your thoughts and emotions are yet even more complex."

Understandably. Jove couldn't help but think. His clone shot him a curious glance as Maré picked up the remark.

You have a strong mind so this is a good thing. Maré continued. *The Incarnate is well known for the control and discipline he or she has over their mental self. You are no different. Like the Merpesces race you too have the ability to read and project aspects of the mind unto others.*

"Why only us?" Jove queried.

It is all within the ability to read and manipulate the electrical currents within the brain. It is an ability every Merpesces has and as such has been passed down until we have evolved into a creature that does not require a mouth. Who would after spending thousands of years under the sea where speech is useless? This is how we communicate. This is how we use our power. Many of your people would scientifically define it as telepathy. Being the Incarnate, you have inherited these powers as well. With the right guidance and control over your development of these skills, we can expand the boundaries of your capabilities.

"Expand how?"

Jove's mirrored figure smirked and moved so close that their noses were almost touching. A glint of excitement burned in his eyes.

Firstly, you can overcome the language barrier. Rather than hearing words and the audio component of language, you can read the representation defined by the word. So rather than hearing the word 'run' in other languages, for example, you will interpret the action or image of a person running when someone thinks or says the word.

"Cool." Jove answered. He wasn't good at foreign language subjects at school anyway.

Secondly, I can teach you to hide your own mind's presence to other life forms. Even now you can feel my mindstream penetrate into yours in order to communicate. I can teach you to disguise your thoughts and probes so that you can roam about in another's mindstream unnoticed. In turn, I will also help you to create defences to strengthen your own mind.

Jove's own excitement built up and was mirrored by the figure that was bursting to reveal the last step.

Lastly, and after years of extensive training and discipline, it might even be possible to create entirely new thoughts and illusions inside another's mindstream. It is only a theory at this stage but may be possible if there is enough power from the host. I have been trying to understand and implement this technique for years.

"Wait, you haven't even tried it yourself before?" Jove queried and a twinge of worry spread through the void.

No-one has. Only the Incarnate would have the power to pull it off. I myself have only just started to understand the basics.

"Has an Incarnate ever been able to do it?"

Well technically there has not been much need for it over the last multiple millennia, so no. It is only since you have been reborn as a human and under these circumstances that we thought we might put this theory to the test. We now live in a world where the discovery of the other races is imminent. Once this happens, there is no telling what will happen and the extent anyone will go through to come out on top. Any action that can be taken to hinder any negative impact must be harnessed as soon as possible so we can use it to our advantage. For instance…

The Global Government plan. Jove's thoughts finished Maré's sentence without meaning to.

Exactly. The Maré version of Jove nodded. *Which is why Auster asked that I come to train you now rather than later with the Ventiera. Human society and their technologies are progressing far more quickly than we first anticipated.*

Suddenly Jove felt the blackness swirl around him and the colours of his memories washed away as water seemingly filled his mindstream. His mirrored figure disintegrated below him and he was thrown back into his body. The water that swirled around his head was now surrounding his physical body and trying to force itself into his lungs.

Almost choking under the water, Jove darted toward the surface. For a second time he coughed up seawater in an attempt to fill his lungs with clean air. This time it took slightly longer to get his breath back. The fact that he now had a pounding headache was not helping.

"We did that all in one breath!?" He gasped.

You held it for a good minute or so. Maré answered while still lurking in the water below.

"That was only one minute!?"

Yes. Brainwaves travel much faster than the physical body's nervous system does. When separated, the illusion of time expands in your mindstream and appears longer than in the physical world.

"That's insane." Jove wallowed toward the shore where his feet could touch the sand. His head was spinning and his body felt almost completely drained.

That should be enough for today." Maré projected from the water. *"I have a fair understanding of your mindstream now.*

Jove still felt uncomfortable at the idea of this Merpesces roaming about in his head.

I suggest you go rest. Maré continued as Jove waded across the shallows. *The first time you enter a mindstream is supposedly the most taxing.*

Jove clambered out of the water onto the empty beach and found it was taking all his energy not to slump down in the sand dunes.

I have already projected to master Auster that you are on your way. He has prepared supper for you. He could feel Maré fade away in the water.

After what felt like an eternity, Jove clambered through the back door and collapsed on the couch.

"How did you go?" Tia perked up as he entered. He looked at her with eyes that could kill.

"Any more surprises and I think my head will literally explode."

Broken In

Another couple of weeks passed and Jove became accustomed to the new routine at Grendun Court. Surprisingly, he found that the highlight of his days were his mind-conditioning lessons with Maré. His thoughts would wander in the cool water and he didn't complain when it caused them to take longer sessions even though they usually left him with exhausting migraines.

After a while Jove became quite used to having his thoughts read. He felt it was useless in preventing Maré from reading them. Nonetheless he was reassured that all his embarrassing and private thoughts, including his feelings for Tia, were kept between them. On occasions where he felt homesick and stressed he would look forward to his mind training. It almost felt like he was seeing a shrink.

As for his training with Auster and Tia, Jove had progressed to the point where he almost matched their own abilities. In their sparring sessions Auster had taken to using more fighting instruments. Jove's particular favourite had been the wooden broadswords.

On one particularly hot afternoon, Jove was feeling especially fast and confident, and it showed. By now he was used to Auster's fighting style and had started to pinpoint the few weaknesses he had.

"Good." Auster stood back as he blocked an onslaught of punches. "What else can you do?"

Jove spun around and swung his leg upwards. As he expected, Auster lowered his right arm to deflect it. At the last moment, Jove twisted his body so that his leg dropped and he sprang up on the other one, catching Auster off-guard. His shoulder was left unprotected and he had no time to react before impact.

"Brilliant!" Auster was impressed as he rubbed his shoulder. Jove found that no matter how hard he managed to strike Auster, he was always able to shrug it off. As a result and as requested, Jove did not hold back in both attack and defence. More recently, however, Auster had been taking more hits than dishing them out.

"Now let's see your defences again."

Jove took a protective stance as he waited for a fresh barrage of punches and kicks. Auster started with a forceful punch to his right flank, Jove slid his arm down and deflected it surprisingly easily. Gliding passed, Auster tried to throw him off with an upward kick to the chest. Expecting something like this, Jove blocked the blow with his wrists and grabbed Auster's ankle to throw him off balance.

Recovering, Auster twisted and tried to swing another punch in order to gain the upper hand.

However, Jove easily ducked to avoid it. He thought he may have Auster in a position where he would finally be able to beat him. He struck at Auster's knees to weaken his stance before preparing a final blow to his chest. At the last moment, however, Auster managed to gain his ground and stop Jove's fist just inches in front of his own ribcage.

"Fantastic. You've definitely improved your reflexes." He commented as he relinquished his grip on Jove's hand. "You've learnt to read your opponent's moves and resourcefully come up with a counter attack."

Jove stood there feeling quite proud of himself. It was about time Auster started to give him recognition for his efforts.

"Although perhaps you and I have been sparring together for too long. You have gotten used to my particular style and fighting habits." Auster pondered as he continued. "I think it's time we took things to the next level."

"Why do I get the feeling I'm not going to like this?" Jove queried. Auster merely smirked in response.

"There is no way that I'll be able to match your youth and agility. So we'll need to cater to that." He walked over to the shed door. "Tia!"

Jove's heart sank.

"What?" Tia yelled from inside the house. It sounded as if she had been sitting in the lounge.

"Come here a minute!"

In a matter of seconds, a disgruntled Tia emerged from the house and appeared at the shed door. Her face brightened slightly as she saw her father's evil grimace. Jove did not like this at all.

"I think that it's high time the both of you fought someone who will be able to match the other's speed and creativity. This way you can help each other develop. It's time for you two to fight one another."

"I don't want to fight her." Jove stood back.

"Yeah Dad this might hurt." Tia agreed.

"I have no doubt you'll be fine." Auster reassured her.

"I wasn't talking about me." Tia jerked her head in Jove's direction.

"Oi!" He retorted, now over whatever reservations he had.

Auster grinned. "Okay, quit your bickering and take your stances."

Jove and Tia took up their positions on either side of the mat and awaited Auster's signal. Their eyes locked and Jove could see the ferocity in Tia's swirling eyes. A playful smile flashed across her lips.

"Go!"

Tia's body was immediately a blur. Before Jove had a chance to react, her fist had almost connected with his right cheek. He ducked just in time to see it whiz past his face. She responded with a left hook to his side which Jove barely managed to block. A third blow aimed at his chest made him stumble back a few steps. Tia allowed him a chance to recuperate.

"What's wrong?" She jeered. "Afraid of hitting a girl?"

"Afraid of making one cry." Jove responded and lunged forward, but she was ready for him. Easily avoiding his fist, she danced underneath his arm and straightened up again behind him. Pre-empting her movements, Jove swung his other arm in a backswing. He almost connected with her shoulder but she somehow managed to block him.

"Better." She commented. "But you'll need to be more creative."

As if it were an instruction Jove twisted his body and swung his other arm around toward her. Tia deflected it with her own arm and retaliated with a sideways kick.

"Good." Auster shouted over them. "Faster. Make the most of your agility, both of you."

Jove noticed that Tia had a very similar fighting style to her father, but her moves had their own unique flare and she had tailored them to suit. Her style combined with her speed made her an extremely tough opponent. The only thing which stopped her from defeating Jove was that she did not know his fighting style. It soon became apparent that she was also not used to battling anyone other than her father.

On and on, blow after blow they attempted to strike each other, taking advantage of each and every opening only to be blocked by the other's defences. Auster's shouts of encouragement sounded distant as both Jove and Tia were engrossed in their bout.

Beads of sweat started to roll down their foreheads and sting their eyes, however neither of them gave in an inch. Every time it looked as if one of them had the upper hand, the other would pull a move to throw them off and it was back to anyone's win.

They raced around fighting from all parts the shed, even using some of the equipment to their aid. Both were ready for the other's moves. Jove started to feel bruises and welts form on his arms as he continued to block Tia's barrages. She seemed to be growing weary as well.

Before long, their movements became more erratic. They revealed more openings for the other to take advantage of but they were losing speed as their energy depleted. In one last attempt to take out the victory, they each raised a clenched fist, ready to dish out the final blow when…

"Enough!"

The order came as a shock to both of them but their bodies quickly relented and they collapsed onto the mat, utterly exhausted.

"That was fantastic!" Auster continued. "Good to see that the both of you have let my advice sink in. Next I want you to fight with weapons. Tia, get your staff."

Tia picked her head up off the mat with an annoyed expression on her face. "Are you serious?

Did you even see the fight we just had? There is no way that I'm going to be moving for a while."

Jove was taken aback by Tia's retort, even though he was thinking the same thing. Auster glared at her for a moment before giving in.

"Very well. We are going to have to work on your endurances as well. Starting tomorrow."

"Thanks." She sighed and dropped her head down again.

"I'll see you both inside for dinner." Auster finished as he walked out of the shed, leaving Jove and Tia to recover in silence. It took quite some time for them to work up the energy to pick themselves up off the floor again.

"You fight good." Tia panted.

"Thanks, you too."

Jove felt like he was asleep for only a couple of hours that night when he awoke to Maré unexpectedly prodding his mind. His presence seemed weaker than usual as he projected from the beach.

It's a bit late for you to be testing my defences. Jove answered unappreciatively. He was still completely worn out from his battle with Tia.

It's not that young master, Maré's tone was riddled with concern. *There is a group of humans on approach to the house.*

Jove sat bolt upright in bed. No sooner had the sentence finished processing in his head when he heard a noise beyond the hall. The sound of someone struggling with the front door made the hair on the back of his neck stand on end. They quickly succeeded in picking the lock.

What do they want Maré? Jove started to panic. He sensed the Merpesces senses flicker uneasily.

I am afraid I cannot venture into a mindstream undetected from this distance. I can merely project and receive.

Jove couldn't help but swear in his head. He felt Maré flinch, not recognising the word in his own vocabulary.

I am confident you are ready to do it yourself. You have a strong mind young sir.

Footsteps sounded faintly from the lounge room as the intruders tried to move about as silently as they could. Also trying not to make a sound, Jove carefully got up from his bed and tip-toed over to the door. A brief scan with his mind told him that Maré had mentally jostled Auster and Tia awake as well.

How many do you think there are? Auster queried when Jove bridged a connection with their minds from his room.

I'm detecting about three but I could be wrong. Jove replied without much confidence after another quick scan.

Sounds about right judging by their footsteps. Auster thought so Jove could hear.

The invaders seemed to have kept to the lounge room and kitchen and had not decided to venture toward the bedrooms yet. Jove opened his door as quietly as possible and peered down the hall. Flashing beams of light darted about in the dark as the trespassers scuffled about raiding the house.

Three, Jove confirmed his suspicions. He turned as he heard a small creak and saw that Tia and Auster had appeared in their own doorways. Even in the dark Jove could tell that Tia's eyes were swirling angrily.

Do you think they know who we are? She allowed Jove to read her thoughts.

Clearing his mind, Jove tried to subconsciously bridge a connection to the invaders' minds. The process was painstakingly slow as he tried not to trigger his presence within their mindstreams. One of them stopped uneasily when Jove's consciousness accidentally brushed against one of their thoughts.

"Oi." They heard him whisper to one of his mates. "Do you guys feel like we're being watched?"

"Bloody hell stop bein' so paranoid." Another one of them hissed in reply. "We would have run into trouble or heard somethin' by now if someone was watchin' us. Here help me with this cabinet. This old coot's got some crazy gear."

Jove retracted his mind as carefully as he could.

Just a group of robbers. He projected to Auster and Tia.

"We can take them." Tia mouthed and almost started walking down the hall when Auster made a grab for her arm.

"No." He whispered. "No matter who these guys are, we cannot reveal your abilities. Not even through hand-to-hand combat. They may spread the word to unwanted sources, even unintentionally."

Then what will we do? Jove projected. He wasn't game to speak aloud in case the robbers heard. They had started ransacking the bookcase and cabinets. Auster, Jove and Tia ducked behind the safety of their doors as a beam of torchlight shone down the hallway. Once it left, Auster poked his head out again.

We need to scare them. I'll handle this. He allowed Jove to hear the thought.

"Should we check down the hall?" They heard one of the intruders whisper.

"Nah, we'll do there last in case they wake up... Hey check out the size of that shed. I bet they've got a heap of decent crap in there."

Jove heard the three of them shuffle over to the back door to inspect the shed.

"Oi Mark, you stay here and keep an eye on that hallway to make sure nobody wakes up. We'll check out the shed."

They heard the back door slide open and two of the thieves walked out leaving *Mark* to keep watch. As far as Jove could tell, he had stayed at the back door so to keep an eye on both the shed and the mouth of the hallway. The bedroom doors were still hidden from view so they were able to poke their heads out of their rooms without being noticed.

"Do you think the two of you could make a noise in the kitchen from here?" Auster smirked.

It took a moment for Jove to understand what he had meant, but he mirrored Auster's smile when it clicked. He nodded confidently.

Both he and Tia started circling their arms, creating a silent stream of wind. They held the pressure and awaited the signal.

Auster held up three fingers to show the countdown. He dropped one finger.

Jove and Tia combined their respective streams.

He dropped another.

They took aim.

When Auster dropped the last finger, Jove and Tia directed the air current down the hall and silently targeted it past the unfortunate robber and into the kitchen. The glass fruit bowl on the bench shifted and fell to the floor, smashing on impact.

Sure that this would have diverted the man's attention, Auster bolted quietly down the hall, dropping his body into a low army roll as he emerged from the hallway lip. Within a second he had made it past the bookcase and straightened up again, grabbing a large book from one of the shelves and hiding from view. Jove was quite impressed that he was able to move so quickly and silently without distracting the lonely thief from the broken bowl.

All at once, Jove heard a metallic *click* and Auster reappeared again. The noise immediately drew the attention of the remaining robber and something in Auster's hand glinted in the revealing torchlight.

"I suggest you and your mates get off of my property right now." Auster's gruff voice rumbled as he held a military grade pistol firmly in his hand. The polished metal shimmered as the thief eyed it nervously. Just seeing it from the side made Jove feel intimidated, let alone seeing it from *Mark*'s perspective.

The robber was rooted to the spot. The torchlight started to scatter as his hand quivered with fear.

"Turn around. Now!" Auster demanded.

The man seemed to stutter and shake for a moment before obeying.

"Now walk out to the shed where your mates are."

Slowly and cautiously the man stepped out the back door and made his way toward the shed. Auster followed him out, keeping an even distance with his pistol aimed in the centre of Mark's back.

Eager to keep their eyes on the scene, Jove and Tia emerged from the hallway and watched on.

Lights flashed from the shed windows as the other robbers emerged, sensing trouble. Both of them held sacks filled with their findings. They too froze as they caught sight of Auster with his gun raised. From the back door, Jove was able to see all three of them clearly in the moonlight.

None of them were smart enough to cover their faces and all seemed only slightly older than Jove. The eldest one, seemingly the leader of the group, eyed Auster with malice. He shone his torch at Auster's face and caught sight of Jove and Tia behind him. As much as it looked like he wanted to make a move against them, it was hard to argue with a raised pistol.

"You little shits better get off my property. Otherwise next time I won't be so easy on the trigger. Now!"

The three intruders dropped their sacks without hesitation and stumbled down the backyard toward the beach. Each of them was putting as much distance between themselves and the house as they could. The leader turned around before disappearing from sight and caught Jove's eye. He gave him a hateful glare which made Jove feel uneasy. Auster kept the pistol raised until the sound of their panicked running faded away over the dunes.

"I didn't know you had a gun." Jove eyed the pistol as Auster picked up the half-filled sacks and walked back into the house.

"I've had it since I left the military. Never know when you might need it."

He dropped the sacks on the couch and looked through them to see what the thieves tried to steal.

The living room itself was almost completely ransacked. Some of the weapons from the cabinets lay strewn across the floor along with some books. One book in particular caught Jove's eye. It was the one Auster grabbed just before taking on the robbers. As he picked it up he noticed that the pages had been hollowed out.

"You keep a gun in the bookcase?" He showed it to Auster.

"I already keep a knife strapped to my person at all times. Handy to keep other forms of weaponry elsewhere." Auster twirled the pistol around his finger and unloaded the clip in a single swift movement. He handled it like it was an extra limb.

"S'pose." Jove looked nervously at Auster. For the first time, he truly saw what years in the army and working for the hidden world had done to train him. It made Jove feel both safe and scared at the same time.

"Did they get hold of much?" Tia started going through the sacks of items that were almost stolen. It was mostly fitness equipment from the shed and weapons from the cabinets.

Jove couldn't think of anything in the house that was worth stealing. The most expensive item in the house was most likely the television and it was probably older than he was.

"No." Auster replied as he starting putting the weaponry back into their cabinets. "Our real fear is if they came across anything that would give them clues about who we really are." He picked up a small, worn out leather book and tucked it gently into his pyjama pocket.

"I'm going back to bed." Auster continued. "I'll deal with this in the morning."

"It's alright Dad we got it." Tia grinned.

Auster thanked them and returned to his room, still holding the pistol delicately in his grasp.

Jove and Tia started to clean up the books and put them back in the bookcase. Jove hadn't really taken much notice of them before but they were mainly old, tattered books. Most of the covers and binding had deteriorated on a lot of them and some were even so faded that the title and text were illegible. One in particular caught his eye.

"What's this?"

He came across a larger book with a leather cover that looked as if it would fall apart at the slightest touch. The cover was faded and worn and small bits of plastic film poked out from the pages. Small golden letters were embossed in the centre of the cover spelling 'Photos'. Jove delicately opened the book, careful not to tear any of the pages.

The first photo he saw was of a little girl whose beaming face stared into the camera with sparkling misty eyes. A river of light brown hair flowed down to her waist.

"What's that?" Tia sounded from behind Jove.

"Looks like an album." He showed it to her as she knelt down next to him.

"I didn't know we had this." Tia ran her fingers over the page and her eyes glazed over. "I

186

must have been about three when this was taken. And this one."

She wiped the dust off the next photo. The same young toddler was being held in the arms of her father. They both shared the exact same smile. This version of Auster Favon seemed about twenty years younger with barely any wrinkles on his face and a head of jet black hair.

"These must have been taken just before Wentra was destroyed and abandoned." Tia pointed out the forest backdrop.

"Wentra?"

"The Ventieran city in the Daintree we lived in after I was born."

"Oh." Jove turned the page and the next photo showed the same youthful Auster standing between two other men. One had dark brown, unkempt hair and hazel eyes while the man on Auster's other side had a lean face with short sandy hair and dark green eyes.

"Who are these guys?" Jove plucked the photo from the page and pointed them out to Tia.

"Dunno." Tia took the picture out of Jove's hands, "Dad did a lot of travelling between the colonies before I was born. They were probably his mates who went with him."

"He's never told you about what he did before you were born?"

"Not much aside from his army days." Tia turned over the photo to see if there was any writing on the back. Written in faded pencil were the names *Auster, Al and Tom*.

"There you go, must've been old mates." Tia placed it back in the album. "I wonder what happened to them."

There were a few empty pages where they saw some photos had been removed and torn from the paper. Eventually they made it to the last page and Jove felt Tia become tense next to him. He delicately picked up the photo.

This one showed Auster standing next to a stunning woman with exceptionally long, light-coloured hair. Her eyes gleamed into the camera with flawless white pupils and her belly showed that she was heavily pregnant.

"This is your mother isn't it?"

Tia nodded slowly and Jove noticed that her face had lost a bit of colour.

"She's beautiful." Jove handed the photo to her.

"I know." She answered softly while staring at her mother's image, "I haven't seen a photo of her this large before."

Jove sat there and watched her quietly until something clicked in his mind. "That thing you have in your wallet, it's a picture of her isn't it?"

Tia nodded slowly. "We don't normally talk about her. Dad never did when I was growing up so I guess I learnt not to as well."

Jove put his hand on hers as she continued.

"When I was little, I found a smaller version of this photo on the floor right here. It must have fallen out of this album all those years ago. I've kept it ever since."

"Does it help keep her close?" Jove tried to comfort her. He was surprised to see her shake her head.

"Not really. I never knew her so I don't know what it's like to keep her around. It sounds silly but having this just helps me realise that she was real. That I actually did have a mother, just like everybody else."

Jove noticed some writing scribbled on the back of the picture. He tilted his head so that he could read it properly.

"Tia?" He read aloud.

"Dad named me after her. It's tradition to name the daughter of a Ventiera after their mother. It keeps their legacy going if they die giving birth, like my mother did."

"I know how you feel. I never knew my dad. Mum said he died before I was born as well. We didn't talk about him much either."

"I'm sorry."

They sat there in silence while staring at the photo of Tia's mother.

"You look just like her." Jove put his hand on Tia's shoulder and she turned to smile at him. A tear began to well up in her eyes and her pupils were swirling. She carefully put the photo back in its original place.

"Thanks." She composed herself. "I think I might go back to bed as well. I'll see you in the morning."

She left Jove sitting in the lounge by himself with the album in his lap. He continued to flick through the pages and inspected each photo as if they were famous works of art.
Eventually he tucked the book away on the shelf and decided to return to bed. It was only a few hours until he had to get up for another full day of training.

Christmas

On an extra hot afternoon in the dying days of November, Jove and Maré lulled about on the surface of the ocean after a mind training session.

What is Christmas? Maré projected out of the blue. Jove had to check that his mind had interpreted the question correctly.

It has trailed in your thoughts for a few days now.

"It's a tradition amongst humans celebrated as a holiday." Jove answered. "Friends and family gather together to celebrate and exchange gifts."

Like a festival?

"Yeah, exactly, a festival."

It's something you miss from home isn't it? You and your friends were going to go to the beach and your mother makes the best bird. Correct?

Jove snickered at Maré's interpretation of his thoughts. "Roast, but close enough. My mates and I had planned to spend Christmas week camping on the beach. It would have been our last holiday together before splitting up to take on different career paths."

Sort of like an initiation?

"I guess." Jove suddenly felt a hole grow in his chest. He was starting to miss his friends again.

Have you discussed anything with Old Master and Young Miss to celebrate Christmas here? Gather together and have a good time much the same?

"No I haven't. It wouldn't be the same though."

You are at a beach now? That's like the plans you had.

"I suppose." Jove pondered.

Great! Maré exclaimed, misjudging the answer.

"Wait, that wasn't a yes."

You were thinking it.

"Fine." Jove relented, "I guess there's no harm in asking. Besides, I think I've earned myself a holiday."

They lay in the water a little while longer while Maré asked more questions about Christmas and Jove's skin started to prune. As usual, the beach was deserted so Maré accompanied him up to the house. Excitement emanated from his body and burst into Jove's mindstream so that he had to block Maré from his thoughts.

They walked through the back door and found Auster sitting on the couch in front of the television.

"Good to see you venture up here in this heat Maré. How'd training go today?"

"Alright." Jove replied bluntly. "Where's Tia?"

"Training in the shed." Auster eyed them suspiciously, "Why?"

She's coming. Maré quickly interjected and soon enough Tia burst through the back door.

"Hey what's up?" She sounded slightly breathless, "Maré called me in the shed. It sounded urgent."

"Not really." Jove answered, raising his eyebrow at Maré.

"So what's going on then?"

Christmas! Maré was bursting to get it out.

"Umm, what about it?" Tia was confused and her father didn't seem to fully understand either.

"Maré wants us to celebrate it this year." Jove clarified.

I've never experienced such a human festival before and would be curious to take part in the tradition.

Auster was taken aback and Tia had to bite her lip to stop herself from laughing. Standing out of Maré's view, Jove also had to stifle a snicker.

"Er, sure." Auster was slightly speechless, "We were just going to have the day off but I guess we can organise something a bit more… festive."

"Does this mean we have to organise gifts and everything?" Tia piped up.

"Sure. How about I give you each fifty bucks and we'll have our own Christmas morning."

Maré shivered with excitement and projected the word 'awesome', mimicking Jove's mannerisms.

By the way, what are bucks and what do they have to do with Christmas?

That warm December passed very quickly and aside from their usual training regime, the slight change in atmosphere was apparent in Grendun Court. Auster and Jove chopped down a baby pine tree from the forest and propped it up in the centre of the lounge room.

Tia had taken charge of the other decorations. Soon the interior of the house was lined with "Merry Christmas" banners and fairy lights that her father had found at the local two dollar shop. She had even woven together a few handmade decorations using debris she found on the beach and in the forest. The one she was most proud of was a dazzling wreath made from pine needles, seaweed and wildflowers.

Finally Christmas Eve came around and Auster decided to give everybody the day off to finish the preparations. With Maré's enthusiasm growing and invading their minds, it was difficult for them to keep focussed. Jove frequently found himself shielding his thoughts to block out the bursts of curiosity and excitement being shot around. Maré took particular interest in the decoration process and was constantly following Tia around, barraging her with questions.

"For the last time, I don't know the full story behind the wreath!" She quickly grew impatient as she hung her creation on the back door. "I guess everyone puts it on their doors to welcome in the Christmas spirit or something."

Her frustration grew as Maré kept up his line of questioning and scoured her thoughts for more information. Jove curiously intercepted the conversation with his mind but all he could pick up was Maré's gibberish and Tia's dim attempt at shielding him. He did, however, manage to translate something in Maré's rant about *Greek mythology* and *Roman tradition*.

"Maré's taking this way too seriously." Jove commented to Auster as they watched on.

"Ah let it go. Merpesces by nature are highly inquisitive and Maré has always been extra… enthusiastic, about human behaviour and traditions."

"Then I guess this will be an experience for everyone."

After a long day of mental torture, nightfall came and they decided to head down to the beach and build a small fire. They had sent Maré down earlier that afternoon; his constant probing became too much to bear, and he was playing about in the water as they arrived.

The three of them watched Maré swim in the night-stained sea, descending back into the water whenever a love-struck couple or a group of kids walked by on a late night stroll. At one point, Maré did a flip as a couple of loud, drunk teenagers approached. Jove and Tia rolled around with laughter at their reaction as the teens ran home to tell their other mates how '*massive*' this fish was.

It is interesting what humans find as humorous.
Maré projected from the water, *Especially Australian ones*.

The night wore on and eventually the beach was completely silent. Maré decided to treat them to a dazzling display of gravity-defying water. Pillars shot up and streams danced around forming various shapes before dispersing into vapour and ice shards that glittered in the moonlight. Jove watched on in awe and wondered if he would ever be able to control water in such a way.

"So can you kids guess what Santa might be getting you this year?" Auster said when Maré had finished.

Just as Tia gave him a *'seriously Dad'* look, Maré interjected showing off his knowledge of St Nicholas. He had developed a theory that the legend of Santa might have derived from Ventieran culture since he had been around for so many years and had pets that granted him flight.

"I was only pulling their legs Maré." Auster rolled his eyes as he regretted bringing it up.

But look at the history, Maré started off again. *He started off as Sinterklaas in Dutch stories and was known for his generosity and his story spread to other continents.*

"Then if he is of Ventieran blood how come his name isn't established amongst their culture?"

The argument continued and Jove and Tia could only laugh. To any passers-by it would have appeared that Auster was having an argument with thin air.

"I'm glad Maré convinced us to have Christmas this year." Tia said to Jove, "I can't remember the last time we celebrated it like this. It's just been Dad and I for so long and we didn't really get into the spirit like everyone else. There wasn't much point. I suppose it must have been really different compared to growing up in your world. "

Jove looked at her and thought back to his own experiences over the years. "Not really. Other than the odd dinner or get together at a friend's place it was just Mum and I. We don't have any living relatives so each year was small and simple. But we made it special in our own way. Her Christmas roasts are awesome…" he paused, "*were* awesome."

Jove suddenly felt an empty hole in his gut. He had not seen his mother in months. He wondered how she was settling into her new life with the Ventiera and whether she fully understood his role as the Incarnate. She must have been just as anxious as he was.

"So I guess our upbringings aren't so different then." Jove finished and stared into the fire. There was a short pause between them before Tia spoke again.

"You know, it's so nice to have you living here with us now." She yawned.

"Why's that?"

"It's good to have someone around that I can talk with and relate to. I was never able to have any real friends travelling around with Dad all the time. I feel like I've missed out on so much growing up."

She leaned over and put her head on Jove's shoulder and he could feel her shivering in the cool night air.

"Thanks." He put his arm around her to warm her up. "I suppose if I had a choice of people who were to kidnap and practically torture me day in and day out, I would pick you guys in a heartbeat."

Tia snickered lightly and yawned again. Jove felt himself grow weary as well and could almost have fallen asleep by the fire. Noticing this, Auster suggested they headed back up to the house and go to bed.

I'll know if you've been sleeping. I'll know when you're awake! Maré projected cheerfully as they left.

"He can really freak me out sometimes." Tia quietly commented as they headed up the dunes, hoping Maré would not detect the thought.

Jove awoke while it was still dark on Christmas morning. He could feel a force subtly pushing in the back of his mind.

Maré get out of my head. I'm awake already.

Excellent young master, I am waiting in the lounge.

"The sun is barely up and it is nowhere near time to open the presents." Jove said aloud as his projection was still groggy.

Oh I know sir, which is why instead I've produced a Christmas breakfast before we start the gift-exchange ceremony.

"It's too early for breakfast as well." Jove pushed Maré out of his head but he suddenly jolted awake, "Wait, how could *you* have prepared food? You don't eat like us!"

Food plays an integral part of the tradition and as such I have prepared it accordingly.

Curiosity got the better of Jove so he jumped out of bed, grabbed a shirt and headed out of his room. Tia met him in the hall.

"I see Maré woke you up as well. Are you as intrigued as I am?" She greeted him.

"Worried, more like. Five bucks says he's brought up raw fish."

"You're on." Tia giggled.

They quickly entered the room and saw Auster had walked in merely moments before them. A tired, perplexed look was on his face as he stood in his pyjamas. Maré was standing proudly over the dining room table.

If Jove's head wasn't still in the process of waking up he would have burst out laughing. Set up neatly on the table were three plates piled with chocolate chip cookies Maré had found in the kitchen. Sitting next to each of the plates was a tall glass of milk.

"I think you misunderstand Maré." Auster didn't particularly want to crush his efforts. "The milk and cookies are what children put out for Santa to eat when he comes and delivers the presents."

Exactly! Maré's eyes were glistening with pride, *This Santa character is the person who gives gifts, and since you have all taken on this role I see it fit to offer milk and cookies to all of you.*

Jove and Tia couldn't take it anymore and roared with laughter behind Auster, who couldn't resist cracking a smile himself.

"I could get used to this." Tia finally calmed down and sat at the table.

Jove took the chair next to her. A faint smell of fish wafted from the plate and he could make out a slimy film covering most of the cookies. Tia wasn't so quick to notice this and had already taken a bite out of one. She quickly realised her mistake.

"Maré did you handle these with your bare hands?" She politely emptied the contents of her mouth into a napkin.

Yes of course. Why is that young miss?

Auster picked up on what Tia was getting at and quickly tried to distract Maré to avoid any insult. However Maré had already read her mind and his eyes and fins drooped sadly.

"It's a nice gesture." Auster tried to comfort him. "I'm impressed that you went through all this trouble, but how about we skip breakfast and get straight to the presents? We may as well now that we're all up."

Excellent! I put mine under just this morning while you were all still sleeping, Maré's mood instantly changed and he raced off into the lounge with Auster, leaving Jove and Tia at the table.

"He's like a small kid." Jove commented.

"Yeah, a small kid at Christmas." Tia was swishing the milk around her mouth to get rid of the fishy taste. "Who woulda thought?"

"You know, your sarcasm isn't at its best early in the morning." Jove teased.

"Nor when I eat fish cookies." She got up to take the plate of biscuits to the kitchen.

"You kids coming or what?" Auster shouted from the lounge.

"In a sec." Tia left the plate in the sink and walked out toward the lounge. Jove got up and joined her.

"By the way you owe me five bucks." She whispered in Jove's ear.

"Worth it." He smirked.

Within moments, everyone was sitting around the lounge in their pyjamas with the exception of Maré who simply sat there wearing a Santa hat. Auster crouched down to the bottom of the tree and inspected the gifts to see which one should be opened first. He picked up a small cylindrical present at the front.

"To Maré from Tia." he read out and passed it to the blue creature. "I know you've probably already extracted from our heads what everything here is but try to keep it to yourself. Surprise is the key."

Jove wasn't sure how Maré could have expressed shock or surprise without a mouth but watched him unwrap the gift anyway.

Human fragrance, He projected excitedly before the paper even tore, *Such an honour to be able to smell like your people. My pores will very much enjoy the scent. But I'm afraid it will wash off while I am in the water.*

"You use it while you're on land," Tia suggested, "to freshen yourself."

"With a can of deodorant?" Auster inspected the can and shot her a dark look, "Such a thoughtful daughter I have."

Much thanks Young Miss. Maré misunderstood Auster's sarcasm and shook Tia's hand in gratitude. An accomplished grin broke across her face.

"Next present, to Jove from Maré."

"Thanks Maré." Jove delicately took the package from Auster. It was tightly wrapped in dry seaweed and was about the size of a cricket ball. He peeled off the seaweed until a clear solid sphere sat in his hand. It was oddly heavy.

"A block of ice." Jove tried not to laugh but Tia giggling next to him was making it difficult.

I can sense your confusion and I figured as much," Maré winked. *"But that's not any ordinary ice. What's different about it?*

He pondered, "It's heavy."

What else?

Jove sat there puzzled for a second. He swapped hands and realized what else was wrong with it.

"It's not cold," he said in disbelief, "and it's not melting in my hand either."

Auster and Tia's eyes widened as they figured out what Jove was holding.

"Is that Everice?" Tia blurted. Maré nodded.

"What's Everice?" Jove was confused.

Everice, as it is known by the other races, is pure water that cannot be directly affected by heat. Maré explained. *So, if it is not manipulated, it can remain in whatever form its user wishes. It is a common item we Merpesces carry if we ever have to venture on dry land and water resources are scarce. Once you begin your training with the water element, this will become invaluable to you.*

"Wow." Jove ran his hands over its surface, "Where did you get it?"

I made it. Maré's fins fluttered proudly. Auster cut in when he saw Jove's confused look and explained.

"Everice is made by constantly expanding then compacting water molecules until they become accustomed to changes in pressure. This makes them immune to the effects of heat and the intrusion of foreign particles. Also, because the molecules have been manipulated so rigorously, you can alter the size and density of Everice to your desire. But the conditioning process can go for weeks before you start to see results. You really outdid yourself Maré. It looks like there's enough here to fill a wading pool."

It was nothing really. I was in the latest project to extend the Antarctic ice sheet to cover for the boost in our population. Most of our housing in those sheets are encased in slabs of Everice.

"So much for global warming and the ice caps melting then." Tia commented.

"I'll say. Thanks Maré that's awesome." Jove delicately placed the ball on the table as if it were made of thin glass. He still had his eyes on it when Auster handed out the next present.

"To Tia from Dad." He handed his daughter a large package. A sweet smell filled the air as she unwrapped it.

"Toffee!" Tia squealed. She eagerly opened the container filled to bursting with candy and threw one into her mouth.

"Dad theesh are amashin'." She said with a mouthful, "Rum-flavoured?"

Rum has a history with Christmas starting with…

"Yeah, that's enough Maré." Auster interjected, "It's your turn for a present. From Jove."

A watch! Maré proclaimed before the wrapping had even come off. He quickly attached the watch to his slimy wrist, *I've always wanted one of these.*

"It's waterproof too." Jove added proudly.

"Open mine nexsht Dad." Tia grinned as she popped another toffee in her mouth.

"Socks and jocks." Auster unwrapped his present and held up the small pile of undergarments, "Again, you've outdone yourself."

"Hey, the amount of times you've complained during our travels that you don't have enough…"

"Thanks Tia, broadcast that to the world why don't ya?" Jove interrupted as Auster checked the sizes. Maré grabbed a pair of jocks from the pile and inspected them carefully. Jove heard the word *fascinating* pop into the Merpesces' head.

"Here's a special one for you Jove." Auster handed him a small package wrapped in a leaf; "It's from your mother. It arrived a couple of days ago."

Jove's heart skipped a beat as he retrieved the package from Auster's hand. A small note was attached to it on what seemed to be a thin slice of tree bark.

Merry Christmas Darling,
Sorry I can't be there with you. May this keep you safe until we meet again.
Love Mum

Jove unfurled the leaf and a small trinket fell into his lap. It was a tiny acorn wrapped in silk string tied to a sturdy woven band. A small feather poked out from under the silk layer.

"What is it?" Tia looked at it curiously.

"That's a good luck charm." Auster became entranced by the small object, "It's supposed to protect you from harm. They're pretty popular in Fervune."

"Cool." Jove played with the acorn in his fingers.

"Doesn't look like it travelled too well." Tia inspected it more closely, "Look, it's even a bit charred in places."

"How the hell do you burn something in transit?" Jove pondered out loud. Tia shrugged.

"And how did she know where to send it too?" He looked suspiciously at Auster.

"Do you think your mother would have let me take you without telling her where we were going?"

"Fair point." Jove slipped the charm over his wrist. Auster picked up a long thin package and handed it to Jove, "This one's from Tia."

Tia smiled as Jove ripped off the paper. It was a long and sturdy strip of wood not unlike a thick broom handle.

"You got me a stick." Jove raised an eyebrow.

"Not just any old stick." Tia replied enthusiastically. "Shoot some air down that hole in the centre."

Jove inspected the wood more closely. Sure enough there was a tiny hole just visible in the grain. He shot a small burst of wind into it and nearly dropped the stick in shock.

As air shot through the hole, an unseen mechanism unlocked two wooden prongs within the staff and they sprang out. They were connected at the tips by a strong, elasticised string.

"What is this?" Jove curiously plucked at the string.

"It's a bo-staff." Tia replied smugly, "Or more effectively, a *bow*-staff. I made it much like mine but with some obvious modifications."

"I can shoot arrows with this thing?" Jove was impressed, "I knew you were good at building stuff at school but this is something else."

"I repeated my senior years around the state, remember? I was bound to pick up something along the line. I've got some arrows and a quiver in my room you can practice with. Only just finished making them yesterday so didn't get the chance to wrap them."

"Well hold your horses on the practice, we haven't finished here yet." Auster interrupted and reached for the next present.

"To Tia from Jove." He passed her a thin package and she eagerly tore it open. Jove held his breath as he waited for her reaction.

"Oh Jove." She paused and carefully inspected the gift, lost for words. It was the picture from the album they found of her mother.

"I figured you might want something better than that thing you have in your wallet. So I got a frame to put that one from the album in."

"This is beautiful." Tia ran her finger over her glass before clutching the frame delicately against her chest. "Thank you." She leaned over and pecked him on the cheek.

"Mind if I see?" Auster perched on the couch next to his daughter and looked at the photo. Jove saw a lump form in his throat and his eyes glazed over as he stared affectionately at his wife. "Where did you get this?"

"We found an album on the floor on the night of the break in."

"I forgot about this photo." Auster smiled admirably, "Believe me when I say it doesn't do her any justice."

He stared at the photo for a time before bringing himself back to the presents, "Actually, I also found something on the night of the break in that I wanted to give you Jove. This one's from me."

Auster handed Jove a small and reasonably thin present. He unwrapped it to find a pocket book of some kind. It was very aged and worn as if it had survived every condition on the planet. It was barely intact.

"What is it?" Jove looked down at it curiously. It was made of the same material as the album.

"That," Auster gestured for him to open it up, "is a journal I've kept with me throughout my travels amongst the races. It has information I've recorded over the years that explains key points on their beliefs and traditions. I've kept it hidden in the bookcase all this time. Well, until the night of the break in anyway."

Jove ran his hand along the delicate leather cover and saw that parts of it were fragile and close to falling off. Being careful not to let any of the pages fall out, he opened the cover and ran his eyes through the pages. They were filled with scribbled notes and loosely drawn diagrams of the other races. In some sections, Jove saw dusty snapshot photographs that had been sticky-taped to the paper.

He saw live versions of the Ventiera living in their forest city, a pair of duelling Draagni, and a baby Olderak playing in a hole it had just dug.

"This is amazing." Jove looked at the pictures with awe. "You did all this?"

Auster nodded. "I was extremely inquisitive when I was younger and loved exploring how the other races lived. Everything I learned, I collaborated right here. It's got some really useful information and insight that I figure may be a benefit to your learning. So I want you to have it."

Jove looked at him with shock, "Are you sure? This is all your work."

Auster nodded, "I think you may have a greater need for it now than I do. Besides, I've learnt all that I can from it. I did write it after all."

"Thank you." Jove drew his attention back to the journal while Auster finished off the gift-giving ceremony. Auster had bought Maré some human clothes and soon enough the creature was sitting in a pair of board shorts and polo shirt.

"Snazzy." Tia commented.

After all the presents had been exchanged, Maré left them for the beach as his body was beginning to dry out while Tia went into the kitchen to prepare a proper Christmas breakfast. Jove was still sitting on the couch engrossed in the journal while Auster tidied up the lounge room.

He memorised such notes as '*32 human years is equal to 1 Ventieran year according to the red moon festival calendar…*' and '*Draagni are able to digest nutrients out of igneous rock for nourishment when food is scarce…*'

Upon closer inspection, Jove noticed there were different styles of writing throughout the pages. It was as if a few different people had added their own sections to the book over time.

Eventually, he came to a section where Auster had marked '*Humans*'. The pages were less cluttered with notes and he saw a large number of question marks scattered around the pages.

"Hey Auster, what made humans so special amongst the five races?" Jove asked curiously. "If they had no powers, how come they were able to become such a threat?"

Auster sighed and retrieved the journal. He inspected the same pages labelled under *Humans*.

Jove curiously probed his thoughts, "Unless they *did* have powers, at some point?"

"That's been a debate that's lasted between the races for centuries. No-one really knows for sure, although many theories have been circulating."

"What do you think?"

"Well I have a theory that humans had control over a fifth element. Some martial art forms and ancient civilisations practise traditions in groups of five. Air, Fire Earth Water…and Aether."

"Aether?" Jove repeated.

"Spirit, void, raw energy." Auster explained. "I believe it's this very power that brought together the other elements in order to bring perfect balance. There is some science and history that implies that humans had at least some kind delegation over something like this. Look at olden day priests and clairvoyants for example; they believe they had the power to interpret the life and spiritual forces around them. If you believe in that kind of stuff."

"Sounds logical." Jove pondered. "So what happened? Did the power just disappear?"

"I dunno." Auster shrugged, "That's where the theory ends and the debate begins. Those who believe in it say it was lost once the Incarnate was created and that's why another cannot be made. Some say that our abilities, if we had any, simply died away. Humans could have even abandoned the power in search of the utopia they're still trying to achieve today."

Auster caressed the page and stared blankly at his notes. "But then again, who's to say the power even existed in the first place?"

Silence fell between them for a moment before Auster snapped back to reality.

"That's getting off topic. You shouldn't worry about ideas that are just that; ideas. You need to be focussing on the abilities that *do* exist. Turn back to the notes on the Draagni."

Auster thrust the journal back under Jove's nose. Jove obeyed and flicked back through to where he saw sketches and photographs of the Draagni.

"I think you may be ready to start learning the basics of their culture soon and develop a respect toward them."

As much as Jove tried to disguise it, he couldn't hide his distaste.

"I know you're not too keen on the idea but I think understanding their way of life will help when it comes to living with them down the track."

"I suppose." Jove was reluctant. He had been worrying about this for a little while now. "But what if they don't accept me into their culture? There's already someone out there trying to hunt me down and kill me."

"That's only a minority." Auster quickly interjected, "I can assure you that there are some out there that support the Incarnate and are willing to give you a chance. But first you have to prove to them that you accept their ways and respect them regardless of your personal opinion. They're a part of you after all."

Jove winced at the thought. Auster smiled.

"I thought the same way when I first learnt of their existence, when I was ignorant. I thought they were a brutal and violent people. But they go deeper than that and are much more than they seem. Read the passage down the bottom of that page there."

Jove looked where Auster had pointed. Faded against the aged paper was a phrase scribbled in another language.

"*Ac sine honore ad ignaviam occidere, occidere non afferent gloriam ignavus.*" He sounded it out slowly then looked questioningly at Auster.

"Roughly translated; To kill without honour is cowardice and to kill a coward shall bring no honour." Auster interpreted. "It's Latin. Used to be the language of the races before humans adopted English and spread it globally. That particular phrase is an ancient saying used by the Draagni which they have upheld for many years."

"What does it mean?"

"It means there should be honour within death. The Draagni don't kill for the sake of it. There has to be purpose and reason. Respect and honour is highly regarded amongst them and often decides their position within their society. They must earn it through their actions."

"Hmmm." Jove inspected the photo of the two Draagni duelling. He was slightly relieved that there was a more civil side to these creatures.

"Oi, shrimp." Tia's voice made them both jump as she snuck up holding a quiver of arrows, "You gonna come try out your bow or what?"

"Hell yeh." Jove closed the journal and jumped up to join Tia. For the remainder of the day, they ran up and down the beach playfully fighting each other and shooting random objects with their arrows while a smartly dressed Maré watched from the water.

All Fired Up

Swim…Swim…SHARK!? Swim…

Jove probed the weak minds of a nearby school of fish. He drew the string on his bow-staff and shot a long sharp shard of ice at them.

It had been a few months since Christmas and Jove's physical and mental power had increased exponentially. Not only had he become more skilled at reading mind waves, but he had also taken to telepathy for communication almost as much as Maré did. Auster and Tia had to do their own mind training sessions just to keep Jove's probing at bay. Even Maré was caught by surprise at times when his guard was down.

Per his usual routine, Auster continued to scan the news for updates on the outside world, more specifically the Global Government Scheme. The lack of its mention seemed to put his mind at ease.

Since receiving the Everice for Christmas, Maré had started training Jove to control water in line with their mind sessions. Jove was able to expand the Everice into a large body of water that could have easily flooded the living room.

Due to the surprising density and mass of the Everice, Jove found it difficult to control and quickly drained his energy and concentration. Mostly he just took to practising with small slivers at a time as he got used to its motions and fluidity.

When he wasn't using the Everice, Jove was able to shape it into a thick spiral that snaked around his upper arm. Even while he trained in the ocean it didn't dissolve into the salty water just as Auster and Maré said.

Jove's air skills were also greatly improving, especially now that he could practice with his new bow-staff. Not only was he able to use it to help stream air currents but Tia was able to train him in using it for direct combat. On a creative streak, Jove also thought of forming small slivers of water from the Everice into sharp arrows. This way, it was easier to manoeuvre the arrows while they were in the air and also meant he had an endless supply of ammunition.

At this pace, Jove quickly felt that he was beginning to master all points of his regime and that he was ready to go further. It was almost as if his abilities were beginning to feel restrained. He pondered this again as another of his Everice arrows pierced yet another unsuspecting fish.

Brilliant! Maré was impressed, *Your skills with water are certainly coming along Young Master.*

Thanks. Jove projected back as he retrieved some of his kill, leaving the rest for Maré to feast on.

Something he had learnt first-hand was that Merpesces ate by shredding their prey and absorbing the miniscule meat particles and nutrients in the water through the large pores in their skin. It was an experience Jove didn't like witnessing so he asked that Maré waited until he was out of the water and up at the house before 'eating'.

"Fish and chips for dinner anyone?" Jove proudly held up his catch as he walked through the back door.

"Yes!" Tia answered enthusiastically and yanked the dead fish out of Jove's hands.

"You're getting pretty crafty with water and that staff." Auster complimented from the lounge as Tia escaped to the kitchen to prepare dinner.

"Thanks, maybe that means we can get out of here soon so I can learn more?" Jove dared to ask.

Auster frowned and before he could open his mouth in reply they heard Tia cry from the kitchen.

"Dad! The damn gas isn't working again!" She whined as she struggled to light the stovetop.

"Here." Auster got up and fiddled with the knobs on the stove. Nothing happened. "Must be a leak. Try and light it again on my signal."

Auster handed Jove the cigarette lighter they usually used to light the stove and disappeared out the back door toward the gas tank. Jove and Tia leant over the plate to wait for the hiss. A warmth spread through Jove's hand as he held the lighter.

"Okay! Give that a go!" Auster called and they immediately heard the gas stream through.

Jove ignited the lighter which set the stovetop ablaze. He stepped backwards as the flame disintegrated to a low, healthy flicker.

"There we go." Jove straightened up but Tia seemed panicked.

"Jove! Your hand!" She pointed at his arm and Jove saw that the back of his hand was also alight.

Reacting instinctively, he grabbed the nearest tea towel and managed to bat out the flames in a matter of seconds.

"You okay?" Tia grabbed his wrist to check for burns. However there was no damage aside from a few singed hairs.

"Yeah." Jove inspected his skin curiously. "I didn't feel a thing, actually."

"Well that's good." Tia dropped his hand again. "Maybe your body knows it'll be handling fire more often soon." She winked.

"Maybe…" Jove eyed the lighter in his hand when Auster walked back into the house.

"Did that work?" His question was answered as he saw Tia place the pan of fish over the flame.

"Great." Auster then turned to Jove. "You should go do a few sets in the shed while that's cooking."

"What?" Jove went to complain but the stern look in Auster's eyes made him think otherwise. He pocketed the lighter and grumbled all the way out to the shed.

It was a hot evening and Jove was not in the mood to do weights or exercises so he simply sat on

217

the mat and started fiddling with the lighter in his hands. He thought about what Tia had said about training with fire, even though he knew she was only joking.

Since Christmas, Jove had engrossed himself in Auster's journal and it left him with a thirst for more knowledge.

As much as he hated to admit it, he had become particularly intrigued with the Draagni. He had seen a roughly drawn diagram that showed one to appear mostly like a stout crocodile that stood on its hindquarters. Another picture had shown a live-action photo of two Draagni in a duel. He remembered that their small eyes seemed to pierce through the other's soul as each were engulfed in large streams of fire that burned with great ferocity.

Jove ignited the lighter and held the flame up against his hand to see if it would burn him. Like the stove before, it had no effect. He felt the warmth but it didn't cause him any pain. For a moment, he was reminded of his childhood when his mother was always getting angry at him and calling him a 'firebug' when he played with candles or matches.

Remembering the notes Auster had written in the journal, Jove knew that the Draagni were able to manipulate and fuel fire through their emotions. The idea was that they could transfer their energy to agitate the molecular structure around them and cause friction. This would then generate heat and eventually the particles would ignite. For some reason the idea mesmerized Jove, and now that it seemed he was immune to burning, he wanted to try it.

He played around with the lighter in his fingers, igniting the tip again and feeling the heat against his palm. The flame danced hypnotically in front of his eyes and he could sense the energy emanate from the lighter in a way he had not felt from fire before. He could almost feel the particles in the air burn and become irritated as they fuelled the flame. With his hand he tried to shape the small blaze. However, it continued to flicker unaffected.

Jove released the trigger with his thumb and the lighter died. The idea of emotion and focus kept on reiterating itself in the journal. The Draagni he had seen in the pictures were perfectly exemplifying this. They seemed to have blocked out everything around them as they duelled. The intensity in their eyes was enough to send a shiver down Jove's spine every time he looked at the photo.

What makes me emotional? He sighed as he clutched at the trinket his mother had sent to him. He hadn't taken it off his wrist since Christmas as it somehow made him feel closer to her. In turn, it also helped him remember life before Grendun Court.

He ignited the lighter again and images started to form in his head as he stared into the flame.

Jove remembered his old life and his classmates from school. They were laughing and having a great time. He pictured himself back at school with them and he couldn't help but smile. He could hear them egging him on as he remembered the high jump contest. His sense of pride that day was unforgettable, and he felt like nothing could stop him. Those were the days.

He wondered what had become of his friends, whether their lives had changed even half as much as his had since leaving. They would have graduated months ago; Cameron setting off to join the army; Ben most likely getting a scholarship at some kind of sporting institute and Mitch was probably still deciding what to do.

Their smiling faces died away in his mind and Jove felt a wave of sadness wash over him. He started to feel very isolated. Now that he let himself think about it, he fully realised how much he had really lost since being practically kidnapped. For a moment, he desperately wanted his old life back as if nothing had ever changed.

The flame started to bulge and flux from the lighter tip and Jove could feel it draw energy from his hand.

He was starting to feel emotions he had kept down since arriving in Grendun Court well up inside. Hatred and anger started to overwhelm him as he thought of how being the Incarnate had cheated him out of everything he had. He started to feel malice towards Auster for forcing him away and pushing him to the limits. What right did he have? Both him and Tia.

As Jove conjured up these feelings, the flame grew larger and more intense. He could feel it draining his energy, feeding off his emotion. The heat in the shed started to rise and Jove could see the air distort as a result. The fire started to gush out from the lighter tip to almost a metre high.

Fear now welled inside Jove as the fire grew beyond his control. It was manifesting into a blazing inferno!

Panicking, he tossed the lighter out the shed door as hard as he could, hoping the fire would dissipate. Unfortunately, what happened next was quite the opposite.

The trailing blaze erupted around him and set fire to the walls and equipment, quickly singeing Jove's clothes. Desperate to get out, he covered his face and bolted out of the shed. He barely made it out with the flames licking his heels. Auster and Tia had heard the commotion from inside and were running frantically towards him.

"What did you do!?" Auster roared over the noise.

Before Jove could answer a loud crash sounded from inside as the roof of the shed collapsed.

"Jove, your Everice!" Tia shouted as she came to stand beside him. She took a fighting stance with her hands raised over fire.

Without hesitation, Jove summoned the Everice from around his arm and expanded it into a large shell of water. He struggled to control the mass as it hovered uneasily in front of him.

Tia frantically waved her arms in backward motions streaming all the air and oxygen away from the blaze like a vacuum. As hard as she tried, it still wasn't enough to stifle the flames and they continued to grow.

"Can someone call out to Maré?" She yelled to whoever would listen.

"Done!" Jove called back as he reached out with his mind.

Auster appeared again with a fire extinguisher from the kitchen and was madly using it to try and dowse the fire. With the extra help, Tia had been able to extract the majority of the air fuelling the fire so it became less intense.

Still fighting with the water, Jove pulled his hands close to his body and thrust them forward again. The water twitched violently before it expelled away in front of him with a force that almost washed away what was left of the shed. Auster had to quickly jump out of the way to avoid being collected by the water as well. It was enough to drench the fire and reduce it to small cinders. A large plume of steam rose into the sky and Auster extinguished the dying remnants of the fire.

Once satisfied that there was no more danger, Jove retrieved the Everice and froze it around his upper arm again. He and Tia sank back onto the ground and each sighed with relief. Something warm and smooth pressed against Jove's spine as he leaned back. The lighter was sitting unharmed in the grass. Hoping nobody else had seen it, he quickly pocketed it.

"You mind telling me what the hell happened!?" Auster turned and advanced on Jove, dumping the empty extinguisher next to the debris.

"It was an accident. I thought I could start learning how to handle fire."

"What made you think you could start fire?" Auster growled and Jove was taken aback. "You've barely got the hang of martial arts let alone wind and the other elements!"

This touched a nerve with Jove. He was still feeling the rage inside of him and retaliated.

"How dare you! I've been busting my arse day in and day out since we got here." He stood up so that he and Auster were at eye level.

"That doesn't mean you've progressed anywhere." Auster retorted, "I'll be the judge of how well you can control your powers."

"That's all you bloody care about isn't it?" Jove edged closer until their faces were just inches apart. Tia sat speechless on the lawn, her mouth open and eyes wide in shock.

"My powers. Your mission." Jove continued to yell. "Forget the Incarnate crap for a moment. You have barely cared about me as a person since we've met. I'm fine by the way, no burns or anything. Thanks for asking."

"Why, you ungrateful little brat!" Auster spat.

"Why should I be grateful!?" Jove cut him off, "I didn't ask to be kidnapped from home and ripped away from everything I knew to come here and obey your every command."

"Well sorry to ruin your perfectly selfish little world. But grow up! The world is full of injustice and conflict. It's time for you to take on some responsibility, Incarnate or not."

"You know, you're just jealous aren't you?" Jove moved in closer. "Since discovering the other races you've wanted to be just like them. That's why you've spent so many years studying them, but obviously that wasn't enough as you wanted to feel more important, like *you* matter."

"How dare you!" Auster roared back but Jove continued.

"So in the pursuit of making a name for yourself you've taken every means possible; even if that involves dragging your daughter across the country. You never gave her a choice let alone a chance to do what she wants."

"You leave Tia out of this!" Auster shook with rage. "I would never force my daughter to do anything she doesn't want to do."

"Well obviously I fall under a different category then. I never asked or wanted to be the Incarnate. Nor to live under the instruction of a sour, broken man like you."

Auster raised a threatening fist to which Jove didn't even bat an eyelid.

"Stop it both of you!" Tia screamed desperately from beside them. Tears were starting to well in her eyes.

Auster lowered his fist and stood back. "Get out." He broke his gaze. "If you don't want to be here then I'm not going to stop you."

Jove stood there and glared at Tia's father. He had never felt so much hatred toward one person before.

"Gladly." He said and turned heel, pushing past Tia. He stormed through the house and quickly made his way out the front door. It slammed shut with almost enough force to knock it off its hinges before Jove trudged down the driveway. He had barely made it to the street when he heard the door open again.

"Where the hell did that come from!?" Tia roared down the driveway, her voice sounded like a cruel mutation of anger and sad desperation. "We were one happy family just an hour ago."

"Just leave it Tia." Jove saw her about to run down the path after him.

"No, I'm not going to leave it." Her voice trembled as she caught up with him. "You're not like this."

"How do you know what I'm like? You're just as bad as he is."

Tia stood there gobsmacked. "We're not as bad as anything. We both care just as much for you as we do our mission." She paused, "*I* care for you."

She held out her hand for him to take. "Please come back inside. Dad wouldn't have meant any of what he said and I know you didn't either."

Jove looked from Tia's hand to her eyes and back again. He probed her mind and found it was bubbling with fear. For a moment he wanted to take her hand, but he did not want to stay around Auster.

"Just leave me alone. I need to get out of here."

He turned his back and continued down the street. He sensed her mind saddening and heard her take a step forward to follow him.

Turning and shooting a glare at her, he projected a thought a bit more forcefully than intended.

Go!!

Tia flinched in shock and withdrew a step. Her eyes started to water.

"Fine." Her voice trembled. "Just promise me you won't do anything stupid." She turned and stormed back up the driveway. Jove watched her as she reached the front door. She gave him one final glare before disappearing into the house.

Jove stood in the street for a moment and watched her figure in the window. Auster was leaning against the wall staring intently at the floor. He sprang to attention when Tia entered the room. He went to comfort her but instead she shrugged him off and walked out of Jove's view toward her bedroom. Auster then walked in the opposite direction and Jove heard a loud crash come from the lounge room. The sound of glass tinkling told Jove that Auster had just kicked in the television.

Feeling another wave of rage surge through his body, Jove stormed down the road and around the corner.

Night fell very quickly and the dank streets seemed very eerie as Jove stumbled through them. Even the quiet houses appeared to watch him judgingly as he passed. The only sources of light came from the newly-risen moon that glinted off the bitumen and the sparse street lights that flickered to life.

Jove rounded another corner and strode by the closed fish and chip shop. Not knowing which way to go, he reared down a nearby street toward the centre of town. As he walked, he retrieved the lighter from his pocket and fiddled with it. Although there was little wind blowing, the flame twitched violently every time Jove ignited it.

More streetlights started to appear the further into town he walked but the roads remained empty. Eventually Jove heard some voices in the distance and, not having anything better to do, decided to follow them.

The noises grew louder as he approached a supermarket building. A group of young men not much older than Jove were gathered in the alleyway. Tattoos covered most of their bodies and their tattered clothes looked as if they had been pulled out of the garbage. They were yelling obscenities and laughing loudly. Jove heard the clanging of glass bottles as they drank heavily. The smell of cigarette smoke wafted about and nearly made Jove choke. Lately he had become more sensitive to impurities in the air.

There was something familiar about the group as Jove passed by. Intrigued, he probed their minds carelessly and one of them, the taller one, sensed his presence.

He turned and Jove got a full view of his face. A nervous twinge knotted his stomach as Jove recognised the malicious expression. It belonged to the same man that had ransacked number nine Grendun Court a while back.

Hoping the boy would not recognised him, Jove turned heel and started walking down the opposite end of the street.

"Look who's walking the streets by themselves." The head of the group stood up and jeered. He pulled the cigarette out of his mouth and pointed with a half-empty rum bottle. Jove kept walking. The gang got up to follow him.

"Hey wait a minute." The leader called out again. "Don't I know you from somewhere?"

He ran ahead so that he was directly in front of Jove and could get a better look.

"Yeah, you're that kid from that punk old man's house. Doesn't look like he's here to protect ya now is he?" He smiled wickedly.

"You're outta luck again tonight guys. I haven't got anything on me." Jove replied while patting his pockets. He hadn't had his wallet on him since moving to Driscoll let alone used it. Auster had been paying for everything for him instead.

"That old coot had nothin' worth stealin' anyway."

"Sucks to be you then don't it?" Jove retorted before pushing past to walk away again. But the group circled around and cut him off.

"And where would you be going in such a hurry all by yourself?" The leader continued and advanced on him again. "We're not scaring ya are we? We might just be looking for new friends."

"Bullshit you are." Jove calmly stood his ground.

"Hmm, this one's got attitude boys." The leader laughed and Jove could smell the booze on his breath. The others snickered and edged in closer, "Maybe we should teach him some respect."

"Just shove off will ya?" Jove went to break out of the circle. He knew this would aggravate them but he didn't care, he could take them. One of the burlier guys stepped in front to block him and the leader grabbed onto Jove's shoulder. The expression on his face showed he wasn't amused anymore.

"Perhaps you don't know what we're capable of you little brat." The man held up a clenched fist. "And you don't have your cranky old bodyguard here to protect you."

Jove couldn't help but raise an eyebrow. He was perfectly capable of defending himself, especially without Auster.

"Oh please demonstrate." He antagonised them. This had done it. Within the blink of an eye the man sent a clenched fist rocketing towards Jove's face.

Jove stepped aside and avoided it easily. As it went whizzing by, he grabbed the man's wrist and twisted it. He squealed with pain but Jove maintained a firm grip. The other gang members charged at him from all directions. Turning on the spot, Jove wrenched the guy's arm behind his back and forced him around to take out the oncoming attackers.

Taking advantage of their drunken state, Jove easily swung blows that forced the group backwards again. The first round of punches left them all shell-shocked and it took them a short time to compose themselves.

They came in again and Jove effortlessly blocked their punches. He could hear their bottles smash as he knocked them to the ground. Another one of the group towered over him and aimed another punch at Jove's face.

Wanting to dish out some revenge, Jove pressurised some air around his fist. Dodging underneath his opponent's attack, he lunged forward and hit his attacker square in the chest, releasing the air as he did so. The sickening crack of breaking ribs filled the atmosphere as he was forced backwards, collapsing to the ground. The rest of the gang stopped in their tracks as they watched their mate go down. Jove could sense fear flash through their minds.

How did he do that? He heard one think groggily.

Then, from behind, Jove heard a single word float through someone's thoughts.

Knife…

He spun around just in time to see the ringleader unsheathe a pocket knife and lunge forward.

Jove ducked just in time and felt the blade brush just inches above his head. Retaliating, he retrieved the lighter from his pocket and lit it while swinging it through the air like a sword. He could feel his anger fuel it as it left a blazing trail of fire. The attackers' eyes widened with horror as Jove brandished the lighter and flames roared from the canister.

The man with the knife still held the blade threateningly but now he was quivering with fear. They eyed each other for a moment before one of the other guys yelled from the sideline.

"Leave it, he ain't bloody worth it." His voice trembled and Jove noticed he was trying to help the guy with the broken ribs up off the ground, "He's got some freaky shit going on here."

The man lowered the knife and glared menacingly at Jove for a moment before breaking his gaze to check on his mate. Jove also looked at Mark who was coughing and spluttering on the footpath.

Mottled and broken warps of air that only Jove could see formed around his mouth as he breathed.

It looked like his broken ribs were constricting his lungs.

"You guys should get the bloody hell outta here." Jove darkened his tone and lifted his finger off the lighter trigger. The fire quickly disintegrated. "Before I do that to you too."

The man with the knife glared at him darkly for a moment before common sense finally kicked in. He and his mates quickly scurried to help their injured friend up.

While they were preoccupied with getting him to his feet, Jove discreetly hid his hand behind his back and focussed on the restricted area inside the man's chest. With a quick flex of his fingers, he forced the air in his restrained lung to expand and push his ribs back into place. He yelled with pain but it was soon evident that he was relieved to somehow be breathing properly again.

Once they had him up and walking, the gang gave Jove a final glance of hatred, to which Jove threateningly held up the lighter again and they frantically scattered out of the alley and out of sight.

Jove didn't relax again until he was confident the group was well out of range. He collapsed onto the footpath feeling suddenly drained, as if most of his energy and anger had literally been burnt out.

He sat there rocking for a time with his head in his hands reliving what had just happened. It suddenly occurred to Jove what he was becoming and it scared him. He couldn't believe that he had gone to such lengths to harm another person.

For a moment, he reminded himself of the Draagni that had attacked him back home. A dark shiver surged through his body at the thought of ever becoming like one of them.

Jove stared at the lighter which was now covered with scorch marks. He now partly understood why the Draagni were as fierce and powerful as they were. A newfound respect toward them, although quite small, formed within him.

Feeling guilty, Jove pegged the lighter down the street with the little energy he had left. He silently vowed not to try controlling fire again until he was ready to train with the Draagni.

He cradled his head in the gutter and mulled over the argument he had with Auster. It *did* seem to come from nowhere. Although Jove figured it formed from every doubt he ever had about himself, it all seemed to burst to the surface at once. He knew Auster was right in how he had to accept his responsibilities sooner or later, but he had no clue what to think for himself.

How should Auster know what I'm supposed to be doing? He pondered. *How do I know what I'm supposed to be doing? Why did I have to be the Incarnate, out of all the people on this planet? I wish I could have someone else who could give me some guidance.*

Jove kept mulling over these thoughts until his head hurt. It was as if he was talking to Maré in his mind.

After what seemed like an eternity of sitting in the gutter, Jove got up again. He wandered down to the end of the street trying to decide where to head from there. He was too ashamed to head back home for the moment.

Instead, he thought he might head down to the beach to clear his head. He hoped Maré would be there to give him some wisdom. Or at least some company.

The Memory

Jove stumbled over the sand dunes struggling to keep his balance from lack of energy. The darkness made his journey all the more difficult as he tried to figure out which streets led back to the outskirts of town.

Eventually he made it to the deserted beach where the sand was cool underneath his feet. He saw Maré in the distance wading amongst the waves. Columns of water snaked around his body in a hypnotic dance as he controlled them with his hands. The midnight moon glistened over the creature's body and as alien as Maré looked, Jove couldn't help but admire the fact that he was indeed a perfect specimen, suited to the water.

Maré didn't react as Jove trudged down the beach. Instead, he probed his mind and bridged their telepathic connection.

I sensed your electrical pulses from quite a distance Young Master. He projected curiously, *You seem troubled.*

Jove put up barriers in his mind so Maré couldn't probe any further.

I've had a complicated evening. He replied without opening his mouth.

I can tell that you have been in conflict with yourself. I have sensed it building up subliminally in your mind since we met, though now it seems that it has taken over.

Jove broke the telepathic bond as he reached the water's edge and started to speak aloud as all his thoughts rose to the surface. "I never asked for any of this and I am constantly being pushed and pushed but it doesn't seem to be getting me anywhere. Or so Auster thinks. This Incarnate stuff is throwing me right out. What if I'm not capable and screw things up? Everyone else is telling me who and what this Incarnate is but how am I to know for myself?"

Maré paused for a second. The water he was controlling crashed back into the ocean and he frowned with concern. *Come into the water. I think you need to clear your mind.*

Jove stood there and stared into Maré's eyes. Feeling exhausted, he agreed and let down his barriers. He removed his clothes and waded into the ocean.

As he followed him out amongst the waves, Jove probed Maré's mind and found an unfamiliar thought in the blue creature's head.

"This isn't going to be a normal mind session is it? You're planning something."

Maré nodded. They were so far out Jove could barely see the shore and the ocean floor was metres beneath his feet.

We're going to go back through your memories.

"Haven't we scoured through my head enough?" Jove moaned sceptically. "I'm pretty sure there's nothing more from the last eighteen years that's going to help." He looked into Maré's head and saw the idea form through his yellow eyes, "Unless something else is locked up somewhere in there."

You're halfway there. I have had a theory for some time now. You have knowledge of this world locked away in your thoughts, but I believe some of it may not be from this lifetime.

"How do you mean?" Jove raised an eyebrow.

The Incarnate has lived many times in many lifetimes. Even though its physical form constantly changes, its spirit does not. I believe all the knowledge and power it possesses gather through each lifetime and are hidden somewhere within you.

"Yeah well I'm pretty sure I've seen none of this knowledge or power that everyone keeps telling me about."

I understand you still doubt your destiny of being the next Incarnate in the cycle. But this is something you have to face yourself and I am going to help prove it to you. Or rather, help you prove it to yourself.

Jove contemplated for a moment while treading water. Eventually he relented.

"Ok, let's give it a try."

Upon coming to this agreement, they slowly descended under the ocean's surface. Jove immediately emptied his mind.

This is tricky. He heard his own tone more clearly as Maré projected it, *These will be your own memories which have transcended through your many lives. To access them you must completely detach your mind from your body and search for them.*

Maré's tone mesmerized Jove and he sank further into his mindstream. *I can only push you so far. The rest is up to you.*

Jove plunged into the darkness and further into his subconscious. He felt Maré sever the connection between body and mind and before long, he was floating in the void of his own mindstream. It was a lot deeper than he had gone before and he started to feel fearful as Maré forced him further down. Soon, even his most powerful memories started to flicker and fade and Maré's presence became very distant. Collecting himself, Jove tried to focus on the task at hand.

Ok what am I looking for? He said to himself. Regular thoughts and memories pulsated dimly around him.

These are recent and from this lifetime. Jove saw blurred visions of his childhood, and fond ones from his school days. *I have to block these out. How can I go back further?*

He pushed them away and they phased out into nothing surprisingly quickly, leaving Jove in a dark and empty oblivion. There was more space and depth now than he had ever seen before. Maré had done well by blocking out all else for him.

Small, iridescent lights of memories started to grow in the darkness below. They flickered feebly as they rose from the depths and floated around him. Jove could not decipher them but heard voices from some and felt their emotions as he approached them.

The more powerful thoughts washed over him with mixtures of fear, passion and power. He could hear laughter coming from some of them. But mostly the memories were filled with a morbid sense of death and despair.

Some stronger memories even showed blurred visions. One in particular that caught his attention made him feel like he was underwater and a small figure in the distance was mocking him. It was blurred and made him fearful. It spoke in a faded voice he didn't recognise.

"I can survive you." The scene raced and twitched violently and Jove felt a surge of pain before the entire memory cut off completely.

These aren't right, he thought, *I have to go further. Deeper.*

These memories began to slowly dissolve as well and Jove soon found himself very alone with nothing occupying the oblivion. It seemed endless.

He began to doubt whether there was anything else in there when something tugged at his conscience. It beckoned for him to go further, to a place hidden deep within his mind that he did not think existed.

Jove journeyed deeper and deeper and eventually a faint golden glow emanated in the distance. His instinct urged him to follow the light. It was starting to feel familiar, like a journey he had undergone many times before. He could tell this memory was ancient and he couldn't even depict a time. It pulsated with a powerful mental energy.

This is so strong. How could I have missed this before?

As he got closer, voices and noises filled the void while lights and colour burst from the memory and he saw shadows of people move about inside. As he approached, warmth embraced his conscience, welcoming him like an old friend. The large orb of light floated in front of him beckoning him toward it. Its defences were strong, especially for this depth.

Just as he was about to reach out and touch it, Jove saw his own reflection staring back at him from the glossy skin of the orb. It was a more developed and flawless version of his own face. The pupils in his eyes were pure white like that of a Ventiera, and his skin shone like armour. He opened his mouth to speak to it and he saw that his reflection bore a set of shiny, jagged Draagnian teeth.

"Welcome back." His reflection greeted him. It instantly disappeared and the bubble thrust itself towards Jove, enveloping him in a blinding light. He spun and tumbled downward as the memory started to revolve and form around him. Just as Jove felt like he was about to explode, images came into focus and silhouettes of people came into view.

As the light dimmed, Jove noticed that he had fallen into a hollowed crevasse in the ground about fifty metres deep and the size of a football field. The cavern opened up to a forest above and he had a clear view of the cloudless sky. The walls were laden with moss that crept down the rock where water trickled into a clear shallow moat that lined the perimeter of the cavern floor.

Along the shoreline of the moat, was a circle of people and creatures standing proudly in formation. Upon closer inspection, Jove noticed they were people from each of the five races standing in order around the crevasse. The sound of mumbling filled the air as they greeted each other.

Five figures engrossed in deep conversation stood on a rocky pedestal at the far end of the cavern dressed in regal garb. In the centre of the five stood a tall, proud woman wearing a royal gown that had been woven entirely of pure white feathers. A river of silver hair flowed from her head matching the length of her dress. Her most outstanding feature, however, was her flawless white pupils. For a moment, they reminded Jove of Tia's eyes. This woman must have been a full blood Ventieran, just as Tia's mother was.

No wonder she's pretty, Jove thought to himself. He finally broke his gaze and observed the rest of the members on the altar.

To the left of the Queen stood a significantly shorter creature that best resembled a stout crocodile standing on its hind legs akin to a human. His crimson scales were gleaming over his stubby arms and legs. Polished armour lined the larger part of his body leaving room for a short but thick tail to protrude from his rear. Its small, beady eyes stared over the cavern emitting the same sense of pride and intense ferocity that Jove had seen in Auster's journal. They sent shivers down Jove's spine.

He then turned his attention to the hunched yet solidly built animal standing to the Queen's remaining side. The mole-like creature's head stooped forward so that his long faded beard almost reached the ground. A thin layer of brown fur covered his entire body, stopping at his paws. These were instead covered in a sensitive skin that he held delicately by his sides.

Jove remembered what he had learned about the Olderak so far. They were simple creatures who drew all their resources from the earth around them in order to survive. Being creatures that lived underground, they relied mainly on detecting movement in the earth to identify their environment rather than sight. Their other senses were heightened by their ability to control and shape the earth around them. It seemed that their way of life was peaceful and modest. This, Jove thought, was the perfect representation of the earthen element.

At the end of the altar stood a familiar figure, this one bearing an uneasy presence amongst the other races because of its mysterious appearance. To Jove however, he felt comfortable looking at the creature. He basically saw an older version of Maré.

This Merpesces however, had a darker blue tinge in its skin than Maré as it stood naked on the altar. Jove was unsure whether the creature was male or female but did notice that it was wearing a large coral necklace to demonstrate its status among its people. The folds of skin on its back and between its fingers started to flex as Jove noticed its skin had started to dry out from being on dry land for so long.

Lastly, standing on the other end of the altar was a dominating figure draped in the finest robes and cloth Jove had ever seen. The Human king looked over the proceedings with as much pride as the Draagni general. He also sensed that the presence of this man, as well as his people, came with great welcome from the other races. This scene was clearly from the time before humans started to take over.

Jove was beginning to wonder what was going on when everyone in the room suddenly went quiet and all eyes fell upon him. Feeling uneasy, he hesitantly took a step back. Much to his surprise and relief, he found they were actually focussing on a small cot made from rock protruding from the ground directly beside him. Surrounding the cot and Jove's transparent figure was a perfect, five-point pentagram carved into the earth.

As he was about to step out of the star, Jove noticed that the cot was not the only thing everyone in the cavern was staring at.

An elderly human woman entered from the other side of the cavern clutching a small bundle of cloth in her hands. The crowd hushed as she approached the pentagram in a slow shuffle. Jove noted the stricken look across her face which was also drenched with tears.

Although Jove was eager to see what was hiding the cloth, he found he was actually rooted within the points of the earthen star. Eventually, the woman made it within Jove's reach and he could see what had caused her anguish.

Unfurling the folds of the cloth, she revealed a lifeless newborn child. Its pale skin was ghost-like. The woman laid the limp body delicately in the cradle and with a silent sob, turned to leave again.

Sadness washed over Jove and he tried to reach out and touch the child's body, only to find his fingers fall through its skin. An unusual tingling sensation ran up his arm as he felt a strange connection between himself and the deceased infant.

Out of the corner of his eye, Jove saw a gentle hand rise into the air, returning all attention to the altar. Once all eyes were upon her, the Ventieran Queen outstretched her arms in a welcoming gesture.

"Welcome one and all from the five races who have come together to bear witness this glorious event." Her soothing voice filled the cavern. "Today we celebrate the birth of a new age as we unite forces and create what will keep our races thriving and at peace for many years to come."

She stepped back as the Olderak beside her hobbled forward to address the audience. His voice was old and hoarse like that of an elderly man.

"Although each of our species have flourished since the time of creation, we believe that in more recent times disparities have arisen between us. Barriers have come to divide us that have the potential to disrupt the delicate balance in which we rely so much."

The Draagni general had stepped out at this point and continued with a loud hissing voice, "Which isss why we are gathered here today to provide a sssolution. We believe that we should create a being; a being that will be born into the world many timesss and will learn and adhere to the waysss of each of the five racesss." He stepped back and the Human continued.

"Its sole purpose will be to serve our people in times of need. It will be a perfect creation of this planet, which will be its duty to protect. It will be granted with all the powers and traits of the five races and will, therefore, become an ultimate creature that will keep the balance amongst us."

Everyone fell silent as the Merpesces prepared to 'speak'. A mental pulse emanated from its head and everyone received the same message in their minds, "*So we, the Council of Five, shall offer these gifts on behalf of our peoples.*"

As it withdrew its grasp from the minds of the audience, the Olderak elder made a swift motion with its paw and a small set of rock steps rose from the ground against the altar. In single file, the five creatures moved down the steps toward the cot. They crowded around Jove and each stood at one of the five points on the pentagram.

Once they had each taken their place, the Queen moved towards the basin and placed her hand on the forehead of the still child.

Jove felt her warmth on his own forehead.

"Along with and by the power of the wind that lifts the birds into the skies and allows them to soar above the land, I offer this element and the longevity of the Ventiera. Our freedom and spirit shall allow you to love and care for all living creatures and treat them as your equal."

She made a swift movement with her hands and a small gust of wind wrapped itself around the baby like a cocoon. Its body rose a few inches into the air before returning safely to the cot.

Jove felt a tingling feeling surround him as if the wind had wrapped around his own body.

As the air became still again, the child's eyes flickered and Jove noticed that its lifeless pupils were pure white, just as the Queens were.

She stepped back into her place in the circle as the Draagni made his way to the cot. His chin stood an inch or so above the basins edge and he placed a scaly hand on the forehead of the infant.

Again, Jove felt warmth on his own forehead.

"Along with and by the power of the fire that lightss our world and warms our bodiess, I offer thiss element and the sstrong will that make the Draagni sso full of ferocity and determination. These qualitiess will allow you to be passionate in your beliefss and fight bravely for them in order to keep the peace among our peopless."

He clenched his fist and an explosion of flames erupted from the cot and engulfed the child. After crackling for a short time, the blaze vanished with no trace of smoke. For a moment, Jove felt his own ghost-like skin burn.

There was no evidence of harm on the child, although its skin had significantly hardened into an armour-like coating and short, sharp talons sprouted from its knuckles.

Looking considerably weaker, the Draagni stood back and resumed his position in the formation as the Olderak elder shuffled forward. Like the Queen and the Draagni, he delicately placed his paw on the forehead of the child. His voice was laced with an array of clicks native to his own tongue.

"Along with and by the power of the earth that provides us with the simple resources of life, I offer this element and the simple beliefs of the Olderak. Like us, you will not be troubled by the complexities of life and you will see the beauty in the basic. You will only demand the essential from the resources we of each race may offer."

He withdrew from the cradle and clapped his paws together. The walls of the cot crumbled and smothered the child in a thick layer of soil and rock, seemingly crushing it.

Jove also felt his transparent body compressed by the pressure.

The elder allowed all the nutrients in the soil to transfer into the child's body before relaxing his fist and bringing the walls of the crib back to their original place. The child now had a soft padding on its hands and on the bottoms of its feet resembling those of the Olderak.

The elder shuffled back to his place and the Merpesces now took its turn. It stood over the child and placed a webbed hand over its face as if to suffocate it. With its other hand, the Merpesces summoned a floating orb of clear water from the moat and dropped it into the cot so that the baby was completely submerged. Jove felt a strange sense of weightlessness as the baby floated in the water.

Extending its mind, the Merpesces reached out so all in the cavern could hear.

Along with and by the power of the water that gives life to all that inhabit this planet, I offer this element and the heightened mental sense of the Merpesces, who understand the feelings of all living things. We pass these gifts onto you so that you too can feel the state of the world around you and heal it when required through the life-giving properties that water brings. Let your emotions flow clearly and calmly, forever changing, so that you can better understand your environment and strive for what is best for all.

The rippling water began to glow brightly before the Merpesces tensed its palm muscle, freezing the water around the child. Raising its arm upwards and relaxing its palm, the ice dissipated directly into vapour and disappeared into the air above them. Remaining on the hands and feet of the tiny child were now small folds of skin imitating the webbed counterparts of the creature standing over it.

Finally, from the remaining point of the star, the Human stepped out to also place his hand on the child's forehead. Its skin, still cold from the ice it had been encased in, was now warmed by his touch.

Jove felt it also.

After taking a deep breath and focussing all his energy into the child, the Human recited, "Along with and by the power of the mind and spirit that make the humans so resourceful and imaginative, I offer…"

Then, without warning, a hush fell over the memory and all Jove could hear was an incoherent mumble coming from the king's lips. Edging closer, he tried to make out the words, but to no avail. For some reason, something in the memory was trying to prevent Jove from hearing what the king had to say.

Just as it looked as if the speech was over, the sound was restored and Jove could make out the last sentence.

"The final element that brings all together…"

As the king was about to utter the final word, a bright light erupted from within the cot and engulfed the entire room. At the same time, a searing pain surged through Jove's head and his conscious self began to writhe and twitch.

As the light and pain died away, Jove composed himself again and peered back into the cot at the mutated child. Signs of life appeared in it as its eyelids started to flicker and its limbs started to twitch.

The other councillors stood forward, watching intently. The ceremony was a success as they had collectively created new life. All five creatures joined hands and stared at the baby who was now squirming restlessly within its cot. Their voices echoed in an eerie chant.

"By the power of the five races, we empower you with all our knowledge and abilities to keep balance amongst our people. You will be reborn in a never-ending cycle throughout the races, serving the world and unifying us as one people. This is your purpose, your duty, watching over us for all of time, until there is nothing left to protect."

As the chant was recited the tiny creature in the cot started to fit and wail as if it was in agony and its eyes sprung wide open. Its white pupils contracted with terror.

"We give all our strength to you, The Incarnate!" The final words of the mantra echoed as a second burst of light engulfed the entire cavern, this time coming from the bodies of the council members.

Jove could feel each of them inside his own body and mind as he and the child fed on their life-forces. He felt sick and disoriented and struggled to stay on his feet. As the light receded, a blur fell over the cavern and the outlines of the councillors could be seen in crumpled heaps on the floor surrounding the cot. No signs of life appeared in any of them.

Darkness started to fill the room and the bodies started to fade away as cries emitted from the baby's mouth. It was now well and truly alive, but not for much longer.

Jove tried to reach for the cot and help the child but the vision moved out of reach and he felt himself falling into a black abyss.

The darkness continued to engulf the scene until nothing was visible. The baby's cries sounded more distant as it died a second time. The Incarnate was now dying with it, waiting to be reborn again.

Jove now understood.

Jove was thrown back through his mind and he snapped into consciousness. Salty seawater choked his lungs and his body thrashed about as he frantically swam toward the ocean surface. Coughing and gasping for air, Maré slowly ascended to join him.

"That was incredible." Jove got his breath back. "How long was I under for?"

About an hour. Maré replied much to Jove's shock.

"What!?"

You journeyed so far down, I lost you completely for a time there.

Jove scrambled to get to shore and out of the water. Maré was furiously combing through his mind and Jove had to block him out just to think straight. His body collapsed with exhaustion on the sand.

What did you see? Maré stood over him.

"It was amazing." Jove felt the urge to tell him everything but something stopped him. The memory retreated back into the depths of his mindstream and out of reach. He could only grasp small details of it.

"I saw my birth, my original one. The beginning of it all." Jove breathed and Maré's eyes widened.

What happened? He continued to probe curiously, but to no avail.

"I don't know." Jove answered, disappointed. He couldn't seem to find it either, "I understand now though." He continued. Maré gave him a quizzical gaze.

"Seeing it left a feeling in me. All this time I thought I had been *chosen* to be the Incarnate as if it was some cruel twist of fate. But I couldn't have had it more wrong. There is no *it* being a part of *me* or *me* being a part of *it*. I *AM* the Incarnate through and through, and it's been my fate even before this life as a human."

A long silence fell between them as they each processed the information. Maré withdrew his mental probe from Jove's mind as the realisation sank in.

"I guess I owe everyone an apology." Jove finally spoke as he suddenly thought of Auster and a wave of guilt wash over him. He looked over to Maré who simply nodded in reply. His eyes sparkled in the moonlight.

"Thanks Maré. I needed this."

It is an honour. He bowed his head slightly, *Now go home and rest. I can sense the house is quiet and Master Favon has left the back door open for you.*

"Thanks." Jove smiled and got up.

And by the way Young Master, Maré projected as Jove walked off, *If you indeed saw your birth down there, I believe I should be wishing you a Happy Birthday.*

Jove couldn't help but break out in a smile as he slowly walked back to the house. He was not surprised to see that it was dark and quiet as he approached. Tia and Auster would have gone to bed hours ago. The screen door had been left open for Jove and he silently crept into the house.

Inside was significantly darker without the moon lighting up his surroundings so Jove moved around slowly as his eyes adjusted. He had made it safely to the dining room table when an unusual shape sitting on it caught his eye. His heart sank as he made out what it was.

Sitting in the centre of the table was a small container filled with some of Tia's toffees. He picked one up and put it on his tongue. A rich taste of rum melted throughout his mouth and ran down his throat.

Guilt erupted in the pit of Jove's stomach and he angrily picked up the container and threw it back into the fridge before retreating to his room.

Collapsing face down on the bed, Jove felt exhaustion wash over him. Although thoughts were dashing through his mind from the night's events, he quickly fell into a deep sleep, his body and emotions finally taking rest for the night.

Jove woke early the next morning but decided not to get out of bed for training. Faded images were flashing in his head as he tried to remember the things he had seen in the memory. Hard as he might, the images were still out of reach and left no trace in his mindstream.

Realising he was not progressing anywhere, Jove contemplated how to confront the Favons. He knew a lot of what he had said was out of line, but he could not think of any reasonable apology. Hopefully Auster had calmed down as well and was ready to face him again. Jove mulled over some choice sentences in his head before eventually pulling himself out of bed.

Suppose I've gotta face them sooner or later, he thought as he reluctantly walked out the door. He was not surprised that nobody had come to wake him for morning training.

Slowly walking down the hallway, he saw Tia on the couch sitting quietly in front of the broken television. Auster, however, was nowhere to be seen. Jove saw that the screen had been smashed in and bits of glass had been ground into the carpet.

"And how are we feeling this morning?" Tia said sternly as she heard Jove enter the room. Her misty eyes were swirling and puffed up as if she had been crying for most of the night.

"I'm feeling a lot better actually." Jove answered sheepishly. He quickly regretted making such a casual statement as Tia launched herself from the couch with a seat cushion firmly in her grasp.

"Well I'm glad you've had a good night while I've been tossing and turning worried sick about you. You…sack…of….crap!!" She bellowed and belted him with the cushion at each word.

"Ok! Ok! Ouch! Tia!" Jove yelled while he shielded his face from her barrage. "Look, I know I owe you an apology! I buggered up big time last night."

Tia stopped and lowered the cushion, only to replace it with a threatening index finger. "Oh, so you realise this now? Why couldn't you have just come back into the house last night when I asked you to? Instead you just had to be a big man with the ego. Both of you!"

"I know, and I completely agree with you. I'm sorry." Jove fidgeted with his hands as he struggled to string words together. "You don't deserve to put up with that."

Tia's face softened and she lowered her finger. Jove didn't have to probe her mind to see that she had conflicting thoughts darting through her head.

"Yeah." She answered.

Jove broke from her gaze to stare at the floor. Tia brought her hand underneath his chin and lifted his face to meet her gaze.

"Although I can't blame you. It's been so long since we've brought you here and you were bound to crack eventually. Plus I know how much of a dumbass you can be at times."

Jove attempted to smile slightly, "I thought the term was *sack of crap*?"

Tia couldn't help breaking into a full smile and she flung her arms around him. "I can't be mad at you. I hate that you've been feeling this way. Apology accepted."

Jove wrapped his own arms around her in return and they stood there for a time before she spoke again.

"Dad may not seem like the most open and caring person I know but he would put his own life on the line for you. Incarnate or not." They broke from their embrace and Jove saw that Tia had started to cry again. Her eyes swirled and glowed as the whites of her pupils shone through, "And I will always be around too."

"Thanks." Jove mouthed softly. She smiled again and wiped her eyes.

"Well I'm going to go train in the forest. My airstreams have been as sloppy as yours lately." She went to grab her bo-staff from the lounge and headed toward the front door.

"Dad went down to the beach a couple of hours ago. I wouldn't be surprised if he's still there. Good luck." She winked at him and then she was gone.

Jove stood there for a short while looking out the door after her. After heaving an anxious sigh, he turned in the opposite direction and journeyed out the back door.

Trudging over the dunes toward the shore, Jove saw Auster sitting on the beach by himself looking out over the water. He took a deep breath before making his way down the sand.

"Hey." Jove walked up and sat down beside him.

"Hey." Auster replied in his usual gruff tone.

They both sat there for a time filtering sand through their fingers.

"Did you have a good time last night?" Auster finally broke the silence.

Jove shook his head, "No. I'm surprised at myself actually. I've never been like that before."

Auster still gazed out over the ocean. "I didn't think so. I thought things through after you stormed out. The fire took control over your emotions."

When Jove didn't answer, Auster continued, "You have to be careful when handling fire. It constantly needs fuel in order to survive. Once it latches onto your energy it does anything to keep burning and growing, so it feeds off your emotions. It is the only element that seems to have a life of its own without anyone controlling it, spreading like a disease."

"I'd believe it," Jove agreed, "but it still doesn't account for all those things I said."

"It wasn't all you." Auster interjected, "Sure you might have been thinking those things deep down, but they were distorted after feeding off your anger and pent up frustration. This, in turn, is understandable. So it was good that you had some time to yourself last night."

"I thought I said the right things." Jove interjected. "Things that I thought I wanted to say. But I felt lousy the entire night. So I came down here last night to clear my head."

"I came down this morning for the exact same reason." Auster answered. "As much as I hate to admit it, I found some truth in your words last night. I guess the fire just gave you the courage to say it."

Auster paused and sighed. "You were right in how I have been preoccupied with the mission at hand. It has been wrong of me not to take your emotional needs into account as much as I should, especially since I practically abducted you from your home."

Jove remained silent. Auster looked at him sympathetically and kept going.

"Truth is, I have basically no experience in raising teenagers. I barely even know how I managed to get Tia through it, the poor girl. She's been so strong and understanding of the mission since she was little. It's the only life she's ever known."

Jove looked over the usually tough exterior that was Auster. It was starting to wane as a tear rolled down his unshaven cheek.

"I've never had the opportunity to raise a young man, especially someone I have only known for such a short time. It's like opening a book and starting the story in the middle. You have to guess what happened in the beginning and are expected to pick up everything along the away, hoping you'll understand the ending."

"Well, I think I know how the story will probably go from here." Jove replied. Auster looked at him curiously. "You were right when you said I had to basically *get over it* and come to terms with my purpose. I am the Incarnate, body and soul. I was never chosen to be this great being, but rather created. It's been like that since before I was born."

Jove took a deep breath, "I gather it's probably a long road ahead, but I would rather have you guys help me get there out of anyone on this planet. I'm sorry I didn't realise it straight away."

A smile cracked across Auster's face.

"Must have been one hell of an epiphany you had last night."

"Yeah, it was a bit of an experience."

"Glad to hear. Maré was pretty excited when he told me about it this morning."

"Where is Maré anyway?" Jove changed the subject as he suddenly realised the blue creature wasn't anywhere in sight, nor in his mind.

"I've sent him to get someone."

Jove turned and gave Auster a confused look.

"I didn't sleep last night after our little discussion and I thought you might need some extra support right now. I gave Maré the mission of collecting your mother and bringing her over to see you." Auster shifted awkwardly, "I imagine she has much to tell you."

Jove's heart excitedly skipped a beat. It had been months since he had last spoken to his mother let alone seen her in person.

"Where is she coming from? When is she getting here?" Jove interrogated Auster who looked back at him with amusement.

"She's coming from Fervune; the Ventieran capital in Brazil. She's been learning about the hidden world, like you. But she won't be coming *here* exactly."

"What do you mean?" Jove frowned.

"I thought it also might be best to take a little field trip. It's high time I took you somewhere we can introduce you to the hidden world first hand.

We are going to rendezvous with your mother there in a few days."

Jove could barely contain his excitement, "So where are we going then?"

Auster got up from the sand and smiled down at him. "The abandoned city in the Daintree Forest. We're going to Wentra."

The Daintree

The summer sun came streaming through Jove's window to wake him. Dawn had only just broken but his room was already starting to heat up. Jove had barely slept that night as his mind bustled with excitement at the thought of seeing his mother again.

Rolling out of bed, he grabbed the bag he'd packed the night before and headed out to the lounge. Auster was already up and making toast.

"I suggest you jump in the shower before Tia gets up. I want to be on the road as soon as possible."

"Right." Jove answered, dropping his pack next to the others. He was fairly pleased with himself for being up before Tia. If only he could do the same on colder mornings when she used up all the hot water.

The weather was already fairly warm so Jove simply turned on the cold tap and let the water run over his body. He thought of how he would soon be reunited with his mother. He had so much to tell her and he could not wait to hear what her life was like since moving to Fervune.

After briefly washing, Jove stepped out of the shower and started to dry himself. Auster had already packed most of the bathrooms contents and only two of the small spare towels remained.

"Bugger!" Jove murmured under his breath as he went to get dressed. He realised that he had packed all of his clothes the night before. Wrapping one of the towels around himself, he walked out of the bathroom to fetch his pack from the lounge.

"Oh! Morning." A shocked Tia was standing in the hall about to knock on the bathroom door.

"Er… morning." Jove greeted her awkwardly. He tightened the grip on the towel.

"Thought Dad might've packed up the bathroom so I grabbed these last night," She held up a couple of towels, "but looks like I left it a bit late."

"Yeah." Jove shrugged. Whether it was because of the warm air or Tia's close proximity, Jove's face was starting to feel hot.

They both jumped as they suddenly heard Auster's voice boom down the hall. "Leaving in half an hour! Get a move on Tia!"

"Sorry." Jove and Tia said together as they struggled to brush past each other.

"Oi!" Tia stuck her head back out as Jove headed down the hall. "That training looks as if it's starting to pay off." She winked and ducked into the bathroom, shutting the door behind her.

Jove went bright red and briskly walked into the lounge to grab the spare clothes from his bag.

A half hour later, all three of them gathered on the driveway. Auster had gone out the day before and came back with a khaki-coloured four-wheel drive that was now sitting on the curb.

"Wow, did you get this from the military too?" Jove queried as they walked out.

"You could say that. Though it's been a while since this baby has been out of storage." Auster ran his hand affectionately over the hood of the car. It still looked a bit old and shaky but Jove was impressed by the improvement to the old yellow sedan nonetheless.

"Geez it's starting to get hot pretty quick." Jove commented as the sun rose higher in the sky. Tia was already sitting in the front after calling *shotgun* and fiddled with the knobs on the air vents.

"Get used to it," Auster replied as they piled into the car, "the air con's busted."

"That's ok." Tia gave up, "We'll just make our own."

She reached down to the pack at her feet and grabbed one of the magazines she had brought for the ride. Ripping of the front cover, Jove saw her fold it into a fan.

"How's this?" Tia turned around in her seat and waved her fan in a single sweeping motion. Instantly, Jove was forced backwards and the back of his head slammed into the car door.

"Far out. You got a setting lower than *hurricane*?" He retaliated, shooting a blast of air at the back of Tia's headrest and sending bits of her magazine flying about the car.

"Oi! Calm down!" Auster climbed into the driver's seat. "It's going to be a long drive as it is without having to put up with you two."

"Sorry Dad." Tia attempted to tidy her magazine pile.

"Now, you haven't forgotten anything?"

"No." Jove and Tia answered in unison.

"And you've both been to the toilet?"

"Yes."

"You sure?"

"Yes"

"Last chance."

"Dad are we gonna have to put up with *you* the whole drive?" Tia retorted.

"Alright, we're off then."

Auster started the engine and pulled out of the driveway. Jove wound his window down and peered down to the beach as they turned into the next street. Hot wind brushed against his face as houses darted by and they were eventually on the highway to the north.

Once the last of the town passed by, Jove lay across the back seat with his head on his backpack. Giving up on his own version of Tia's fan which was only brushing hot air onto his face, he formulated a continual stream of fresh air that passed through the back windows. Tia turned around and was somewhat impressed with his handiwork.

"Bet you wish you didn't have the front seat now." Jove jeered. Tia shot a taunting burst of wind at him before he laid back and closed his eyes. Eventually, the gentle rock of the four-wheel drive and the cool breeze on his face made Jove fall into a light sleep.

A couple of hours later, Jove awoke and sat up. He peered out the window and noticed that the trees had grown significantly denser and towered over the car. The breeze he conjured before falling asleep had faded to nearly still air. The temperature had become much cooler with the extra shade from the surrounding forest.

"Morning sunshine." Auster heard him rustling.

"Where are we?" Jove yawned.

"We're just past half way, only a couple hours to go." Auster replied quietly, "I was going to make a rest stop but I didn't want to disturb you two."

Jove looked over to the front passenger seat and saw that Tia had fallen asleep with her earphones nestled in her ears. Her head was resting against the window.

"She opened the vents and made herself a breeze then conked out just after you. Gotta say, neither of you are very exciting company."

Jove snickered and yawned again. The breeze that Tia had made was still faintly streaming through her side of the car and through her hair. He couldn't help but notice how pretty she looked with

266

the speckled light coming through the trees and reflecting off her face.

Jove suddenly realised that Auster may have been watching him and quickly averted his gaze.

"Amazing how she can keep it going even while she's asleep." He uttered.

"Well she had enough practice growing up. Hasn't changed much over the years though. Once she sticks those earphones in she's out for most of the trip."

"So I see." Jove answered with a softer tone. "It must have been hard for you guys to uproot yourselves so often."

"To a degree. I was used to travelling around the world but things changed when Tia was born and Wentra was abandoned. It's not fair to deprive a kid of a normal life."

"It's all you guys have known though isn't it?"

"Yeah, but I guess she's always known that she was different from everyone else. We have had moments where we both just wanted to have a normal life and live like a normal family. But at the end of the day we had responsibilities and we were depended on. We knew our place in the great scheme of things."

"Yeah." Jove felt a twinge of guilt in his gut as he recalled their argument earlier that week. Auster noticed it in his expression.

"Although, believe it or not, I don't think we'd have it any other way. How many fathers and daughters get to say they've travelled around the country together? I think it's brought us as close as we can be, and to have found you has just made everything we've sacrificed worthwhile."

"Guess you've been looking for me for a long time."

"Yeah. Well honestly we weren't all that confident in finding you at all. We were just one of so many teams around the world and you could've been born anywhere. You can imagine how over the moon we were when we found you. And you of all people."

"What do mean me of all people?"

"Well, I mean," Auster hesitated, "you could have been some punk teenager that would be really hard to get along with. But honestly, I'm proud to have you join our little family, and eventually your mother as well."

Jove raised an eyebrow, "You and Mum sound like you hit it off really well."

Auster smiled, "Not that she had much choice in the matter but it did take a bit of convincing to let us kidnap you for your training."

"Yeah, you must've been quite the talker to help her understand. I'm still getting used to it myself."

"You'd be quite surprised at how understanding she was. Remember, you were knocked out for quite a while too."

"Right." Although Jove wasn't entirely convinced, he decided to drop it anyway. He still felt like he was walking on eggshells since the other day.

Auster felt the rising discomfort and turned the conversation to stories about himself and Tia during their past travels. He even spoke of some embarrassing moments which Jove thought would be wise to remember in case he ever needed to use them against Tia.

Eventually they stopped at a fuel station a short way from their destination. The sudden stop in motion was enough to stir Tia awake and take out her earphones.

"How far away are we?" She yawned.

"A while away yet." Jove answered while Auster was fuelling up. He held a cheeky grin on his face.

"You been up for long?" Tia eyed him suspiciously.

"Long enough." Jove jeered. "Your Dad and I have been having a good chat."

"Oh great, the two of you in casual conversation. Should I be worried?"

Jove simply answered by widening his grin. By this time Auster had paid for the fuel and extra supplies and returned to the car.

"Water?" He tossed them a bottle each and packed some extras in his bag in the back of the car. "Drink up, once we park up nearer to the forest the hike is going to take a fair bit out of you."

The next couple of hours saw them travel further north where the towns and properties became scarce. At one point, Auster turned off the main road onto a vast network of dirt roads and bushland. The trees grew dense and eventually the roads started to fade away to the point where they were practically off-roading through the forest.

Just as Jove was starting to be jolted around the cabin from the bumpy road and wondering how far they had to go, the car screeched to a halt.

"Alright. Everybody out." Auster opened his door and disappeared from the driver's seat. Jove and Tia followed. They had stopped in a tiny clearing that would have been easily missed had Auster not already known it was there. Dense shrubs covered the road they had just driven in on and a small ridge was blocking the path ahead leading into a dense wall of rainforest trees.

"I don't remember it being this thick." Tia stood beside Jove, also marvelling the scenery.

"Well it's been a while since we last had to come through this way." Auster was already unpacking the four-wheel drive and tossing their bags across the ground.

"Back then you were too young to be carrying your own weight so you didn't take much notice of the surroundings. In fact, if I remember correctly you were asleep most of the time." He picked out one of the three larger packs and passed it to Tia to take to the top of the ridge, "So suck it up princess, this time it's all you."

Tia shot her father a dark look and blushed when she caught Jove snickering.

"And don't think *you're* going to get it easy." Auster turned to Jove and threw another pack over. "Once you've taken all the bags up, grab some loose greenery and come back down. We need to cover the car up."

It didn't take long to gather enough loose shrubbery and large tree fronds to cover the four-wheel drive. Since it was already khaki coloured, it was fairly easy to blend it in with the surroundings. Even if a person were to pass through the area, it still would have been difficult to notice the car's presence.

Once Auster was satisfied that it was sufficiently hidden, they all climbed up the ridge and picked up their packs. After making sure they were all watered and did not need to go to the toilet, they headed into the forest.

The path they followed was barely visible in the vast ecosystem. Jove was surprised that Auster was somehow able to navigate through it. Focussing solely on getting through the forests various obstacles, the group remained fairly silent throughout most of the journey. Jove and Tia had packed their staffs and they now conveniently doubled as walking sticks.

The landscape constantly sloped over ridges and chasms, testing their endurance. At one point they were trekking in a low valley where their feet started to sink into the moist ground. They had to tuck their pants into their socks to keep their legs dry and safe from leeches.

They kept up a steady pace for most of the day only stopping for toilet breaks or a short snack before continuing. Otherwise they powered through the forest. Any average explorer would have gone mad from lack of direction and exhaustion. However, since all three of them had followed a strict fitness regime for some time, they had an almost superhuman advantage.

After what seemed like an eternity of walking, the sun started to set and fatigue began to sink in. Eventually, there wasn't enough light to continue along the track and Auster signalled for them to stop on a flat piece of land on the downside of a hill. It was the first piece of level land they had seen in a while.

"This'll do for the night." Auster finally threw down his pack. Jove and Tia eagerly followed suit.

"Thank god! My feet are killing me." Tia collapsed on the ground and leaned up against a nearby rock.

"Same." Jove ripped off his shoes and socks and flexed his toes in the fresh night air. Blisters were starting to well up between them.

"Don't make yourselves comfortable just yet. We still need to set up for the night."

"Shotgun dinner then." Jove leaned over and grabbed his bow-staff.

"Deal. I'll get the swags out." Tia unzipped her pack.

"Then I'll set up the fire." Auster finished.

Jove reluctantly put his shoes back on and struggled to get back up. He summoned some Everice from his arm and moulded it into a long, sharp arrow before walking off down the hill and into the darkness.

The cold, moist air pressed against Jove's eyes as he tried to detect any movement in the treetops. He could feel them swirling as they tried to read the atmosphere and identify air currents. Jove silently triggered the bowstring out of the staff and loaded the ice sliver, aiming it upwards.

Finally, he heard a rustle above him as a possum tried to jump between the branches. He could see ripples of a slipstream form behind the animal as it scattered amongst the leaves. Focussing his energy, Jove stilled the wind to make for an easier shot.

With his eyes on the movement and tensing the bowstring, Jove aimed and fired. The ice-arrow sliced through the air with unnatural silence and hit dead on target. The unsuspecting possum fell to the ground, dying instantly.

Satisfied with the hunt, Jove retrieved the still animal from the forest floor. The ice sliver stuck out from the side of its skull.

Amazingly, he thought, there was barely any blood spilt on the ground. He liquefied the water, making sure he summoned only the pure Everice and froze it again around his upper arm. Then, slinging the possum over his shoulder, he returned to the makeshift campsite. As he left, the wind picked up slightly and the forest went on as if nothing had happened.

"That was quick." Auster greeted him upon his return. A fire was now crackling healthily and shining its light on the three swags set up around it.

"Moving target, first go." Jove boastfully dropped the dead creature by the fire.

"Good job." Auster replied, "I felt the wind drop as well. Nice touch."

"Yeah, yeah. Nice work." Tia was eyeing off the possum, "Can we get this feast going already? I'm starving."

Within minutes, the three of them were sitting around the fire in their swags dining on free range possum.

"Sweet, sweet meat." Tia was stuffing her face, "I've been craving this all day."

"Yeah compliments to the chef." Jove chewed the bones getting every last bit of meat. "So how much further have we got to travel tomorrow?"

Auster finished his mouthful, "There should only be a couple of hours' worth of hike left before we hit the barrier. Then it's easy sailing for about another league or so."

"Barrier?"

"Most of the major Ventieran cities are surrounded by a boundary line where the air is significantly thinner. Anyone passing through it would get violently ill from oxygen deprivation and would be forced to turn around. It's quite an ingenious form of defence if you ask me."

"Clever." Jove commented but was a little worried, "How are *we* going to get through it?"

"Yeah Dad I don't think either of us are skilled enough to create a pocket with a sufficient amount of breathable air in it." Tia had swallowed the last of her dinner and tossed the bones into the bush.

"No worries." Auster reassured them. "The barriers have deteriorated somewhat since the city was abandoned. The worst we will feel is probably nausea. So when you start feeling sick it means we're getting close."

"Righto." Jove lay back on his swag and let his body relax. "You know I don't think I've ever walked so far in all my life."

"You and me both." Tia agreed and started digging through her pack for something.

"It's been a while for me too." Auster tossed his bones into the fire, "I haven't made this trek in years. I mustn't be as fit as I used to be."

"Maybe you're starting to get old then Dad." Tia teased and finally emerged from her bag with what she was looking for. Any retort her father had was quickly interrupted by Jove.

"Marshmallows!?" He eyed the packet in her hand.

"Yep. What's a camping trip without 'em?" She ripped open the packet.

"I don't remember buying those." Auster said accusingly.

"Of course you don't. I did, then smuggled them into my bag last night." She popped a raw one

275

in her mouth and then grabbed three skewers from the front pouch of her bag.

"You are every bit as devious as your mother." Auster took one of the sticks and smiled.

Tia smiled childishly back, "I've heard."

The three of them only managed to cook up a few marshmallows each before exhaustion completely set in and they were ready to turn in for the night. Tia packed away the marshmallows and starved the fire of oxygen until it was down to a smoulder.

They crawled into their swags and after only a few moments the three of them were fast asleep. Even the nocturnal voices of the rainforest weren't enough to disturb them for the entirety of the night. The sun had fully broken over the forest when they awoke the next morning. Jove lay there for a time as he felt his muscles aching from their epic trek the day before. He could hear Tia stirring on the other side of the fire pit and figured she was also making the most of these last moments of relaxation before they had to get up and start again.

Eventually Auster gently kicked at their swags, instructing them to get up. After some defiant moans the fire was out, the swags rolled up and their bags repacked. Once they had eaten a quick breakfast of energy bars, they set off again through the rainforest.

Although they were still feeling exhausted, they managed to maintain a consistent pace and covered a fair amount of ground before lunchtime.

However, as they continued to trek, their endurance started to test them.

"I don't feel so good." Tia said suddenly when Jove was beginning to feel slightly queasy, his breathing became strained. At first he thought exhaustion was getting the better of him but then he noticed the forest was becoming quite different.

Around them the trees were slightly brown and there was no evidence of animal inhabitants. In fact, the normal noises of the forest had simply died away.

"I take it this is the barrier." Jove panted.

"Yeah." Auster sounded just as breathless, "It's slightly stronger than I had anticipated."

Jove looked back toward Tia and saw that she was very pale in the face. The lack of air seemed to have a more drastic effect on her.

"Are you al…" Jove didn't get the chance to finish his sentence as Tia turned around and spewed against a nearby tree.

"I'll take that as a no."

She was unable to stand upright to answer so instead she replied with a rude finger gesture. As funny as Jove thought this was, he started to taste vomit in his own mouth and his stomach became uneasy. The previous night's possum was putting up a vengeful fight.

Realising that staying there would only make everyone feel worse, Tia composed herself and motioned for them to keep going. She held her hand in front of her mouth as they walked.

After what seemed like ages of slow and shaky walking, the forest became lush and green again. Fresh, cool air filled their lungs and they stopped for a moment to regain their energy. They regenerated reasonably quickly with every breath

"Is there any way we can avoid going back through there?" Tia breathed heavily and her body collapsed on the ground. "That felt like crap."

"Unfortunately no." Auster doubled over trying to catch his breath as well, "If I'd have known it was going to be that bad I would have packed oxygen masks. Every time I've ever had to go through here I had an escort. Never knew what it was like to journey without one."

Jove washed the taste of sick out of his mouth with water and passed his bottle over to Tia.

"So now that we're through there we shouldn't be too far from the city then, yeah?"

"That's right." Auster pointed through a gap in the forest ahead of them, "There's an uphill ridge just through those trees and the outskirts of Wentra are just beyond it."

A wave of relief and excitement washed over Jove and he felt the urge to run in the direction Auster had pointed. Tia seemed eager as well and stood up again.

"Race ya." She winked.

Their excitement quickly grew as Jove and Tia raced ahead through the forest and up the ridge. Auster kept a steady pace behind them. They noticed that the trees around them were growing significantly larger and walkways began to appear and branch out in different directions.

Taking the route directly ahead of them, they almost fell head first down the other side of the ridge before reaching a large clearing at the bottom. Their jaws dropped as they gazed at the sight of the city in front of them.

"This is it." Auster called from behind as he caught up to them. "Welcome to Wentra."

<u>Wentra</u>

The atmosphere was still and silent. Even the normal noises of the forest died away as if they had entered a graveyard. Fifty foot high trees choked the canopy and blocked out almost all signs of the sun and sky above. Thick vines and branches intertwined above to provide a large network of worn walkways between the trees. Some of the trunks were metres thick and hollowed out at the base. The thicker ones had spiralling stairwells and pathways that led up to the canopy levels above.

The air was cool and refreshing on Jove's skin. But it was different, like something was missing. It was stale and the forest looked as if it was starting to die.

"It's so," he struggled to find the right word, "lifeless."

"When the Ventiera still resided here, they had become a part of the ecosystem." Auster explained, digesting the scene before them.

"The community provided a rich and flourishing atmosphere which the forest thrived upon. They gave the land protection and nourishment and in return the land gave the people shelter and the resources to build their community. Eventually the two parties became completely dependent on one another for survival. When the Ventiera were forced to abandon this place, the forest could no longer support itself naturally. So it's dying."

"But it's only been about what, eighteen years?" Tia was inspecting the hollow of a nearby tree. "Should it all be disappearing this quickly?"

"I don't know." Auster replied, "I've never seen it for myself before now."

They walked further along the outskirts of the city as the scenery sank in. More and more hollowed out trees and canopy roads appeared and the forest was looking more like a deserted urban city. Jove could faintly hear the sound of running water and before long they came across a large clearing with a river flowing right through it.

"This one will do." Auster walked inside one of the hollowed trees not far from the riverbank. Carved into the wall inside were horizontal alcoves barely big enough to fit a full grown person.

"That's where we sleep." Auster was already unrolling his swag into the alcove adjacent the hollow's entrance. Jove and Tia followed suit on opposite sides of the tree wall.

It took a few minutes to unpack and set up their sleeping gear before they collapsed onto their beds. Jove's feet and back ached more than ever. He was about to doze off when he heard Auster get up and walk outside.

"I'm going to get started on the fire pit. Feel free to contribute."

"Don't worry Dad. You set up the campsite while we go get some firewood." Tia called out after her father before turning to Jove.

"That gives us a chance to explore." She winked and looked up the tree.

He groaned at her and glanced upwards along the hollow. It quickly dawned on him what Tia was thinking.

"Oh come on." she said getting up, "It'll be fun."

"Fine." Jove got up out of his alcove, squatting slightly to gather a wind boost, "Ready when you are." He smirked.

Tia was too quick for him. She darted upwards in the blink of an eye and almost forced Jove backwards. A split second later he shot up after her, bounding off the inner walls of the tree. There were hundreds of tiny bulges along the hollow between the alcoves like the handles on a rock climbing wall. He saw Tia leap from one to another using them as footing before eventually jumping out through a hole near the top of the trunk.

Jove followed, aiming for the same exit. However, as much as the extra footing was helping, he could feel the wind deteriorate beneath him. Struggling to keep himself aloft, he made one last jump. He could see Tia standing at the opening just above him before... SMACK!

He face planted into the wood at Tia's feet and bright lights danced in front of his eyes. He was about to fall back down when he grabbed one of the handles and found his feet on another one below. Tia was snickering above him.

"Shut up!" he called up at her. If his face wasn't already turning red from the impact, it would have from embarrassment.

"I'm sorry, here." She was still giggling and put her hand down to help him up.

"Thanks." He replied in a low rumble.

Jove brushed himself off and they both stepped out into the sunlight. They were standing on a thick branch in the canopy where a multitude of pathways spread out before them. Vines fell from the branches and were shaped into what seemed to be dishevelled hammocks hanging high above the forest floor.

"That's where the middle class would sleep." Tia jumped down into a more secure hammock. "The lower class or younger families would sleep below where we've set up. The upper class resided in chambers in the trunks in the centre of the city. Come on, let's go check 'em out."

Tia leapt forward and started running along the branch. "Keep up! I want to see how much this place has changed."

Jove bounded after her, rustling the leaves in the canopy behind them. The forest seemed to liven up at their presence. The ground far below rushed past in a blur.

"You've gotta be light on your feet around here." Tia called from ahead.

"I see what you mean." Jove replied as he stumbled across the walkways.

"Yeah, back then I was never allowed up here without supervision." Tia yelled back. "No one here to save you now though so, you know, don't slip."

They darted throughout the treetops. Jove awkwardly leapt from path to path but was quickly getting the hang of it. A few branches and leaves smacked him in the face as Tia bounded past and they recoiled.

He started to catch up to her when she suddenly changed course. She jumped off the path and grabbed a nearby vine hanging from the canopy.

"Come on, they should be safe." She called back to him, but he was already hot on her trail. Jove spun and boosted off the nearest trunk, shooting himself into the vines swinging in front of Tia.

"Smooth move Tarzan." She scoffed. "Try this."

She spun and jumped to another vine and boosted towards a thick trunk ahead. Her speed increased to a blur as she raced towards it. Just as Jove thought she was going to crash head on into the solid wall of timber, Tia quickly changed course again. She whirred around the tree at breakneck speed and wrapped the vine around the trunk, gradually circling down. As the vine shortened, Tia ran sideways along the bark until there was nothing left and rolled onto a lower branch.

"Show off!" Jove yelled from his vine as she regained her balance.

He spun around in mid-air and formed an air boost at his feet and shot off toward the same tree. His wind stream blasted vines and branches out of his way. Like Tia, he darted in the other direction just as he was about to collide with the trunk and spiralled downward. The forest around him whirled past as he spun faster and faster... too fast. The trunk grew closer and he started to panic.

"You're going way too..." SNAP!

Jove heard the vine split and he started hurtling towards the forest floor. He tumbled through branches and turned his head toward the ground to see it rapidly racing up at him.

Thinking instinctively, Jove spun his arms and shot an air stream straight at the ground below him. A cushion of air instantly expanded and shot up towards him. His fall slowed immediately but his aim threw him across in another direction.

"Whoa!" His limbs started flailing as he slid across the ground, rolling a little way before colliding with a nearby trunk. Debris and branches rattled from above and fell on top of him.

Jove lay face down in the leaf litter as Tia jumped down from the branches above.

"Geez are you ok?" She landed and rolled him onto his back. His arms and legs ached as she did so.

"Ow." He groaned, "Yeah, but you're no help."

Tia giggled and put an arm around him to help him stand.

"Come on get up. That was really quick thinking with the air cushion."

"Thanks. I wish there was a less painful way of breaking the fall though." Jove slowly got up and brushed the dirt and leaves from his body.

"Ah well, live and learn. Still good for your first try though." Tia let him go. "My first fall, I landed flat on my face. Mind you it wasn't from that height. Nor with that much speed."

"Well good to know it is only going to get more painful." Jove groaned sarcastically.

"Wait until you start playing with fire again." Tia snickered. "Speaking of which, this stuff would be good to get one started."

She bent down and picked up some of the dead branches that had become dislodged in the fall. Groaning from the aching in his limbs, Jove knelt down and started making a pile of his own. Before long, they had both built up large armfuls of kindling.

"Some of these dead leaves would be good as well." Tia bent down and gathered as much of the litter in her arms as she could. Standing up again, she condensed the pile of dead leaves by sucking the air out of it like a vacuum seal and propped it on top of the firewood Jove was holding.

"You got it?" She left it balancing on his pile.

"Yep." Jove steadied his hands and started walking back towards the campsite. He only managed to take a few steps before stumbling over a tree root protruding from the dirt.

"Dammit!" He tried to regain his balance but to no avail. Jove fell face first into his pile of sticks and landed with a thud in a thick pool of mud.

"You're a real clutz, you know that?" Tia had turned around at the sound of the thud. Jove would have retorted but he had a mouthful of dirt and twigs.

"After all the training we've done you've still managed to keep the lack of grace you had in school."

Jove coughed the dirt out of his mouth and sat back against the trunk of the nearest tree.

"Well thanks for your sympathy." He said sarcastically and tried to get up. Tia suddenly doubled over with laughter and dropped her kindling.

"You should see yourself!" She said when she caught her breath. "Your entire front is covered in mud!"

Jove stood upright and inspected himself. Sure enough, he was coated with thick clumps of mud and leaves. He couldn't help but start laughing as well. Then he got an idea.

"What are you doing?" Tia straightened up as Jove scraped a large ball of mud off of his arm.

"Seeing what this looks like on you." Jove smirked and pegged the ball of mud at her.

"No!" She squealed and attempted to dodge but she was too late. The clump clipped her side and splatted across her shirt. A look of playful shock broke on her face as Jove scraped another load off his other arm.

"Don't…you…dare." Tia waved her finger at him, trying to maintain a serious tone.

"Or what?" Jove edged towards her and reared his hand up.

"This." Tia shot a gust of air at his chest forcing him backwards and into the dirt again. He wiped his eyes and heard her laughing in front of him.

"Right." Jove dug his hand into the puddle and launched a spray of mud at her. She jumped to dodge and Jove launched himself off the ground. Tia squealed loudly as she darted behind a tree.

"Naw, I'm sorry." He came at her and embraced her in a bear hug.

They rolled around in the dirt trying to slap mud in each other's face and hair until they eventually collapsed against the side of a tree trunk.

"You're filthy." Tia was still giggling and edged over to wipe the grime from Jove's face.

"So are you." He reached up and picked a leaf out of her hair.

"You're making it look good though." Jove said softly and ran his fingers through Tia's hair. She leaned in close, placing her hand on Jove's cheek.

Her pupils started swirling, completely mesmerising Jove. The skin on his face tingled as her hand ran over it. The rest of the world died away as he edged towards her.

Before either could think about it, their lips brushed against each other's. Tia's were soft and Jove's heart raced as her hair fell against his face. Their breathing hastened and synchronised.

Without warning, she broke away. Her eyes were wide with shock and her face flushed bright red.

"We shouldn't have done that." She stood up. Jove sat there equally embarrassed. He tried to interpret her thoughts but quickly retreated when her mind blocked him.

"We'd better get back to camp." Tia quickly composed herself and picked up her pile of firewood, "Dad's probably wondering where we are."

"Erm, right." Jove didn't know what else to say. Tia was already briskly walking back towards the campsite. He followed sheepishly.

They slowly trudged into the campsite trying to look as innocent as possible. Auster was tending to his fire pit.

"Bout time you guys got b... What the hell happened?" Auster turned and saw how dirty they both were.

"We went exploring and thought we could fit in some training while we were gone." Tia replied quickly.

"Okay." Her father said with a stern tone and raised his eyebrow. "Well you both have to wash yourselves before dinner."

"Right." Jove and Tia answered simultaneously. They walked towards their packs to grab a fresh set of clothes each before heading off to separate spots in the river to bathe.

"One at a time!" Auster called after them. Tia turned and gave him an *'obviously Dad'* look which he apparently ignored.

"Jove, come here and help me with the fire first."

Jove felt a knot tighten in his stomach and saw Tia blush before he quietly turned back toward Auster. Without making eye contact, he helped to get the fire started and they quickly had it flaring nicely.

For the rest of the evening they sat quietly around the fire and feasted on food Auster had packed from home and scavenged from around the forest. With Jove and Tia still feeling slightly awkward and tired from their trekking, they decided to turn in early for the night.

"Morning!" Tia woke Jove so suddenly that he hit his head on the roof of his alcove.

"Dammit! Is this gonna be a regular thing?" Jove rubbed his forehead until the lights in front of his eyes disappeared. Tia was smiling devilishly down at him.

"Naww, did I disturb your beauty sleep?" She threw his pack to him.

Jove was surprised at Tia's cheerful tone. It was as if the previous days' events had never happened. He figured he'd play along as well.

"Come on we've got training to do. It will be heaps better around the forest here since there's more room."

"What about breakfast?"

"It's taking a bit longer for Dad to master outdoor cooking. Not exactly his forte. Besides, I figured we might work with something you have been waiting to use for a while."

Jove gave her a confused look. She gestured to something she was holding in her hand.

"The whip!?" Jove sprang wide awake.

Tia answered with a nod. "I've seen you eyeing it in the cabinet so I thought to pack it. Up here we don't have to worry about attracting any attention or disturbing the neighbours. Only the local wildlife."

It only took a few seconds for Jove to get ready and soon enough they had darted up the inside of the trunk and out into the canopy. Rather than walking anywhere in Wentra, the two of them quickly grew accustomed to racing through the trees.

Tia had decided they would train in the centre of the city where there was more space between the trees. This would make it easier to manoeuvre the whip.

In a surprisingly short time, they reached the heart of the forest where the largest tree stood and spread its branches to the surrounding trees. Jove stared in awe at the sheer size of the trunk. It was as thick as a grain silo and stretched highest above the forest canopy.

"Apparently that tree and these ones surrounding it are the only ones that have actual housing chambers and stairwells intertwining through them." Tia explained. "This is the upper class district and that tree in the middle is where the royal family used to live."

"I wonder if your parents lived somewhere around here." Jove said still marvelling the scenery.

"Would be cool to think so wouldn't it? I really only remember running through lots of trees as a kid. Everything else is a bit sketchy."

Tia slid down a nearby branch and dropped to the ground. Jove followed.

Tia continued, "Knowing that my mother and father might have played an important part so as to earn enough respect to live here is a comforting thought."

"Yeah." Jove agreed. He suddenly thought of his own family heritage. His upbringing seemed so simple and bland. He had nothing against his mother but Jove did feel sorry that she seemingly gave up on achieving anything in her life. Jove felt guilty that her sole purpose for the last eighteen years was to keep a roof over their heads and food on the table.

His father didn't sound as if he had managed to make a name of himself either, especially if his mother never spoke about him.

For a split second, Jove wished he could have known what it was like to grow up in Tia's world. Being proud of your heritage and knowing that your parents were able to make a difference.

"Are we gonna start training or what?" He tried to distract himself and his eyes trailed to the whip in Tia's hand.

"Of course." She unravelled it and walked through the trees where there was the most room. Jove stood out of the way waiting for her to demonstrate.

"You know how the average whip works and makes the cracking sound, right?" She started.

"Yeah, the sound is the tip breaking through the sound barrier."

"Correct." Tia spun around and flicked the whip. As expected, it made a cracking sound.

Jove continued, "Because the whip is travelling through the atmosphere so quickly, it disperses air faster than normal. We have the power to enhance this movement."

"Someone's been studying." Tia reeled the whip back behind her. "The displacement of air is most concentrated at the point where the sound barrier is broken. The force sends shockwaves through the atmosphere and, if controlled right…"

She whirled the whip above her head and Jove could see the air warp and stream behind the tip.

Quickly building up momentum, Tia flicked the whip upwards toward the canopy and cracked it. A strong burst of air erupted from the tip, forcing Jove backwards and blasting a small hole in the forestry above.

"…you can produce a sonic boom."

"Wow!" Jove straightened up again. A small circle had formed on the ground around Tia where the wind pushed away the leaf litter and a thin layer of top soil.

"Do you want to give it a go?" Tia held out the stock of the whip.

"Hell yeah!" Jove couldn't get up fast enough. He let the whip trail around him.

Tia began to eye him nervously, "Have you ever even held one of these before?"

"I've picked up this one when you weren't looking." Jove joked. Tia gave him a worried stare.

"C'mon, it can't be that hard. You see stuff like this on television all the time, and those guys can't control air currents."

"Right, well you think that. I'm just gonna stand over here a bit." Tia took a few cautious steps toward the cover of a nearby trunk. Then she motioned for him to go whenever he was ready.

Jove widened his stance and started swinging the whip around his body, quickly building momentum.

"Good. Now start focussing on your air stream." Tia called from behind her tree.

As instructed, Jove started warping the air around the tip and he felt the pressure starting to grow. Thinking it was ready to *crack,* Jove whirled the tip to his front and yanked the handle back.

Tia was almost rolling with laughter as the whip instead doubled back and wrapped around Jove's body, almost making him fall over. He felt slightly foolish.

"I didn't expect you to get it first try." Tia calmed down. "Give it another go."

Jove untangled himself and started a second attempt. After whirling the whip around for another few seconds he flicked it again. There was still no sound from the tip but at least this time he didn't entangle himself.

"Again."

Another couple of tries and Jove managed to start getting the whip to crack. He felt the air pressurize around the tip like he thought it should but he still wasn't able to make a sonic boom like Tia had.

"You're almost there." Tia encouraged him from a distance. "Just focus on the space where you're going to crack it."

Jove reeled the whip back and started waving it around again. Thinking it would help him focus and build the air flow, he closed his eyes and felt for the wind streaming around his arm. He swung harder around himself and built up momentum. The pressure quickly grew around his hand and he sent it down the whip. Eventually, he couldn't hold the tension any longer and, eyes still closed, he flicked the whip in front of his body with all his might.

CRACK! The force threw Jove backwards so hard that he crashed onto the ground and rolled a distance before hitting a tree trunk. His eyes flickered and he could feel a painful lump form on the back of his head.

"Do you ever try to land on anything other than your head?" Tia jeered.

"I don't *plan* to hit my head. Crap that hurt." Jove rubbed his head furiously. Tia combed through his hair to check for any blood. They were both relieved to see there was none.

"Where's the whip?" Jove asked when the lights subsided from his vision.

"Over here somewhere." Tia got up and spotted it further around the trunk. "Got it."

Jove picked himself up off the ground and looked over to where Tia was standing. A strange expression covered her face as it suddenly turned pale. Her body had frozen and her eyes became fixated on the trunk.

"What's wrong?" He approached her curiously.

"I know this place." Her voice was almost breathless. She shakily pointed to a spot at the base of the tree, "Look."

Jove looked where she was pointing. Engraved roughly in the bark and still barely visible from years of wear was a single word. It seemed to be carved by a child that had just learned how to spell her own name. *Tia*.

Tia knelt down and ran her fingers over the letters, "I can barely remember carving this. Dad and I must have lived here."

She got up again and Jove followed her as she slowly stepped through the archway leading to a spiralling stairwell. Dust swirled around their feet as if they were the first visitors in decades. They made their way up the stairs and passed by small chambers within the trunk. Tia stopped and inspected each of them carefully trying to find something that would jog her memory.

Jove remained quiet and looked over the rooms as well. They seemed fairly upper class compared to the housing he had seen in the city so far. There were worn cabinets and drawers carved into the wood and timber beds lay against the walls. Some of them even had old silk sheets strewn across the floor.

"These guys must have left in a hurry." Jove broke the silence as he noticed the cabinets had been ransacked, leaving most of the rooms in a mess.

"They had to." Tia replied without looking at him, "*We* had to. The city was under threat of discovery and invasion. Apparently there were time constraints because Dad said someone on the outside had revealed this location."

"Yeah, I remember him telling me something about that." Jove had been told the story when going through some notes in the journal. "The city council decided to summon a cyclone as a diversion. It was enough to cover the entire population so they could escape and migrate to Fervune."

Tia nodded and they continued to walk. "I was only a toddler when it happened. From what I remember, it was pandemonium as everyone was rushing to get out. We were some of the last to leave because Dad was helping everybody else get out. There was one lady near us who was going hysterical. I think she was pregnant, poor thing. And someone had just died. She and Dad got into a massive fight before he convinced her to leave. The storm was about to hit and everything was going dark. We crossed the border just as the rain started to pour. Next thing I knew, the lady was gone and Dad and I were at the abandoned house in Grendun court with just the clothes on our backs. It was a while until Dad managed to wire some money over from Brazil to get us set up and going again."

Just as Tia finished speaking they stepped onto a landing near the top of the tree. The walkway split into two and each led to a room on either side of them. Tia paused at the entrance to the chamber on the left. She didn't have to say anything to make Jove realise that this was her room.

It was larger than all the other chambers in the stairwell and had a large bed pushed up against the wall. The sheets were tattered and infested with mites while the window above had been smashed. Shards of glass were scattered about the room, shredding a set of lace curtains as a result. The shards crackled under their feet as they entered the room and Tia made her way over to the remains of the curtains.

"Mum made these before I was born." She ran her fingers through them. "She was a seamstress."

"They're beautiful." Jove said. Tia merely answered with a smile.

Jove turned around to see what else was in the room. His attention fell upon something that was wedged in a tiny alcove next to the doorway. Walking toward it, he realised it was a large wooden cot carved into the trunk of the tree itself. Thin roots dangled from the ceiling above it with roughly carved shapes tied to it like a child's mobile.

He peered into the cot which was filled with a soft bundle of blankets. Something was caught up in them and poking out the top. Jove drew the sheets back and saw a small, handmade doll lying amongst the covers.

"Flora! I'd forgotten about her." Tia walked up behind him with a twinge of nostalgia in her eyes. She picked up the doll and caressed it in her arms. "The lady that lived in the next room made it for me."

A small gust of wind blew through the window and something hiding under the bed caught Jove's eye. A sheet of paper fluttered in the breeze. The movement also caught Tia's attention.

"What's that?" She said as Jove reached under the bed to grab it.

"It's a... book." He pulled out a thin book bound with leather. It had nearly two decades worth of dust and wear and the pages were starting to fall out. Trying to keep it from falling apart, Jove opened the front cover. Stuck to the paper pages were small photographs. Familiar photographs.

"These are the same as the ones at home."

"What?" Tia stood beside him, still clutching Flora.

"Yeh look. There's the one of you and your Dad." Jove flicked through the pages, "Your Mum. Your Dad again with those two guys." Then the pages suddenly went blank and Jove noticed that the remaining pages had been ripped out.

"Where's the rest of it?" Jove looked under the bed and Tia helped him search around the room. She quickly found something.

"Here."

Jove looked where she was pointing. A single page was caught in the doorway. The wind picked it up and dragged it towards the room on the opposite side of the stairwell.

"What's it doing way over there?" Jove got up and walked over to the other room. Tia was right behind him, eyeing the chamber as they entered.

"This room is exactly the same as ours." She said as Jove picked up the page.

She was right. The room was a mirror image right down to the lace curtains. There was even a cot carved into the wall. However this one was significantly smaller and looked as if it was never used.

"Look, here are the other pages." Tia walked ahead and picked up more sheets of paper strewn around the room. Most of them were torn as if someone was trying to destroy them. Jove looked down at the one he was holding.

The dark haired man from Auster's photo was standing proudly next to a heavily pregnant woman. The two were lovingly caressing her baby bump and beaming at the camera. Jove's heart skipped a beat as he ran a finger over the photo, wiping the dust away from the woman's belly.

"I don't know these people." Tia scrutinised the photos in her hand before handing them to Jove. His heart began to race as he glanced over the photos. The same woman was appearing in them again alongside the dark-haired man and Tia's parents.

"I know who this is." Jove came to a photo of the woman standing by herself with her hands resting on her pregnant stomach.

"That's my Mum."

Reunion

The afternoon sun was streaming through the forest as Jove stormed back into the campsite with Tia in tow. He had spent the previous couple of hours scouring through the photos trying to digest their contents.

Auster was sitting by the river with a makeshift fishing rod trying to catch their dinner. Tia shot a gust of wind at him to alert him of their presence. He had barely turned around to ask them where they had been when Jove cut in.

"How long have you known my mother?" He demanded. Auster gave him a surprised look and Jove immediately felt barriers springing up in his mind. They were especially powerful this time.

"I met her just before I met you." He hesitated slightly.

"Really?" Jove replied with no hint of believing him. He flashed his mother's photo in front of his face.

Auster's mouth flapped open and shut as he tried to utter a reply. He glanced at Tia for support but she was standing beside Jove awaiting his answer with her arms folded.

"Where did you…?"

"That wasn't the question."

Auster struggled to find words. "I am not in a position to tell you."

"Why?" Jove demanded.

"Because your mother swore me to secrecy."

"And why the hell would she do that?"

"Jove, you have to trust me. She has her reasons." Auster said trying to calm him down. "Yes I've known her for many years now. Please mate, you must understand that I have wanted to tell you ever since our paths crossed in Boonda."

"What about me, Dad?" Tia piped up. "Sounds like you've kept me in the dark as well."

"I know and I am so very sorry to both of you but my hands were tied. It's up to your mother to tell you everything Jove. She's just been waiting for the right moment."

"So that's the real reason we're here isn't it?" Jove deduced.

Auster nodded slowly. "She initially wanted to wait until you met again in Fervune. I did offer for her to initially come with us to make your transition a lot easier for you but…"

"Instead she ran off because she didn't want to face me." Jove finished the sentence for him. Auster's eyes softened and he put his hand on Jove's shoulder.

"Jove. Sandra Boyd has gone through more than you will ever know. It has been killing her for years. Being thrown back into this world again is probably taking its toll. Just please spare some sympathy for her. I have no doubt that she has your best interests at heart. As do I."

They all stood there silently for a moment with Auster's hand resting firmly on Jove's shoulder. His eyes remained fixed on the photos.

"But how could she keep this from me?"

Auster remained silent and Jove shrugged off his hand. Turning on the spot, he started to head out of the campsite.

"Jove." Tia ran up behind him but he shrugged her off as well.

"Sorry Tia. I just need to go clear my head."

He walked off and left her silently standing there. Auster came up behind her and motioned for her to come back and sit by the fire pit. Ignoring him, she watched Jove disappear through the trees before turning in the opposite direction towards her swag. She shot her father a dark look as she disappeared within the trunk.

Night started to fall by the time Jove walked all the way back to the city centre and up the timber staircase to his mother's chamber. He glanced over the ransacked room for a while as if he was seeing it for the first time again. The shards of glass on the floor sparkled in the rising moonlight beginning to shine through the window.

Jove walked over to the unused crib and ran his hand over the woodwork. It was meant for him all those years ago. He was meant to be born into this world, the real world. He could have grown up alongside Tia and the Ventiera and known earlier that he was the Incarnate. His upbringing would have been completely different.

A wave of fury surged through his veins as he wondered how his mother could have left it all behind and ignored it for such a long time. In anger, Jove conjured up a whirlwind that raced around the room, picking up all the broken glass and loose debris. The pressure built until it started to crush his body and he couldn't contain it anymore. Yelling into the wind, he shot it out of the window, smashing everything that remained. The room became quiet again.

Exhausted, Jove collapsed onto the bed and slowly pulled out his mother's crumpled photo. With his other hand he removed the trinket she had given him for Christmas and rolled it through his fingers.

"Who are you?" He ran his finger over her pregnant belly.

Her face simply smiled at him in return.

Jove woke to a gentle breeze on his face and the sun streaming through the shattered window. He watched the dust and leaves dance across the floor for a moment before the previous day's events flooded back to him. Groaning, he rolled out of the bed and walked over to the window, looking over the forest as it basked in the morning light.

It seems current events have intensified Young Master. Jove nearly jumped out of his skin as a familiar voice rang in his head.

"As if things haven't been intense already since all this started." He spoke aloud to amplify his thoughts for Maré to read.

I understand. The voice calmly responded, *We are almost at your position. I suggest you return to greet us. I sense master Auster is anxious as he is pacing alongside the river. And your mother is eagerly awaiting this forthcoming reunion.*

"More like confrontation." Jove answered darkly.

Young Master I urge you to give your mother a chance. There is much of which she desperately needs to inform you.

"And what would she have to say now which couldn't have been said ages ago." Jove interjected.

Just come down. I sense her knowledge has been paining her for longer than you know. She is just as frustrated with herself as you are.

Jove fell silent while Maré calmed his mind.

"Fine." He answered aloud as he stepped out the window and launched himself into the canopy.

"You know, I always hear of people complaining about little voices inside their head telling them what to do."

Glad to be of service Young Master. Maré jeered in response.

Within minutes, Jove made it back to the campsite. As Maré had said, Auster was impatiently pacing along the riverbank. Tia was sitting in front of the dying ashes, staring into the embers with the remaining photos sitting beside her. It seemed that she had been looking at them until it became impossible to dissect the images any further.

Upon Jove's entrance, Auster stopped pacing and came to greet him.

"Jove, it's so good to see you," he was struggling for words, "your mother will be here in a mo…"

"I know." Jove interjected. "Just please, don't say anything. I want hear what she has to say, and everything else I should know about."

Auster opened his mouth to answer but Tia beat him to it.

"Me too." she said coolly.

Her father frowned. "Fine."

Jove felt Maré's presence coming closer. "They're here."

An enlarged raft emerged from around the riverbend. Maré was steering it gently through the water with a current he had conjured himself.

Sandra Boyd stood eagerly in the centre of the raft, her whole façade was completely different to how Jove had ever seen her. Her hair was significantly longer and she was wearing a garb of leather and feathers. They were similar to the Ventieran clothes he had seen in Auster's journal. However the biggest difference was the unbreakable grin across her face.

Maré docked the vessel in the shallows alongside the shore and Sandra launched herself onto the bank. Before either of them could speak, she caught her son in a strangling embrace.

As angry as he was with her, Jove couldn't help but be happy and relieved to see her again. Over the last few months he had missed her and wondered how she had adjusted to the sudden changes in their lives. She seemed so content and healthy now, as if she was living back in her own comfort zone.

"It's so good to see you again, Jove." Sandra said proudly while holding back tears, "I've been so worried and cannot imagine what you've been going through. Auster and Maré have filled me in on everything that has happened. I hate that I had to leave you to bear it all on your own."

"He hasn't been alone." Auster piped up beside them. "It's good to see you again Sandra."

Sandra loosened her grasp on Jove and moved on to Auster and Tia.

"You too. Thanks for looking after him," she looked over to Tia, "both of you."

Throughout these greetings, Jove's thoughts were niggling at the front of his mind. He wanted answers and he wanted them now. He attempted to peer into his mother's head, but to his surprise he found it difficult to navigate his way in. Her mental defences were akin to Auster's barriers, as if they had been built up over many years.

"Mum, it's good to see you and all but I've got to know…" He walked over to the campfire and picked up the pictures to show his mother. Struggling to finish his sentence, the fading expression on Sandra's face told him he didn't have to.

Her eyes softened and glazed over as she stared into the pictures. Years of secrets she had tucked away resurfaced and were staring back at her.

I think I shall go explore. Maré projected gently and retreated back to the river. He left the four of them in silence.

"How about we sit by the fire." Auster gestured toward the pit.

"Good idea." Sandra replied softly and followed his direction. Jove and Tia sat opposite their respective parent as Sandra gently ran her fingers across the first picture.

"I haven't seen these in years." Her eyes started watering. "We were so happy back then."

"What are they?" Jove demanded, "You guys have a history don't you."

"Yes," Auster's hands were restless, "going back longer than you might think."

"I've always known about the other races Jove," Sandra cooed softly, "since long before you were born. Your father and I were part of a reconnaissance team that travelled between the different races as representatives for humans. We would be part of attempted peace treaties and lived among each of the races to promote diversity and understanding in their societies. There were many such groups based around various parts of the world."

She held up an older photo that consisted of four young adults smiling, "Ours in particular consisted of myself, Auster, his old army friend Albert, and your father, Tom."

"So you guys were a bridge between the races?" Jove clarified.

"In a nutshell." Auster answered. "Within the last century or so the human population has grown exponentially making it almost impossible for the other races to remain in hiding. That's where we came in. We were able to educate the Ventiera to mingle inconspicuously in the human world where necessary. We were quite the group, and after doing it for so long we adjusted more to Ventieran life and started to settle in."

Auster stared into the fire pit. "As we all grew older, we started to veer apart. Albert started taking on more personal and precise missions concerning foreign affairs, I took over the supply of equipment and resources for the colonies and your parents continued to educate the hidden population about the human world. Eventually, we all decided to take some time off and settle down. I met Tia's mother here in Wentra and retired so we could live together and raise a family." He smiled proudly at Tia.

"Having worked together for so long, your father and I were also quite close Jove." Sandra continued. "We were married here in Wentra and wanted to start a new life together amongst the Ventiera, staying close to Auster and his new wife." She paused and looked directly at Tia. "You and your mother share so much more than just a name, Tia, you have no idea how alike you are. She was a valuable friend and I was proud to have the privilege of knowing her."

Tia blushed as a tear rolled down her cheek.

"So what happened to change things?" Jove was still puzzled, "If this is all true then shouldn't I have been born into all this? How come you moved back into human society and left all this behind?"

Sandra's face hardened, "It wasn't something I planned to do. It had been a couple of years since Tia's death and we had begun to move on with our lives when Albert returned to Wentra. He had been given a new assignment and asked for us to come out of retirement."

"What for?" Tia asked.

Auster stepped in to answer, "Albert had been making trips to the Draagni colonies in attempts to bridge the connections between themselves and the humans. Shortly before then, Triton, the previous Incarnate of the Merpesces, was killed when humans discovered and honed in on their capital, Atlantis. Since Tritons death, the Draagni knew that the new Incarnate would be born a human and there was an argument as to how this would affect their survival. Plans were formulated to hunt this human and kill them so the cycle would continue onto the

Ventiera instead. Some Draagni still maintain those beliefs."

Jove was briefly reminded of the two previous attempts on his life. Both by the same Draagni, Gahnarg.

Auster continued, "Albert, still being on the frontline and experienced in army training like myself, had volunteered to be the head of negotiations. However, due to his violent history with the Draagni, their peoples didn't take to his presence too kindly and he thought reinforcements were needed. Naturally, I had to refuse because my sole focus was to raise Tia."

Sandra interjected, "And I had to decline as I had just fallen pregnant with you." Jove's heart skipped slightly. "So that left Tom. Albert promised that this mission was vital in maintaining the safety of humans."

Sandra breathed a heavy sigh and her eyes started to tear up. "If I had known the negotiations were going to go sour I never would have let him go."

"What happened?" Tia asked curiously. Auster stepped in to speak instead as he noticed Sandra beginning to get upset.

"From what we gathered, things turned violent. The Draagni turned on the both of them. Albert went missing after but Tom wasn't so lucky."

Sandra sobbed softly and Auster put a comforting hand on her shoulder. Jove felt a lump well up in his throat.

Auster continued. "The Draagni then decided to turn on humans associated with the other races. Here in Wentra, the population contained many such people. People like us and hybrids like Tia, so one of their targets was here. Word spread that a Draagni attack was imminent and we were still concerned for the secrecy of the population. So we devised a plan to abandon the city under the cover of a cyclone created by the Ventiera."

"Wait, so it wasn't humans that forced everyone out of here after all?" Tia pondered. Auster shook his head.

"We had to lie so that nobody would panic. There's enough separation in the world without the hidden races turning on each other as well."

"So what happened to everyone that used to live here?" Jove questioned. Sandra answered this time.

"Most migrated to Fervune which has more secure defences and diversity within their colony. Thanks to us and a few others, the introduction of technology combined with the Ventiera's ability to read air currents has made the city virtually undetectable. No human would ever dare to venture that deep into the Amazon jungle anyway."

"What about the rest of you?" Jove queried although he already knew the answer.

"We blended into normal human life."

"As if nothing happened?"

"It was safer, Jove. Draagni forces were out to get rid of the humans helping to bridge the other cultures. To go into hiding was the only option."

"But why totally forget about it?" Jove retorted. He couldn't hide his rage and curiosity any longer. "How could you just whisk me away and raise me knowing we would be totally cut off from it all. Didn't you think that it would come back to haunt you? For the last eighteen years you've been lying to me when we could have been out there doing something like Auster and Tia were."

"I didn't want that life for you." Sandra replied sternly. "Your father and I lived dangerous lives as it was. Back then with things becoming riskier I wasn't about to put my child in any danger."

"But why keep it all secret?"

"Because I knew that if you were anything like your father you would have taken the first chance to be on the front line. It was too dangerous. Losing your father was hard enough for me. I wanted to take every action I could to make sure you would never suffer the same fate."

Sandra's voice started to tremble but Jove remained angry. "Well, whether you wanted me to or not, I *am* a part of it. A big part it turns out. It would have helped to have known all this growing up rather than having it hit me all at once and turn my life upside down. I left everything I knew!"

"You think I don't know that same feeling!?" His mother retaliated. "I sacrificed everything and left it all behind, to protect you." Tears were streaming down her face. "I abandoned everything I knew and everything I had worked for. I left my closest friends," she glanced at Auster, "and worst of all I lost the love of my life. Thomas Boyd was my entire world. Please understand my darling, I gave it all up. For you."

The whole circle went quiet and Jove found himself speechless. He had never seen his mother in this state before. Tears were streaming from her eyes and her body shuddered uncontrollably. Eighteen years' worth of conflicted emotions had finally surfaced.

"I didn't sleep for years over that decision and have always wondered whether it was the right thing to do. But in the end it was the best decision I could have made at that time." Sandra reached over and grabbed Jove's hands in her own. "I never would have believed in my wildest dreams that you would be the next Incarnate. Ever since Auster told me back home, I have regretted every single day that I never told you about the real world. I am so frustrated that I missed the chance to prepare you for all this."

Jove felt all the rage in his mind subside and returned his grip on his mother's hands. She managed to compose herself before continuing.

"That charm I gave you for Christmas," she nodded at Jove's wrist where he always wore the trinket.

"That was actually your father's." Sandra delicately slid it over his hand and played with it in her fingers. "He gave it to me on our wedding day to ensure that we would live a long and happy life together. I gave it back to him the day he left with Albert for the Draagni colonies, to bring him good luck." She paused as she fought to get words out. "But it was the last I ever saw of him. When Auster journeyed over to retrieve his body, this was all that was left."

She pressed the woven acorn back into Jove's palm. "And now it will bring you luck and protection."

"Mum…"

"I will never forgive myself for depriving you of all this. But right now I just want you to know that I am and will always be so very proud of you. You are without a doubt your father's son and I truly believe that you are capable of doing great things for this world, Incarnate or not."

Sandra jumped up from her seat and took her son in a full embrace. By this point Jove's eyes were also watering.

"Thanks Mum."

The campsite went completely silent while they hugged. When Jove broke away he noticed that Tia was tearing up as well and Auster was sitting on his log with a proud smile. It took quite some time for them to compose themselves again.

"So how did you get into it all?" Tia queried to brighten the mood. "I mean, I know Dad's story but what about you?"

Sandra began to smile softly. "I was probably about the same age you are now Tia, many years ago. Back then I wanted to travel around the world and see all its glorious sights. After I graduated from uni, a group of friends and I saved up to go overseas to South America. We couldn't resist the culture and sense of adventure. And the parties."

She picked up the photo of Tom and a faint, nostalgic smile broke across her face.

"Anyway, we were about a week into our holiday and were sitting out the front of a café one day when we noticed three young men sitting at the next table. Naturally, we thought they were cute and eventually plucked up the courage to go and talk to them."

Auster smiled to himself as he remembered the day as well.

"Your father was still as handsome in this picture as he was then," Sandra grinned fondly, "and boy did he and his friends know how to compliment the girls too. We chatted to them for a good hour or so. That was all the time it took."

"Tom was quite smitten with your mother." Auster added. "We weren't used to girls coming up to us for a chat, but somehow they hit it off like they had known each other for years."

"Love at first sight." Tia sighed.

"It was," Auster agreed, "unfortunately the timing was really bad. The three of us were supposed to be meeting up with our guides to be escorted to the Ventieran capital. We soon had to say goodbye to these girls. Though it was all too soon for Tom and Sandra."

Sandra blushed sheepishly. "Naturally I didn't want to just leave Tom and not see him again. So I decided to break away from my friends and follow them."

"Slightly stalker-ish." Auster added, "What we didn't know was that our plans had been compromised and there was a Draagni ambush waiting for us at the rendezvous point."

"I saw the whole thing from around the corner." Sandra continued. "Large men in dark capes jumped the group in an empty alleyway. A fight broke out and bursts of wind and fire were shooting everywhere. I couldn't make out what was going on."

"So how did you all get out?" Tia questioned her father.

"Well back in the day I was more agile than I am now and we were all fairly well trained to defend ourselves. Al was especially vicious in a fight and never really got on well with anyone from the Draagni race. He always carried a dagger on his person and on this particular occasion he managed to slip it through the scales of a Draagni and killed him. The other attackers were outnumbered and forced to back off as the noise would have attracted unwanted attention."

"It was all a pretty horrific sight from my hiding spot." Sandra piped up. "Seeing the strange creature fall and spill blood everywhere made me panic and I gave away my cover. My presence somehow scared away the attackers but not the three men I had just been speaking to. I immediately thought they were criminals and that they might come after me next. I just froze and it was fairly easy for Tom to corner me before I could call the authorities. Naturally, it wasn't easy to explain what had just happened."

"And to Tom it didn't seem right to abduct this girl and hold her until a Merpesces arrived to block her memories. So he went against protocol and told her everything once our location was secure."

"At first I thought he and the rest of them were absolutely crazy. It's not easy to believe a story coming from someone covered in blood and bruises. But there was something about your father that made me believe everything he said and I held onto his every word."

"We had to wait a few days in the city until we were sure it was safe to trek back to Fervune again. But we couldn't hold your mother for that long otherwise her friends would get suspicious. We had to be sure she wouldn't spill the beans once we let her go."

"I trusted Tom, and he trusted me. So I never spoke a word to anyone else. But I had to know more. Over the following days, I snuck away from my friends and we would meet up. He would tell me more about the other races and everything he had experienced while amongst them."

Auster spoke again. "Eventually the time came when we were given the all clear to leave for Fervune and Tom and Sandra had to say goodbye. Much to Al's and my disapproval, they met again supposedly for one last time."

Sandra sighed heavily as she recalled the moment. "In that last meeting, your father asked me something that changed my life forever, and by that stage we both knew I wouldn't turn him down. He asked me to join him and go to Fervune." She smiled fondly, "I simply couldn't resist. As torn as I was to leave everything behind, the idea of adventure was far too tempting. So, of course, I agreed. And I have never regretted it."

"Wow." Tia cooed.

"It is an amazing world out there, darl." Sandra continued. "You are going to just love seeing it and experiencing it for yourself."

"Once he's finished his training here of course." Auster added.

"Ah yes, trying to survive under your rigorous regime I'm sure." Sandra smirked at her old friend. "Speaking of which, I would love to hear how it's all going."

For the rest of the week, Jove and his mother shared stories of how their lives had changed over the last couple of months. He showed her what he had learnt and she was thoroughly impressed. She seemed particularly fascinated by the bow-staff Tia had made him and his newfound abilities in controlling both air and water.

In turn, Sandra would tell stories of all the places and people she had met around the world. She also admitted to contributing some work to Auster's journal. Jove found that she had further knowledge about the hidden races that Auster had missed in his notes.

On the clear nights around the fire, Auster and Sandra would reminisce about their golden days while Jove and Tia listened with awe. Jove was particularly fascinated by the stories of his father and felt a flicker of pride as he pictured the great things he had done alongside his mother.

In Jove's opinion, the entire trip was the closest thing to a family holiday he'd ever had. The five of them, Maré included, lazed about the forest and kept their training to a minimum during their stay.

Eventually, the day came when their holiday had to end. With their bags packed, they bade each other farewell. Jove begged for his mother to come and stay with them at Grendun Court but she assured him that she had business to tend to back in Fervune.

"I think we're almost ready to meet over there anyway." Auster promised them. "Let's just head back for another week or so and then I'll book the tickets."

"For real!?" Tia squealed excitedly.

"I think so." Sandra winked. "It's about time you started living amongst their people. And your timing over there couldn't be better."

"How do you mean?" Auster was puzzled.

"I assume you've already heard of that Global Government scheme, yeah?"

Auster nodded.

"Well, when I stopped over in Rio on my way here, I heard a rumour that the American military had already joined forces with other countries and were moving in on opposing governments. Before I left the city, I noticed that an army barracks was under construction. These forces must be targeting South American parties next."

"That's moved along quickly." Jove commented.

"Yeah," Auster sounded nervous, "and it's closer to Fervune than I would like. Have there been any other movements?"

"Not that I know of." Sandra replied. "I'm going to check in again on my way home. But like I said, the sooner you guys get over there, the better. You don't want to arrive in the thick of it all."

"Mmm…" Auster grumbled.

Once they were sure that all their stuff was packed, Maré escorted Sandra onto the raft and back down the river toward the coast. As soon as they disappeared around the bend, Jove, Auster and Tia cleared the campsite and made their way back through the forest.

The journey didn't seem as long and exhausting as it did on the way in. Although they were carrying all the same gear on their backs, they felt somewhat relieved and relaxed as if half the weight of the packs had fallen away. Even the incoming tropical rain was not enough to douse their spirits.

In a little over a day, they were back at the undisturbed four-wheel drive and had just managed to throw their bags in the back as the first flash of lightning illuminated the sky.

Ambushed

"So it's really happening?" Tia said excitedly during the drive home. "We're going to Fervune?"

"Yep." Auster nodded for the umpteenth time. "Once I've organised everything here first."

Neither Jove or Tia could contain their excitement. They spoke about what Fervune would be like and the different things they would do when they finally got there. Auster merely smiled from the driver seat.

By the time they made it to the outskirts of Driscoll, the rain was falling harder and had grown into a fully-fledged tropical storm. Lightning flashed across the sky and the thunder that followed made the frame of the four-wheel drive shudder.

It was nightfall when they eventually pulled into the driveway of nine Grendun Court. Exhausted from the journey and ready for bed, they grabbed their bags and ran for cover inside. Jove stopped for a brief moment as another bolt of lightning lit their surroundings, scaring off a creature in the nearby bushes.

"Damn." Auster flicked the light switch as they entered and found it didn't work. "The power must have blown while we were gone. You guys mind getting out the candles from the kitchen cupboard?"

Jove and Tia nodded in reply and retrieved them, placing a candle in the kitchen and lounge. Tia grabbed some matches and lit them. The small flames emanated a dim orange glow around the house. Auster had disappeared back out to the car to gather the rest of their things.

"You know, you might be able to control fire better now that we're back." Tia suggested as she noticed Jove staring into the candle flame.

"You reckon?"

"Yeah, I'm sure you're more wary of your emotions now. I reckon you could make the flame larger so we can see a bit better." She winked. "Just sayin'."

Jove nodded slowly. He was pretty sure he was not going to make the mistake of burning a building down again. Besides, he was only going to feed it a small amount of energy.

Concentrating, Jove attempted to make the flame bigger and smaller by feeding it power from his hands. He focussed and tried to manipulate the intensity of the small lick of fire. Slowly, the flickering yellow flame grew slightly larger and the heat intensified beneath his palm.

"You've gotten better." Tia watched curiously.

"I still don't want to make it any larger," Jove continued and watched the licks of fire flicker.

The rain continued to roar as Auster walked in carrying their remaining luggage. Jove absentmindedly played with the fire and his eyes were now fixed on the two yellow lights the candles reflected in the window. They rippled as a heat haze started to spread throughout the house.

"Is it just me or is it really hot in here?" Auster asked as he threw their bags on the couch.

Tia looked questioningly at Jove. "Is that you?"

"I don't think so." he looked at his hands which remained unaffected by the heat.

"Let's go fix that bloody fuse box and get some fans going." Auster grumbled and motioned for Tia to help him.

Jove's attention was still on the small reflections in the window until something very odd happened. In the blink of an eye, the yellow glints disappeared and shifted before reappearing, almost as if they were alive. Curious, Jove extended his mind toward the outside of the house.

All of a sudden, his mental probe hit a wall of resistance and more glints appeared at the window. His eyes widened with horror as he realised what was bearing down upon them. He yelled for Auster and Tia to take cover. But it was too late.

An explosion erupted from the candles, engulfing the entire house in flames. Streams of intense fire burst through the windows and surrounded the three of them.

Having perfected their reflexes, Jove and Tia immediately jumped toward each other so that they were back to back. They swung their arms in sweeping motions, expanding the air and forming a cocoon around them to keep the swirling flames at bay. Glass flew around the room as Jove saw four stout figures jump through the windows aiming more blasts of fire at them.

The Draagni circled the room and raided the house, grabbing all of Auster's weapons from the cabinets. One immediately took Auster captive by clasping his hands behind his back. As much as he struggled, Auster could neither overpower the Draagni nor land a hit that could cause damage to its armour-like skin. Two of the great reptiles kept firing at Jove and Tia. They were barely keeping the flames out of reach with their bubble of circulating air.

Through the fire, Jove could see that they were all dressed in black cloaks. His heart sank as he instantly recognised the fourth stout figure.

"Ssstand down." Gahnarg hissed over the commotion. The sound of his voice sent a cold shiver down Jove's spine. It sounded as if it should have belonged to a hoarse snake.

The two attacking Draagni relented and the fire died down to burning embers. Jove and Tia kept their wind-barrier in place and held their arms in a fighting stance. Tia moved around so that she was blocking Jove from the Draagni in case they decided to attack again.

"We don't want you, little girl." Gahnarg took a step forward and Jove could see Auster struggle more viciously as he approached. "We only want the Incarnate."

Tia angrily shot a burst of wind at the ground, picking up broken shards of glass and debris. She aimed the stream of air at Gahnarg and the shards followed, slashing at his face and cloak.

The Draagni frowned and brushed off the attack as if it were dust.

"Fine." He said in a darker voice, "Come quietly…" He walked over to Auster and held up a clenched fist. Sharp talons protruded from his knuckles and he pressed them against Auster's neck.

"…Or elssse." He finished.

"Don't do it. I'm not worth it." Auster growled.

Tia twitched uncomfortably and turned to face Jove. A mixed look of desperation and anger swirled through her misty eyes. Jove understood. He didn't want anything to happen to Auster either.

Jove gave her a nod and they both lowered their arms. Immediately, the loose debris dropped to the ground and the room went quiet.

"What are you doing!?" Auster glared at them as they let down their defences. Gahnarg took no notice.

"Thatsss better." He nodded and motioned for the remaining Draagni to take them hostage as well.

The one that took hold of Tia dragged her over to join her father while the other that grabbed Jove held one of Auster's steel broadswords to his neck. He could feel the cold, rigid edge of the blade press against his chin and his heart started racing as Gahnarg stood in front of him. Jove stared back into the piercing yellow eyes that had haunted his memories for the past six months.

"So here iss what iss going to happen, human." The heat from Gahnarg's breath felt as if it could singe Jove's eyebrows. "We know who you are and we're taking you with usss. A large number of our people would love to ssee you perish."

"You can't take him!" Tia exclaimed from behind them, "If you kill him things will only get worse for all the races!"

The grip of her captor quickly tightened and she stilled. A scaly hand covered her mouth to muffle her voice.

"Life cannot posssibly become worssse for our peopless." Gahnarg snarled and unsheathed a long talon, pressing it against Jove's cheek. "Only when the humansss fall will we all become free again."

"What of them then?" Jove jerked his head in Auster and Tia's direction. "There are other humans out there trying to help."

"They are sstill of human blood. The diseasse will keep sspreading and take over no matter who standss in their way. But do not fear youngling," a malicious grin flashed across Gahnarg's snout revealing a jagged set of teeth, "your execution shall not be a lonely one."

Gahnarg moved his gaze to Jove's captor about to give an order. Jove quickly scanned his mind and saw that he was about to be knocked unconscious. His mind raced as he thought of a way to break free.

In the split second it took for the Draagni to raise the hilt of Auster's sword, Jove lunged a mental probe into his captor's mind, instantly sending his weak defences into a scramble. The distraction was enough to buy Jove a few seconds.

He sucked as much air into his lungs as possible, almost making his ribs crack. Just as the thick metal handle of the sword was about to strike the side of his head, Jove opened his mouth and released the pressure as if it were an almighty sneeze.

The force sent Gahnarg flying backward, crashing into the bookcase while Jove and the mind-fazed Draagni were flung into the opposite wall.

The impact briefly left them in a daze and Jove quickly took advantage of the moment by knocking the broadsword out of his Draagni's grip. He saw that both Auster and Tia had also broken free in the commotion. Their own captors retaliated by sending more waves of fire swirling around the room.

In another swift movement, Jove took his blade and swung it around, deflecting the flames that came raging towards him. He dealt one of the Draagni a blow to the head with the hilt of the sword, knocking him out and leaving him lying against the wall.

Jove swung blows left, right and centre, landing as many strikes as he could on the other Draagni. Tia had managed to find her bo-staff and was fending off the Draagni in an impressive display of strikes and movements. Auster immediately made a break for Gahnarg and tried to move his attention as far away from Jove as possible.

The heat was scorching Jove's body while he deflected jabs from his surrounding attackers. The sounds of wood and metal colliding with scales filled the room. Jove found it difficult to penetrate their steel-like skin with the blade. He called upon every kind of move and technique he could think of just to avoid getting hit by stray fists and jets of fire.

At one point, a clenched fist found its way through Jove's defences and he felt a sharp talon puncture his cheek. He yelled with pain as he fell to the floor.

Hot blood ran down his face and sweat built up on his brow. Fatigue started to set in as Jove's reactions became slower. Gahnarg and Auster were nowhere in sight.

Suddenly, a bloodcurdling shriek filled the room and Jove saw Tia fall to the ground in a plume of flames. Her bo-staff lay in front of her with burns and splits running along its length. Tia looked up at her opponent and Jove saw that she had blood gushing from her forehead and down her cheek.

The Draagni lifted her over his head by her arm. Tia flailed about trying to resist in vain. Gaining momentum, the Draagni threw her with superhuman force into the emptied weapons cabinet on the lounge room wall.

"Tia!" Jove screamed as she fell to the ground in a heap of splintered wood and glass. Her limp body lay in an awkward position and her hair was stained with streaks of crimson, covering her face.

Immediately Auster came flying from nowhere towards Tia's Draagni.

"How dare you touch my daughter!" He roared as he picked up Tia's staff smashing it over the lizard's head. His attempts at taking the Draagni down were futile and he was merely brushed aside before the creature turned its attention toward Jove.

As opposed to the other two combatants Jove had been fighting, this one meant business. In just two sweeps he had knocked Jove's sword out his grip. Another blow this time to his head forced Jove off his feet and he was slammed into the wall.

Pain surged through his body as he felt a cold, scaly hand close around his neck and push him further into the wall. He shot weak blasts of wind in every direction trying to throw off the Draagni but instead his grip tightened around Jove's throat, crushing his windpipe.

The Draagni slowly raised his fist and prepared to deal Jove the final blow. His sharp talons were glinting in the firelight. Jove closed his eyes and waited for impact.

A deafening bang like a gunshot filled the house and everything fell silent. Jove opened his eyes. It *was* a gunshot.

Gahnarg was standing in the centre of the room with a pistol pointing straight at Jove's face. He quickly recognised it to be the gun Auster had hidden in the bookcase which now lay shattered and burning across the floor.

The bullet had lodged itself in the wall barely a centimetre above Jove's ear. The sound it had made was enough to stir Tia back into consciousness.

"Don't you dare kill him." Gahnarg hissed maliciously. "If anyone iss to take hiss life it'ss going to be me."

The Draagni holding Jove turned to face Gahnarg with a questioning look, his clenched fist was still in the air. At Gahnarg's request, he released his hold on Jove's neck.

Jove immediately fell to a crumpled heap on the ground and started gasping for air. The taste of blood filled his mouth and he spluttered as he tried to clear his throat. Looking up, he saw Gahnarg bearing down on him with the barrel of the pistol pressed against his temple. With his other scaly hand, Gahnarg made a grab for Jove's hair ready to drag him to his feet.

"You're coming with me."

Then all at once, Jove heard a yell come from behind Gahnarg followed by the sound of a large wooden object colliding with the Draagni's shoulder.

Auster had swiftly grabbed one of the dining chairs and smashed it against Gahnarg's body. The impact threw him off balance and the pistol dropped from his hand. Auster immediately jumped onto the creature's scaly back and held him in a strong headlock.

"Get out of here! Both of you!" He roared as Tia stood up and tried to come to his aid. The other Draagni were quickly finding their feet and advancing upon them again. Gahnarg started thrashing about dangerously while Auster started landing punches out of the headlock whenever and wherever he could.

"But Dad…"

"Now!!"

Tia obediently snapped into action and wrenched Jove up off the floor, dragging him toward the front door. She had barely a fraction of a second to swipe something from the wreckage before one of the other Draagni made a grab at them. Tia was too quick for him. They narrowly made it out of his grasp and disappeared out of the house just as they heard another crash come from the back door.

The rain was now pouring down in a thick curtain. By the time the two of them had made it to the curb they were completely drenched. Still clutching Jove's arm, Tia led them toward the forest. As they heard a roar sound from the house they turned to see if the Draagni were in pursuit. Not yet.

Jove managed to power through the pain as they charged towards the forest. Once they had reached the safety of the trees, they retreated upwards into the branches where they could safely watch the house.

Peering through the rain, they saw light flickering through the windows as small fires burned within the house. Every few seconds they heard the scuffling from the brawl as the house interior was demolished. Tia shivered anxiously as the sounds quickly died away into an eerie silence.

"Your Dad's going to be fine right?" Jove nervously broke the silence.

"He's dealt with the Draagni before. He's faster than they are. He's probably managed to pick up the pistol again before Gahnarg." She tried to reassure herself. "Besides, it's not him they're after…"

BANG!

Tia was cut off by the sound of a gunshot coming from the house. Her face instantly paled. The air became silent aside from the crashing rain.

"He wouldn't shoot to kill." Tia breathed. She clutched Jove and was almost shaking him, but Jove knew all too well that it was not Auster that fired.

"I…I've got to go back." She started to sob and it was Jove's turn to grab her by the arm.

"And do what?"

"I don't know." She shuddered. Jove went to take her hand but was surprised to see that she was already holding something. It was what she had grabbed from the house as they ran out. It was Jove's bow-staff.

"Then we'll just have to wait for them here."

Jove grabbed his staff out of Tia's hand and crouched down amongst the branches. Shooting air down the wood, he loaded up the string with a sharp sliver of ice made from the incoming rain. He and Tia knew the forest better than the Draagni did, and the rain would surely have put them at an advantage. These thoughts seemed to help Jove focus as he squinted through the water and darkness back toward the house.

Suddenly, the door swung open and a large, slouched figure burst out onto the driveway. Gahnarg paused and his piercing eyes scanned the street through the rain. Jove pulled back the bowstring and took aim between the Draagni's eyes. This shot would kill him instantly.

Finally, Jove saw his chance and released the lethal sliver. The ice-arrow went soaring through the rain in silence. For a moment, it seemed that it would strike dead on target.

His prey, however, sensed the oncoming danger. Gahnarg caught sight of the icicle and at the last second he raised his thick, heavily scaled arm in an attempt to block it. The ice shattered into hundreds of tiny shards and cascaded harmlessly onto the concrete. Gahnarg lowered his arm and looked for where the arrow had come from. Jove felt his heart leap into his throat as his eyes rested directly on their hiding spot.

The Draagni charged down the road toward the forest. He had barely made it to the curb when he started launching giant orbs of fire towards Jove and Tia's branch. They had just enough time to jump over to the next tree before the flames hit and scorched their ankles.

Pain seared through Jove's body as he landed on the adjacent branch. His body was already starting to give in to exhaustion and the rain made the tree bark all the more slippery. With their reflexes and movements dulled, it was only a matter of moments before Gahnarg followed the sound of their rustling and caught up to them in the forest.

Thinking it might help for them to split up, Tia darted off in another direction making noise to lure Gahnarg away from Jove. It would have worked had Jove not have dislodged a loose branch before the Draagni was out of earshot.

"Get down here you coward!" He screeched as a wave of fire caused Jove to clutch the nearest trunk for shelter. Gahnarg raced towards the tree and slammed his knuckles into the wood. The bark shattered and cracks raced up the trunk, shaking it so vigorously that Jove had to jump down to a lower branch, dropping his bow staff.

Jove spun his arms around himself as he landed and sent an invisible jet of air at Gahnarg. A huge thud sounded over the rain as the great lizard was knocked off his feet and slammed into another trunk.

As Gahnarg found his footing and was about to launch another attack, Jove saw a large, sharp splinter of wood rocket out of the darkness. Tia had reappeared and snapped off a nearby branch sending it racing toward the ground with a powerful slipstream. Gahnarg barely had enough time to react and swiped it aside with a rock hard fist, shattering it into a shower of splinters. However, a small chunk of wood still managed to pierce his scales and he winced as he pulled it out of his arm. Dark blood dripped down his armour-like body and Jove took advantage of the distraction to race back into the treetops.

Viciously retaliating, Gahnarg wildly shot another blast of fire into the canopy. Dodging and weaving through the fire streams, Jove and Tia narrowly avoided the blaze licking at their bodies. The shots were getting wilder and wilder as Gahnarg grew even more furious.

Within moments, the surrounding trees were blazing and Jove and Tia had no choice but to fall back to the ground in front of the insane creature. They were both trapped within a ring of fire that Gahnarg was feeding with his own anger. The heat was so intense that the heavy rain quickly formed a thick cloud of steam as it fell within the battleground.

Desperately trying to defend the both of them, Jove summoned the Everice around his arm and immediately formed a river of water that snaked through the air. A look of shock flashed across Gahnarg's face. He shot another burst of fire at them but Jove managed to dissipate it with the water.

The stream twitched furiously as Jove struggled to keep control. Finally deciding to throw an attack back, he hurled the large body of water toward Gahnarg and hardened it into a spear of ice.

Reacting defensively, Gahnarg shot a powerful blast at the ice-spear. It shattered into a mass of tiny crystals just inches before his chest. Before Jove could recover and launch another attack, Gahnarg charged toward him for a full body tackle that had the momentum of a moving train.

Jove braced for impact but was surprised to see Tia lunge at them from the side. Instead of colliding with Jove, Gahnarg struck Tia with enough force to send her rocketing backwards, hitting her head against a nearby trunk and knocking her out.

This was more than Jove could bear. He built a pressure within his hands that felt like it was going to explode. He felt it twitch and swirl angrily as it expanded into a force Jove could barely control. He expelled it forward in a forceful burst of wind that sent the Draagni hurtling backwards into a flaming trunk.

"Enough!!" Gahnarg screeched as he got up again. His cloak hung from his body in tatters as he pulled something from within the folds of cloth. It was the pistol.

Jove froze rooted to the spot with both eyes on the barrel of the gun. He wasn't ready for a move like this.

"I will kill you here and now if I have too!" The Draagni yelled, "I don't care if thiss goess againsst our ruless! After all that you humanss have done to the resst of uss, there is no honour in killing such a thoughtlesss creature anyway."

Jove knew what was coming. His heart started pounding. The gun was aimed straight at his chest. His brain snapped into action as Gahnarg's finger pressed against the trigger. The bullet narrowly missed his foot as Jove launched himself back up into the canopy.

Furious, Gahnarg shot more and more rounds from the pistol, shattering tree branches and narrowly missing Jove's exhausted body. It was only a matter of time before Gahnarg ran out of bullets.

A noise sounded from the forest floor as Tia came to. She coughed and spluttered and her body shuddered as she struggled to get up again. Jove could sense a sickening thought flash through Gahnarg's mind.

"Maybe you can evade me," he lowered the gun barrel so that it was pointing at Tia, "but *she* can't."

Jove saw Gahnarg's scaly fingers flex around the handle.

"No!!" He launched himself from the tree between Gahnarg and Tia, straight into the pistol's line of fire.

In slow motion, Jove felt the rest of the world fall into silence. Even the sound of the gunshot was hushed as Gahnarg pulled the trigger. Jove's eyes stayed focussed on the bullet as it came toward him. But it was moving so slowly, almost as if time had completely stopped. Jove could see the air warp around the bullet as it hurtled straight at his chest.

The warping was crystal clear unlike anything he had ever seen before.

Every muscle in Jove's body tensed up and he felt all his energy leave him. In that same moment, he felt a powerful force emanate from his body, wrapping around him like a solid, spherical cocoon. It pressed aggressively against his chest, almost crushing his ribs. The pain grew more intense as the bullet tried to penetrate the barrier and break through to Jove's body.

Finally, Jove couldn't bear the pain any longer and let out a loud yell that almost shredded his lungs.

Instantly, the pressure lifted and expanded away from his body with so much power that it ripped the nearby trees out of the ground and extinguished the fire into smouldering piles of ash. Gahnarg had been flung backwards, dropping the gun as he fell into the debris of a fallen tree while Tia remained unharmed behind Jove's feet.

Jove felt his body cave in and he fell onto his hands and knees. He breathed heavily as he tried to figure out what had just happened.

Slowly lifting his head, he saw Gahnarg sluggishly crawling out of the wreckage. The pistol was now lying on the ground between them. They locked eyes before moving as quickly as their pained bodies would carry them toward the gun. Jove was closer but Gahnarg seemed to have more energy as he pushed himself up. A sickening crack filled the air as the Draagni suddenly fell to the ground. His leg was broken.

Jove pushed himself from a crawl onto his feet. A strange sensation coursed through his body and in his eyes. He felt everything going on around him as he picked up air currents on his skin. He felt the bugs floating on the breeze and the birds circling above their now destroyed home. He could even pick up Gahnarg's exasperated breathing.

Step by step, Jove inched closer to the gun while Gahnarg desperately crawled along the ground toward it. Getting there first, Jove picked up the pistol from the dirt and aimed it directly between the Draagni's eyes. He froze as Jove's finger wrapped around the trigger. Anger still flashed across his face as their eyes locked.

"Go ahead. Do it." Gahnarg tormented. "Killing iss in your human blood."

Jove gave him a look of malice and his hands tightened firmly around the pistol. He heard rustling sounds coming from behind him but he still remained fixated on Gahnarg.

"Do it!!" Gahnarg yelled and Jove flinched. He tightened his finger around the trigger and clenched his teeth. But still he did nothing.

"No…" he finally said and lowered the gun barrel, "I'm not like that, and neither are most humans."

Gahnarg's face retracted and became laden with shock.

"Neco vacuus veneratio est ignavus. Neco ignavus addo haud veneratio." Jove recited. He unloaded the remaining bullets and threw them to the ground in front of Gahnarg.

"There is not much difference between us, you know." Jove continued, "Right now you're just as brutal and unforgiving as you say we humans are. But we are all stuck in this world together. If people like you could just look past our differences and give some of us humans the opportunity to prove ourselves, then maybe there's a chance for peace after all."

Jove loosened his grip on the pistol and it fell to the ground with a thud. Gahnarg merely exchanged confused glances between Jove and gun.

"Spoken like a true Incarnate." A gruff voice came from behind them. Jove spun around to see Auster grinning proudly from the edge of the battlefield. Jove was relieved to see that he was alright. A slight limp in his leg showed that the bullet shot earlier had merely left a shallow gash in his shin.

Next to Auster was a taller Draagni cloaked in high quality armour and leather garb that had metal spikes poking out from around the neck. He seemed superior to the other Draagni that were now standing obediently behind him.

"Ssstand down Gahnarg." He ordered. "Thisss human hass proven himself worthy."

"Dux." Gahnarg stuttered and could not bring himself to answer further, so he merely bowed his head.

"What's going on?" Jove eyed the new Draagni.

"Thomasss Boyd." He spoke as he eyed Jove. "My debt iss repaid."

Jove looked at him nervously. He was so confused that his head started to ache. All at once, his limbs ached and pulsated with pain. It was all too much for him. Swaying heavily on the spot, his body finally gave in and he fell to the ground in an unconscious heap.

Travel Plans

It was mid-afternoon when Jove finally awoke in his own bed. Every muscle in his body was aching and his cuts and grazes were seared with pain. He slowly sat up to find that someone had tended to his wounds with stitches and bandages.

He could hear movement and muffled voices coming from outside his room. Swinging his legs over the bed, he painfully got up and slowly walked outside toward the lounge. He was careful not to step on any broken glass or splinters of wood as he walked.

Auster was sitting at the dining table in deep conversation with the strange lead Draagni Jove saw before he passed out. He had to rub his eyes to make sure he was seeing the strange scene correctly. The rest of the Draagni were nowhere in sight. Not even Gahnarg.

"You're awake!" Tia yelled from the couch. Her head was also covered in bandages and streaks of dried blood ran through her hair. She appeared to have only just gotten up as well.

Instantly, everyone fell silent and turned to face Jove. He felt a bit nervous standing there with everyone staring at him.

"Hi." Jove said awkwardly. He shifted uneasily at the sight of the Draagni sitting calmly in their house, "What's going on?"

"Pleasse forgive me." the large reptile replied in a low yet soft hiss as he got up from his chair. "I am Durzven. Dux of Draagni Alae K-D."

Jove still eyed him nervously and backed away as he approached.

"It's alright Jove. That means he's a Draagni commander. He's on our side." Auster reassured him.

"It iss ssuch an honour to meet you in persson," Durzven bowed, "and alsso a relief to ssee you are alright."

"I don't understand." Jove replied. "Where are the other Draagni?"

"I have ssent them away. Resst assured they will be severely punished for the actionss they took lasst night. For that, I apologisse."

Jove still wasn't convinced "Why are you here?"

"I wass tracking down my ssoldiers. They were meant to bring you to me alive sso we could take you back to our colony to passs judgement. I wass waiting on the beach for your arrival until I heard gunfire. I arrived here at the houssse just as you escaped."

346

Jove was surprised to hear the Draagni talk so contently. He had basically just admitted that he was about to abduct him and potentially have him killed at the hands of other Draagni.

"Pleasse forgive Gahnarg's actionss. He had taken a personal vendetta against your life outsside of my orderss. He hass had a dark passt involving humanss, like mosst of our people."

Jove still felt anger towards Gahnarg and this apology was not making him feel any different.

"I'm afraid I can't accept your apology." He said sternly. "Not after all he has done to me already."

Instead of seeming disappointed with this answer, Durzven showed a small hint of a smile.

"I ssee it takess much to ssway your will. You have good fire in your belly. Like Draagni."

As hesitant as Jove was of this creature, something about Durzven's tone made him slightly more at ease.

Auster interjected and offered them both a seat. Jove let out a groan of pain as he sat.

"I don't understand. How did you find us?" Jove queried.

Auster gave Jove a stern look. "Turns out someone that had exceptional fighting skills and a lighter attacked a group of local hooligans. The brawl was caught on the supermarket CCTV and aired on the news."

Jove's face flushed with guilt as Auster continued. "I would have seen it on TV but I kicked it in on the night of our argument. Durzven and his crew followed the story and the trail ended here."

Jove digested the news but still did not understand why a Draagni was sitting calmly next to him. "Then how come I'm still alive? I thought you guys were out to kill me like the rest of your race?"

"It isss true that majority of my people would like to ssee you dead youngling." Durzven answered. "There have been many feudss amongst our tribe. I however believe that you may very well be our ssalvator."

Saviour, Jove's mind translated the Latin as he probed Durzven's thoughts. His intentions were genuine.

Auster butted in, "Many believe that the human Incarnate can do one of two things. Either save the other species from total annihilation or…"

"… be the causse of their destruction." Durzven finished Auster's sentence. "Like Gahnarg, I alsso thought that a Human Incarnate would destroy usss. But you proved lasst night of your intention to help our causse. For thisss reason, I give my word that your life will be sspared and resspected by my people."

Durzven got up again as this time, he prepared to leave, "I shall tell them you have great honor and a sstrong fire burnss in you."

He held out a scaly hand which Jove took before making his way out of what was left of the back door.

"I look forward to sseeing you train with uss ssoon youngling." The Draagni turned heel and pulled the hood of his cloak over his head, covering any exposed parts of his scaly body.

"Durzven?" Jove called out after him. He turned before Jove continued.

"Before I passed out, I heard you mention my father's name. Did you know him?"

The great lizard sighed and small licks of fire flared from his snout. "I was briefly amicusss with Thomasss Filiram. He proved worthy to me a time ago. I expect the same of you, Jove Filirmas."

The Draagni vanished over the dunes before Jove could question him any further. His mindstream quickly retreated out of Jove's reach.

"Filirmas?" Jove turned questioningly to Auster.

"It's a title a young Draagni inherits when they earn the respect of their clan." Auster translated. "They earn the rite to be called the spawn of their parents. Filirmas, child of Thomas."

A sense of pride welled inside Jove. For a moment, it helped him ignore the pain coursing through his body. He looked up at the sky which had completely cleared as if the storm from the previous night never took place.

He noticed something was different as the sky seemed more alive. Jove had grown accustomed to seeing the wind warp and other distortions in the air but for some reason he could see them more clearly now. Rivers of wind currents snaked high up in the atmosphere and Jove even saw small streams form behind birds as they flew by.

"Something's different about you." Tia approached him from behind. "That barrier you made last night to protect us from that bullet. That was amazing."

"Lucky break I suppose." Jove turned and looked straight at her. As he did so, he noticed her face immediately light up.

"What?"

"Your eyes!" She squealed, "Dad come look!"

"What is it?" Jove asked again.

"Your pupils! They're pure white!"

"What!?" Jove immediately ran to the mirror in the bathroom, nearly knocking Auster over on his way past.

Sure enough, his eyes stared back at him. Though this time his pupils shone a pure, bright white as they inspected him with wonder.

Auster limped up from behind and grabbed at Jove's face to inspect his eyes more closely.

"What does it mean?" Jove asked anxiously.

Auster beamed in reply. "It means you're ready for Fervune."

A fortnight passed and Jove's wounds were almost fully healed. Tia's were not far behind. Maré had returned after being informed of the Draagni attack and tended to all their injuries. Even Auster's bullet wound seemed to have almost completely disappeared as if nothing had ever happened.

On the day of their departure, Maré surprised Jove by gathering and returning the Everice that had been lost during the battle in the forest. It would forever be a reminder of the night Jove proved himself worthy to the Draagni.

They had been packing over the last couple of days getting ready to leave the country. Auster was constantly going through the house making sure there was nothing left. Most of the furniture had to be burned as most it was almost destroyed during the ambush. They even threw in Auster's books and weapons in case anyone else came across the house and uncovered its secrets. Eventually all that was left in the house was the most basic of contents and appliances.

"We're not coming back here are we?" Tia asked as the three of them stood at the front door for the last time.

"I don't know." Auster replied, giving the place one last look over. "From here on in we don't look back. We will all hold our own responsibilities and will go wherever we are needed."

Everything was sinking in for Jove. This was his new reality. Taking one last look at the place he had come to call home, he realised he was about to set foot on a global scale journey. All the decisions he made from this point would no longer affect just him, they would influence the entire world and all five races.

"Come on, let's go." Auster turned towards the car. He glanced over the house before locking the door behind them.

Out of the corner of his eye, Jove saw him place the key delicately under the welcome mat before they left for the local airport.

A few hours and a domestic plane ride later, the three of them were standing in customs at Sydney airport waiting to board their flight to Brazil.

"Now remember, you two are brother and sister and we're visiting family in Rio." Auster briefed their story. "Make sure your sunnies are on and secure."

Jove and Tia were dressed as casual teenagers and each had a set of earphones to add to their 'disguise'. They both wore dark sunglasses to cover their pupils.

"You guys pack light." the customs officer said as he put their bags through the detector.

"Most of our luggage is already over there." Auster answered quickly.

This was partly true. Maré had taken most of their things to Fervune himself so not to arouse suspicion at the airport. Jove had to unwillingly part with the bow-staff Tia had made him. With enough convincing however, he managed to keep the Everice on his person. Instead of sitting it in its usual place around his upper arm, Jove condensed and disguised it in a regular water bottle as drinking water.

"We're being fairly well taken care of." Auster concluded.

This seemed convincing enough to the officer and he let them pass through.

"Nice one Dad." Tia shot him a quiet compliment.

"This isn't my first time." Her father smirked back.

Eventually they made it through and were sitting in their seats on the plane. They had a group of three seats together between the aisle and the window. Tia let Jove sit next to the window as she knew it was his first time leaving the country while Auster sat beside the aisle.

"I think I'm going to go use the facilities before take-off." Auster got up again as the last of the passengers filed in. Jove stared out the window onto the runway. A churning feeling was growing in his gut.

"I suppose it's all nerve-wracking for you." Tia leaned over. "To take on all this responsibility and not be able to turn back."

"Partly." Jove continued to stare out the window, "A small part of me wants to go back and forget that all this has happened. I still think that I'm gonna wake up and be late for another school day. A few months ago I would've given anything for that to be the case."

"What does the other part think?"

Jove turned to face Tia and took his sunglasses off. Tia removed hers as well and her mottled misty gaze met with his pure white one.

"The other part knows I was born to do this and that I'm now ready to face it. Plus how many teenagers can say they're about to travel around the world to experience different cultures and learn how to control the elements. It's the chance of a lifetime. I just hope I don't screw it up."

"For you it's the chance of *every* lifetime." Tia grinned, "And you won't screw it up. You're everything the Incarnate should be; compassionate, strong-willed, and you have a tremendous sense of justice and equality. You are all these things and you have barely even begun learning about the other cultures. I think you will be a great Incarnate and with Dad's and my help, I reckon you'll be one of the greatest in history."

Jove smiled and leaned over, "Thanks, I wouldn't have it any other way."

Tia's misty eyes started swirling and she leaned in as well. Their faces were only inches apart when Tia suddenly turned away and retreated backward, "I'm sorry Jove."

He paused. "For what?"

"That… *moment*, we had in the forest. That wasn't supposed to happen."

"Whatdya mean?" Jove backed into his own seat, slightly disappointed.

"Well look at us, we've been cooped up together for so long now. Doing the same thing day in day out is enough to play tricks on us and allow for certain… feelings."

Jove felt awkward by the seriousness in her tone. "Are you saying we shouldn't be getting so close?"

Tia shook her head defensively as she struggled to find the words. "Of course we should be close. I like that we get along this well. What I mean to say is that we can't afford to have something go on between us. You're the Incarnate, you're destined for big things while I'm… well, I don't want to jeopardise any of that or our friendship. There are more important things."

"Right." Jove replied dismally. "Mission first then huh?"

She nodded. Her eyes lulled into a depressing grey. A painful silence crossed between them until Auster finally returned.

"Should be about time to take-off soon." He sat down and fastened his seatbelt. No sooner had he done so when the overhead speaker buzzed.

"Please ensure all seatbelts are fastened as we prepare for take off." The flight attendants voice echoed through the cabin.

Auster plugged his complimentary earphones into his seat and tuned into the radio. Jove distracted himself by watching the land fall away below. It was quickly replaced by the coastline as they flew out to sea.

After a time, Jove thought he might try and start another conversation with Tia but she abruptly cut him off.

"Well I'm gonna catch some shut eye. See you in Rio." She tilted her seat back and slid the complimentary mask over her eyes, giving Jove no chance to answer.

He looked out the window again. Behind them the land sank away over the horizon. Jove suddenly felt his stomach lurch as he thought of where they were headed and what he would experience once he got there.

The Incarnate was about to be reintroduced to the hidden world, and he was ready for it.

Pronunciation Guide

Jove – *"Jōve"* (rhymes with "cove")
Tia – *"Tee-ah"*
Auster – *"Os-tah"*
Maré – *"Mar-ray"*
Ventiera – *"Ven-tee-air-rah"*
Draagni – *"Drarg-nye"*
Olderak – *"Ole-der-ahk"*
Merpesces – *"Merp-see"* (sing) *"Merp-sees"* (plural)
Gahnarg – *"Guh-narg"*
Durzven – *"Durj-ven"*
Mendoza – *"Men-doe-zah"*
Wentra – *"Went-rah"*
Fervune – *"Fur-vyoon"*

Acknowledgements

Much appreciation and thanks goes to those who gave me such great feedback and help with getting Jove to where we are now. Tara for your priceless input with the editing and publishing expertise. Jake for the incredible artwork that brought the character and vision to life. Also to my 'test readers' for your valued feedback and opinions. Most notably Greg, Clotilde, Nikki and various members of the family who weren't afraid to tell me what was good and, more importantly, what wasn't.

Cheers guys.